Shocking Crimes

ALSO BY MICHAEL HAMBLING

THE SOPHIE ALLEN BOOKS
Book 1: Dark Crimes
Book 2: Deadly Crimes
Book 3: Secret Crimes
Book 4: Buried Crimes
Book 5: Twisted Crimes
Book 6: Evil Crimes
Book 7: Shadow Crimes
Book 8: Silent Crimes
Book 9: Ruthless Crimes
Book 10: Brutal Crimes
Book 11: Hidden Crimes
Book 12: Vicious Crimes
Book 13: Heartless Crimes
Book 14: Shocking Crimes

Michael
Hambling
SHOCKING
CRIMES

JOFFE BOOKS

Joffe Books, London
www.joffebooks.com

First published in Great Britain in 2025

© Michael Hambling 2025

Cover art by Nick Castle

ISBN: 978-1-80573-317-1

FOREWORD

This is a work of fiction, and none of the characters and situations described in this novel bear any resemblance to real persons or events. Some of the locations in this novel do exist but are used fictitiously.

For convenience, a short glossary appears at the end of this book, which includes the main ranks within the UK Police Force. You'll also find a short introduction to the area in which the novel is located.

CHARACTER LIST

Wessex Regional Serious Crime Unit (WeSCU):
Detective Chief Superintendent Sophie Allen
Detective Chief Inspector Barry Marsh (Dorset)
Detective Sergeant Rae Gregson (Dorset)
Detective Constable Tommy Carter (Dorset)
Detective Constable Jackie Spring (a trainee detective on loan from Somerset)

Dorset Police Officers:
Detective Inspector Lydia Pillay (Bournemouth CID; newly appointed to the role of DI)
Detective Sergeant Jimmy Melsom (Bournemouth CID)
Detective Constable George Warrander (Bournemouth CID; newly appointed)

To the memory of Gaia Pope-Sutherland; a life cut tragically short.

PROLOGUE

I hurt all over I got cuts and bruses and sors on my arms and legs
thay stub out fags on my back and stomick and laf at me
Why
Why they so crule
I didnt mene to gras em up honest
They say they gonna kill me and stik me in a sootcase and chuk it in the sea
help me plees
im jan im only 10
plees help me

* * *

Holly couldn't understand what was happening to her. Her mind was drifting, her thoughts were woolly and unfocussed, no matter how hard she tried to concentrate. Strobe lights were beginning to shake and swirl, arcing across her line of sight. Faces were distorted and voices echoed eerily, resounding in her brain. The floor wouldn't stay still. One moment it was sloping up, the next tilting and sliding away from her.

Her legs felt spongy and insubstantial. She wanted to scream a warning to her friends, but her face felt all wrong. She was slipping downwards and sideways. Everything faded to a misty grey and then went dark.

CHAPTER 1: NASTY SLUG

Saturday

Detective Inspector Lydia Pillay's phone rang. She was feeling tired and under pressure, having been up since the early hours, and was trying to clamber out of her car. Did she have time to answer it? Could she even be bothered? Sighing, she pulled it from her jacket pocket and glanced at the screen. Sophie Allen. One of the few callers who deserved an immediate response.

'Hi, boss.'

'Lydia. I hear congratulations are in order. An arrest already? You don't hang about, do you?'

Lydia laughed. 'Luck, really. And the fact that she was a bit of a moron, dropping clues like confetti.'

'Even so. It's a great start, Lydia. I just wanted to let you know.'

'Thanks, I appreciate it. Sorry we didn't need WeSCU. It was obvious from the start that it was a pretty cut-and-dried case, and we didn't want any delay. She works at the airport as a cleaner and there was a good chance she'd do a runner, off to far-away climes, if we gave her half a chance. We had to move fast.'

'Where are you now?'

'With Dave Nash. We've just arrived at a property she inherited, sixty-eight Crawley Terrace. Forensics are due soon. It belonged to her, but she didn't live there, not in recent years. We're just about to get kitted out in the suits and take a look-see before they start the detailed stuff and throw us out. Jimmy and George are here with me.'

'That's great. Look after George, Lydia. He's got the makings of a good 'un.'

Lydia rolled her eyes. 'You've said that before, boss,' she said quietly, so she couldn't be overheard by her colleagues. 'You and Barry, both. About a hundred times. Stop mothering him. George is just fine.'

'I'm suitably chastised. Okay, I'll leave you to it.'

The phone went dead, so Lydia slid it into her pocket and walked back to her two colleagues. 'Okay, let's move. Dave, did you say we've got about twenty minutes before another forensic unit arrives?'

Dorset's forensic chief nodded. 'I'm only here because I happened to be nearby when you called me. We've just about finished the initial check of the exterior, but we still need to do the thorough search.'

Lydia took another look at the house's grubby facade and peeling paintwork before entering. The air in the hallway smelled musty and dry. Dust lay on most of the surfaces around them, a grey powdery layer that stirred as they moved slowly through the room.

'She said that she hadn't used this place much. It was left to her in her uncle's will,' Lydia told her colleagues. 'Once she moved in with that poor guy, she didn't need her own place. Parasite.' She almost spat the word out.

She accompanied Dave in taking a quick walk through the cramped downstairs rooms. Tired air. Weary décor. Faded and torn furniture. Dispiriting. The house seemed to have the same effect as that strange creature from TV's *Red Dwarf*. What was it again? The Despair Squid? She smiled to herself. Fancy remembering that at a time like this.

Upstairs, Jimmy and George were moving in a similar way through the poky rooms. Two bedrooms and a grubby bathroom. Stained bathroom fittings. A filthy bath. A row of old medicine packets on a shelf, most of their labels missing, probably the uncle's. Bedrooms with beds that looked at least half a century old, covered with moth-eaten throws. Rickety wardrobes with doors that stuck.

DC George Warrander was in a single bedroom at the rear of the property, poking at a low hatch set into one of the walls. The room had a small dormer window and a sloping ceiling. The hatch looked as though it would open into the eaves, and a less observant person might well have missed its presence. The cover suddenly fell open in a cloud of filthy dust. He leaned in and shone his torch into the gloom. There was very little to see, just masses of cobwebs and yet more dust. He directed the beam of light to the far end. The area had no flooring, but a few planks laid across the rafters would allow someone to crawl along the short length and might give some access to the search teams. He swept the beam back towards where he stood. Something caught his eye in the gap between two joists near his feet, slightly paler in colour than the surrounding filth. He took a photo on his phone, then extracted a pair of tweezers from his pocket and managed to grip what turned out to be an old bit of paper, yellow with age and covered in dirt. He pulled it out and slid it into a plastic bag, then tried to read it in the beam from his torch.

* * *

Dave Nash wasn't particularly happy. 'You should have left it, George. My people like to see all evidence in situ.'

'Sorry. I'm new to this. But at first I didn't think it was important.'

'It must be decades old,' Lydia said, carefully directing the conversation away from George's mistake. 'The writing's so hard to make out and the paper has that dried-out, crumbly

5

look about it. It's a child's writing, I would have thought. Might be someone fairly young, like it says. Wouldn't you say so, Dave?'

The forensic chief took another look. 'Could be, though some adults have childish handwriting, particularly if they have learning difficulties. It's poorly written, isn't it?'

DS Jimmy Melsom spoke up. 'It's worrying, however old it is and whoever wrote it. It's describing torture, isn't it? Plain and simple.'

Lydia was frowning. 'I didn't expect this. Pippa Chandler's only had this house for a few months. This predates her.'

'By some years, is my guess. Even decades.' Dave looked at his watch as he heard the sound of several vehicles drawing up outside. 'That's the squad,' he said. 'Right on time. To be honest, I don't think we'll find much that's relevant to the case, Lydia. The dust in this room hasn't been disturbed for at least a year.'

Lydia frowned. 'That's about when Chandler shacked up with that poor man. So did she ever live here before she inherited it? It would be useful to know.'

'What's the connection with this note that George just found?' Jimmy asked.

'There probably isn't one. But it gives us an extra incentive to check the place out thoroughly.' Lydia turned to Dave. 'We'll be off now. Keep me posted, won't you?' She paused. 'On second thoughts, I'll leave George here with you, just as liaison. He probably needs the experience of seeing a detailed forensic search close up. Happy with that, George?'

'Of course, boss.'

'Come on, Jimmy. We've got a murderer to interview.'

The two senior detectives returned to their car, leaving George, the rookie, in the capable hands of Dorset's chief of Forensic Services. As Dave Nash had predicted, little was found in the first stages of the sweep, looking for fingerprints, bloodstains and the like. George thought the place was like a mausoleum. It quite obviously hadn't been cleaned much even before Pippa Chandler had gained ownership. Had she told Joshua Quick that she owned this property? Probably not. She was a devious, manipulative schemer with a foul temper and a sadistic streak. It had obviously suited her to have a compliant man in her life, looking after her every need, even if he was disabled. Right up until he'd started to rebel and push free from her constraints. Quick hadn't survived her reaction to that.

* * *

Lydia and Jimmy were back in Bournemouth Central police station about to enter one of the interview rooms. Lydia flicked some non-existent dust from the shoulders of her jacket and Jimmy attempted to smooth down his fair hair, but to no avail. It had a life of its own and one or two curls would always go their own way. Jimmy opened the door, and they entered, joining Pippa Chandler and the duty solicitor.

Lydia looked at the woman opposite as she sat down. Her eyes appeared smaller, more piglike than when she'd first been brought in, and every pore in her round face seemed to seep a damp oiliness. Her hair looked dank and greasy. Her narrowed eyes darted between the two detectives.

'Ms Chandler, have you had a chance to think things over, as we suggested?' Lydia said after the interview formalities were over. 'You need to face facts. Your landlord and ex-partner, Joshua Quick, lodged a written declaration with a staff member at the Citizen's Advice Bureau. It was signed and witnessed. It details a long list of incidents, including assault and intimidation, stretching back for several months. We've found traces of saliva on his face from the final assault. We'll get DNA from that. There are fingerprints around his neck from where he was strangled. Your fingerprints, in fact. There were traces of blood in the kitchen. Again, your fingerprints were recorded in those marks and doubtless we'll identify the DNA from it. There's a clear CCTV shot of you leaving his block of flats late on Tuesday night, in a hurry. Your car has traces of blood on the clutch pedal, transferred there from a shoe. Your left shoe had bloodstains on it.' She waited but there was no response from Chandler. 'It's all looking bad for you, isn't it? This *no comment* charade is going to get you nowhere. That approach may work in a case with little evidence, but this? No chance. Your only hope of getting a lighter sentence is to co-operate with us and tell us everything that happened. It will help. It will be taken into account. Judges listen to what we have to say when they're deliberating before sentencing. Come on, you know it makes sense.'

The woman didn't speak but her constantly flickering eyes gave a clue as to the uncertainty that must be swirling around in her head.

'There's a man dead here, and we know you killed him,' Lydia continued, sensing that this wasn't the time to let up on the pressure. 'The evidence shows it without a shadow of doubt and any court will convict on just half of what we have. Be brave, own up to it and tell us.' She looked the woman straight in the eye, holding her breath but not showing it. It was a knife-edge moment, but she wanted to appear calm, relaxed and in control.

Chandler kept her eyes fixed on Lydia. Her voice finally came out in a near hiss. 'You think I'm sick in the head, don't you?'

'I don't know, Pippa. Only a specialist doctor could tell us that. All I want is for you to make things easier on yourself. And you can do that by answering my question. Did you kill Joshua Quick?'

There was a long silence. Chandler remained hunched, her shoulders sagging.

'He never did what I fuckin' told him. I told him I still needed him. He was still goin' on about chuckin' me out.'

Lydia watched her closely for a few more seconds.

'Did you kill him? Joshua Quick?'

Those small, dark eyes, sullen now, stared back at her. 'Yeah, but well, I never meant to.'

'How did you get into his flat? He'd changed the lock.'

'When he was at the doctor's last week. I got the spare from his neighbour. Put on a boilersuit. Carried a toolkit. Pretended I was an electrician calling to fix a fault. Made a copy then handed it back.' Pippa was boasting now.

'It was that simple?'

The woman merely nodded and smirked.

'I don't really understand why, Pippa. What had he done to upset you that much?'

The woman shrugged. 'He tried to chuck me out, didn't he? He found someone else. Someone at work said she'd seen him out with some young bit of stuff. And then he went and told my mother about me and . . .' Another shrug.

'You'll need to explain, Pippa.'

'Junk. Shit. Stuff. You know what I mean. Crack. Mum went berserk. I told her I'd been clean for months, so's I could get some cash from her. She's gone and demanded it back. Why'd he tell her? It weren't nuffin' to do with him. She says she don't wanna see me ever again.'

'And you think that's a good enough reason to kill him?'

Another shrug. 'Well, he got on my tits, doin' that. I mean, show a bit of loyalty, for fuck's sake.'

'He was disabled, Pippa. He could only move around by using an elbow crutch. Couldn't you have given him a bit of leeway? And the younger woman he was seen out with. We think it was his occupational therapist.'

There was no response. It looked as though Pippa was beginning to regret telling them so much. They wrapped up the formalities but, just before they left the room, Lydia asked one last question.

'You've got a house, Pippa. In Crawley Terrace. How long have you owned it?'

She shrugged. 'I dunno. Only found out about it a month or so ago. Maybe less. I been waiting for lawyers to contact me and confirm it.'

'How did you come to own the place?'

'It was my Uncle Gus's. Left it to me in his will. Dunno what to do with it. Too rundown. I ain't got the money to do it up. Anyways, I've always preferred to move in with a man. Better that way.'

There was a manipulative glint in her eye. What a nasty slug, Lydia thought.

'See, that's another thing. I needed some cash to start gettin' it fixed up. But Josh weren't interested. Fuck him, I thought. He could've helped but he didn't.'

Lydia wondered about the state of the woman's brain. Surely coming into the ownership of that property would have solved her financial problems? She could have put it up for auction and pocketed enough money to last her a good few years. Some people were just downright weird. That was the problem with drugs. They addled the brains of far too many users. She'd need to find out about this uncle of Pippa's though, just to check on the legitimacy of what the woman had said.

CHAPTER 2: DESICCATED

Monday

Within two days, the forensic squad had finished their search of the property in Crawley Terrace and was beginning to pack equipment away. As usual, the unit leader, Dave Nash, carried out a final trawl through the house. On this occasion, Jimmy Melsom, the newly promoted detective sergeant in Lydia's unit, was with him.

'I just want to take a last look through the hatchway,' Jimmy said, as they climbed the stairs to the upper floor. 'That was where George spotted that old note. Has anything come to light about it?'

'Our paper expert thinks it's about twenty years old, give or take a few years,' Dave replied. 'It's not an exact science. The ageing of cheap paper depends on a lot of factors. The ink also suggests that kind of timeframe. It's up to you and Lydia to pursue it any further, like getting a handwriting expert in to analyse the style. It looks like a child's efforts, but a clever adult could mimic that.'

They entered the small bedroom and walked across to the hatch. Jimmy leaned inside and shone his torch around the musty interior. They could hear the scratching of sparrows nesting under the eaves.

'A second brood, I expect,' Dave explained. He was watching the area illuminated by Jimmy's powerful torch as the beam swept across the underside of the roof, from left to right. He suddenly put a hand on Jimmy's arm.

'Hold it there.' He peered into the gloom. 'This is why I do this check,' he added, a note of exasperation now evident in his voice.

He walked out of the room and Jimmy could hear him berating a junior member of his team. He was soon back, this time carrying a much more powerful flashlight. He proceeded to shine it to the left side, where they could make out the filthy vertical brick wall separating the loft from its equivalent space in the neighbouring property. Dave then swung the beam through 180 degrees to the equivalent wall at the other end, holding it there for some time.

'Do you see?' Dave asked.

'It isn't brickwork,' Jimmy replied. 'What's the surface?'

'I can't be sure from back here. I'll need to get closer. Push those planks this way. I think I can create a makeshift crawl-way.'

By now, several other forensic team members had come into the room to watch. Dave crawled along the narrow eaves area and was approaching the far wall. Jimmy could make out his body shape and saw him raise his arm. He began tapping the surface. After several minutes he crawled back, his forensic suit filthy with grime and old cobwebs.

He ignored Jimmy and spoke to his team, his voice sharp and controlled.

'It's hollow,' he said. 'My guess is that it's been put up a few inches in front of the solid wall. Get some stronger flooring in here, then get that partition down. It's plasterboard. We need to check behind it. For goodness' sake, we were within a whisker of missing it!'

He moved back and allowed several of his juniors to organise the laying of more substantial flooring lengths and the hanging of brighter lights. Then he and Jimmy watched as two figures used a small crowbar to lever the board away.

'Something's here!' one of them called.

'Get photos before you remove it,' Dave shouted back. 'What is it?'

'An old suitcase.'

Jimmy suddenly felt uneasy. What had that child's letter said? That someone had threatened to kill them and use a suitcase to dispose of their body? Jimmy felt a lump in his throat. Surely not?

A small square of timber board was found and pushed through the hatch. When it reached the far end of the enclosed space, the grubby suitcase was pulled onto it before it was slowly drawn back towards the hatch on its makeshift sled. Dave and Jimmy helped to haul it out onto the bare floorboards of the bedroom.

There it stood, a grey fabric zip-case, lying on its side, zip side uppermost.

'Do you want to do the honours, Jimmy?' Dave asked.

'Bloody hell, Dave. Why me?'

Nevertheless, Jimmy reached forward and tugged at the zip. It resisted for a few moments, then he felt it begin to move. Was that a tragic sigh that escaped into the air or just the sound of the zip, opening for the first time in many years? Jimmy couldn't be sure.

And there it was. The dried-up, desiccated shape of a small body, wearing what appeared to be a child's shorts and T-shirt, crammed inside the small interior of the case. No one spoke for several moments.

'Jesus.' The voice of one of the forensic workers finally broke the silence. 'Sorry, boss. It was me who missed it.'

'Get everything filmed. Get back in there and see if there's anything else. Check all the other walls in the house for partitions like it. When we leave, I want to be absolutely sure there are no more horrors like this lurking in hidden gaps or shadowy cubbyholes. I think it's shocked us all. To use a hackneyed expression, this is the pits.'

* * *

Lydia and George hot-footed it to Crawley Terrace after Jimmy contacted her with a hurried call.

'What exactly has happened, Jimmy?' she asked as soon as she climbed out of the car.

She covered her head with her hands when he told her the details of the horrifying discovery. 'Bloody hell! And there I was thinking we had a nice simple murder case all wrapped up within a couple of days without needing to call on Sophie's squad. I should have known better.'

Jimmy grinned. 'Cheer up, boss. It'll be like old times, won't it? You, me, Barry and the chief super. Those were the days!'

Lydia lowered her hands and scowled at her number two. 'You've only just got promoted, Jimmy Melsom. There's time to reverse that, you know. Or find you somewhere else to go, like the public toilet inspection squad.'

George Warrander looked backward and forward between his two superiors, then quietly slid away to join the forensic team, who were about to enter the house for the second time, but on this occasion under orders to tear it apart in the search for other hidden nooks and crannies. Behind cupboards, under floorboards, inside old chimney breasts.

Meanwhile, Lydia took out her phone and made the call to Sophie Allen. The murder of Joshua Quick might have been a straightforward domestic, able to be handled efficiently by Lydia's own Bournemouth-based CID unit, but this one certainly wasn't. It had WeSCU written all over it.

* * *

The whole of the Dorset-based section of WeSCU arrived within two hours, assembling in the narrow confines of

Crawley Terrace, taking up every unused parking space in the process. A motley collection of neighbours stood behind the police cordon, generating a mood of nervous fascination. Whispered words passed between onlookers, spoken with hands to lips. The atmosphere wasn't cheered by the weather. The normally balmy Bournemouth climate was experiencing a few days of grey drabness, with a misty coastal drizzle hanging in the air.

Sophie Allen only stayed for ten minutes. Her mobility was still limited by her elbow crutches. She looked around, as if trying to place the location. This was one of Bournemouth's most rundown areas, a backstreet jumble of old houses that were the epitome of social deprivation. Outsiders might assume the town was uniformly prosperous, the embodiment of middle-class affluence. They'd be wrong.

'We were just round the corner from here all those years ago, Barry. On that first case. Remember? Susie Pater's flat was only a few hundred yards away. The area hasn't changed much, has it?'

'That's what Jimmy said. He's as pleased as punch though, acting like a youngster again, according to Lydia. Apparently, he thinks it'll be just like old times. I don't think she's very pleased.'

'No, I can understand that. It's her patch now, isn't it? And here we are, muscling in. I assume you're happy to be SIO, Barry?'

'Of course. We'd better get started. The sooner, the better.'

'I'll be off, then. You and Rae get the low-down. Lend me Tommy to drive me back to HQ, will you? Let me know where you'll be setting things up. And keep Lydia sweet, Barry. You know she can be a bit touchy. I know you outrank her and we'll be running things, but do your best to keep her onside.'

Barry frowned. Did he really need reminding? 'You worry too much. We've always got on really well. And I don't think we need the full team here, not yet anyway. Maybe

Jackie? Ade's on a case in Taunton that needs his expertise. And Stevie's on holiday somewhere with his family. Back next week.'

'Fine. We'll call them in if we have to. It might not come to that, though. Not with Lydia, Jimmy and George around, and Tommy still with us. Though there might be a fly in that particular pot of ointment. Lydia told me on the phone just now that there was a serious incident of drink-spiking around the student pubs and clubs last night. Jimmy and George will probably run the probe into what went on, but she'll want to keep an eye on it. She sounded worried, as if there might be more to it. But she was off the phone before I could ask more.'

Barry waited a few minutes after Sophie left, then entered the old house with Rae Gregson, his DS. They needed to get a feel for the place, to soak up its atmosphere. Sometimes these joint investigations worked well, but too often inter-unit rivalry got in the way. That shouldn't happen for this particular case. After all, he and Rae knew the trio of Bournemouth detectives far too well for that. But better to be prepared. And he knew just how prickly Lydia could be at times, despite the reassurance he'd given Sophie Allen. He'd been Lydia's immediate boss once, in those dim and distant days when they both worked for Sophie. He knew the reason for the two women falling out all those years ago. Not that he'd ever breathed a word of it to anyone, not even to his wife, Gwen. Some things were best kept firmly hidden.

CHAPTER 3: DRUG SPIKE

'What are the details, boss?'

George steered the car away from Crawley Terrace and towards the town centre, a mile or so away.

'A bit sketchy,' Jimmy replied. 'An incident of drink-spiking over the weekend. In one of the new bars down by the cinema complex. The uniformed lot who were first on the scene were uneasy about it. Someone's in a coma up at the hospital. We'll need to check that out. Someone else reckons it wasn't just drink-spiking. One of the victims appears to have been jabbed late on Saturday night.'

'That's bad. I know it went on when I was a student here, but it sounds a lot worse now. I just don't understand it.'

'Some people are beyond rational understanding, George. You can try and take precautions against drink-spiking — you know, with your friends. Everyone agreeing to keep an eye on drinks. But jabbing is different. How do you go about preventing it? That might make it a targeted assault.'

George stayed silent, trying to remember if any of his student friends had been caught up as victims of so-called date-rape drugs. He couldn't recall any specific incidents, but he had been aware that the young women within his friendship group had tended to make joint arrangements when out clubbing. The problem had been that such plans often broke down once the group had consumed a few drinks and were in a venue with particularly good, upbeat music. The lure of the dancefloor had often been too strong. He recalled the sense of anger felt by his female friends. Why were such precautions necessary? Shouldn't people be free to enjoy an evening out without worrying about being drugged and attacked? It was a totally unacceptable situation, which had only got worse during the intervening years. He was aware that his own girlfriend, Jade Allen, currently faced the same problems in Oxford.

They reached the hospital entrance and quickly made their way to the main reception desk. They were expected, and were directed to the Intensive Care Unit. They spoke to a nurse who seemed very downbeat, then found themselves in the presence of a doctor. He was frowning.

'Holly Evans is on life support,' he told them. 'Things don't look good, to be honest.'

'Any idea what it was?' Jimmy asked.

The doctor shook his head. 'Still waiting for toxicology reports. The poor kid has got a weak heart though, probably since early childhood. She's been on medication for it for years. Nine out of ten people wouldn't have reacted in this way, to be honest. Maybe just passed out. But her? No chance, not with her heart already compromised.'

'We heard it was a jab rather than her drink being spiked. Is that right?'

'We think so. There's a pinprick on her upper right thigh. That's all I can say. Bibi, the nurse you met just now, spotted it. Bloody outrageous, if it was that. Drink-spiking is bad enough, but she wouldn't be in this state. It takes time to be absorbed through the stomach lining. But this? Straight into the bloodstream. The full whack, instantly.' He shook his head. 'Her parents were here until half an hour ago. They've gone back home to collect some stuff but will be back tomorrow. I think they intend to stay over in a local B&B for a few days. They live in Basingstoke.'

'Okay, thanks for your help.' Jimmy passed across a contact card. 'Can you keep us informed? We might be treating it as attempted murder, going by that information, though that'll be up to my boss.'

Jimmy suddenly realised that the DI making decisions was no longer the cautious and careful Kevin McGreedie. Lydia was in charge now, and rather more belligerent and confrontational than her predecessor. This particular incident would enrage her. He and George carefully noted all the details from the nurse, then he called her. Lydia's reaction was exactly as he'd expected. Anger, almost personal in its intensity. He could feel it pulsing within the way she spoke and the words she used. He closed the call and they made their way outside.

'Where to now?' George asked, as they walked back to the car.

'Witness statements from the people she was with. We keep our eyes open for discrepancies, according to the boss. *Sometimes predators masquerade as friends.* That's what she said. *Look out for the wolf in sheep's clothing.'*

They drove south from the hospital towards the town centre, then west to the university campus.

'You're the expert here, George. Weren't you a student at Bournemouth? Will it have changed much?'

'I wouldn't have thought so. It's only been a few years since I graduated.'

'What subject did you do?'

'Business and Finance. I had great hopes of becoming a financial whiz, playing the markets.' George laughed. 'Then reality hit home. It was okay once I started work but it didn't have much buzz. Then I met you lot when you were investigating Donna Goodenough's murder. It kind of intrigued me, what you were doing.'

'Who interviewed you? It couldn't have been me. I'd have remembered.'

George gave a wry smile as he guided the car into an empty parking slot. 'You and the boss. The chief super. She was a DCI back then. I don't think you said anything. She asked all the questions.'

'God, she was scary. Well, she still is.' Jimmy looked a bit sheepish, as if he'd momentarily forgotten that George was dating Sophie Allen's daughter. 'I didn't mean that the way it sounded. You're still with Jade, aren't you?'

George nodded warily. 'Yeah.'

'Don't take it the wrong way. The chief super's always played everything as straight as a die. But she's so totally in control, so efficient. I know this is a bit nosey, but how does it affect her dealings with you? I mean, with you dating Jade?'

George shrugged. 'It doesn't. At work she's the boss, the chief super. We don't cross paths very much. Then, when we're not at work, she's just my girlfriend's mum. It really isn't a problem. I'm used to it anyway, the double role. When I was at school, my own mum was a teacher there. French. I was in her class for a couple of years. Everyone was relaxed about it, even my friends. I had a few comments from some nutters, but I just ignored them and they stopped. I suppose this is similar.' He looked around him as they entered the administration offices. 'Still the same. Even some of the staff names.'

'It's a bit quiet in here, isn't it?'

'Monday,' George explained. 'Most of the students not at lectures will still be in bed.'

A member of staff appeared and looked at them enquiringly.

'DS Jimmy Melsom, and I'm DC George Warrander,' George said. Jimmy wondered if he was hoping for some recognition from the receptionist. It looked as though George remembered her face, but it didn't appear to be reciprocated.

'We were told to expect you,' she said. 'If you can just sign in, I'll take you to the Business Faculty office. I think the poor woman's fellow students have been asked to assemble there.'

'I know my way around,' George replied. 'I was a student here a few years ago, in Business. No need for you to come if you're busy.'

She gave him a cool look. 'I've been given clear instructions,' she replied. 'It's not a problem.'

The two detectives dutifully followed her across the campus and into the Business building. A small group of worried-looking students were clustered outside a seminar room and fell silent as they saw the trio approach. An older woman wearing a dark blue trouser suit stepped forward.

'Heather Munro, senior student welfare officer. I've done the best I can in getting the group together. Shall we go in? I'd like to stay, if that doesn't upset your plans.'

'That's fine,' Jimmy replied. 'We're just fact-finding at this stage.'

'What's the latest news about Holly? Is she going to be okay?' one of the women students asked.

'Still in a coma,' Jimmy replied. 'Let's all hope that she pulls through. And you are?'

'Josie Osegu,' came the reply. 'Holly was my best friend here. I was with her Saturday night. Well, we all were. That's why we're here. It's totally sick what happened. Something needs to be done. It's made us all feel unsafe. Well, the women anyway.'

'Men can have their drinks spiked too,' one of the male students said. 'It happens all the time. It's these morons who think it's just a bit of a laugh. They're sick in the head.'

Jimmy spoke up. 'Well, you're both right. But just now we have a serious assault against Holly to investigate, so can we focus on that, please? Let's get ourselves settled. I'm DS Jimmy Melsom. My colleague, DC Warrander here, will be taking notes, so I need to ask you to only speak one at a time to give him a chance. Anything to add, George?'

'Just that I was a student here until five years ago. I did a degree in Business and Finance, just like Holly and some of you, I expect. So I know my way around the local pub and club scene.'

Jimmy took over. 'Maybe you can start, Josie? Tell us how the evening started, where you were and who was there.'

'We met up in a pub first, up at the Triangle. Just for an hour or so.'

'What time was that?' George asked.

'About nine. Then we walked down to Suki's.'

'Is that by the cinema complex?' George asked.

'S'right. It's got a great DJ. Drinks are quite cheap too. That's where it happened. We were still in there at around midnight. We were having a really good time. Me, Holly, Daisy and Katie have a kind of plan, where one of us is always with the drinks. It's worked okay up to now. It means none of us has been spiked.'

'Sounds good to me,' Jimmy said.

'Yeah, but what we're worried about now is that if someone's dead set on spiking one of us, they'll use a jab, just like they did with Holly, 'cos they can't drop something in our drink. Surely it's worse?'

'Don't overthink it, Josie. You can't try to second-guess a nasty thug. All you can do is take sensible precautions. Which is what you did. So, what happened next?'

'Holly, me and Katie got up to dance. Oh, and Simon over there too.' One of the male students raised his hand. 'We had to push our way through a group of people stood around the dancefloor. That's when it must have happened. We'd just started dancing and Holly fell over. She couldn't get up. We called for help and the DJ stopped the music. Some security guys came across. We turned Holly onto her side. Her eyes were rolling. She was dribbling and shaking. Just like she was having a fit.' By now Josie was sobbing, her head in her hands. 'It was awful.'

'Are you saying that the jab you think she got may have come from someone in the group you had to push through to get to the dancefloor?'

'I guess so. That's what I kind of assumed. I didn't see it happen, though.'

Jimmy turned to the group as a whole. 'Did anyone see anything suspicious? Did you spot anyone appear to touch Holly at any time in the minutes before she collapsed?'

Simon spoke. 'I don't think any of us saw anything unusual.'

'Have you tested the drinks?' one of the other women said.

'The ones at your table were all secured by the club staff. They're under lock and key, and we'll be arranging forensic tests as soon as we can manage it. Anything else to add, anyone?'

There was no response, so Jimmy continued. 'In that case, we'll need all of you to supply us with your personal information. Full names and dates of birth. Term-time addresses. Home addresses. Phone numbers. Anything else you think might be relevant.'

There was a slight grumble from one or two of the group.

'This sounds more like a murder enquiry, like you see on the telly,' Daisy said.

Jimmy chose not to answer. He hoped it wouldn't become a murder investigation, but his instincts told him otherwise.

CHAPTER 4: SUKI'S BAR

'Where to now, boss?' George asked.

'The nightclub. Suki's, was it? I think I've been there once or twice. What about you?'

George shook his head. 'The name doesn't ring a bell from my time here. It's probably new.'

'It's in that development above the gardens, by the cinema. Places change hands there quite often.'

They were there inside twenty minutes, parking in a nearby cul-de-sac. The bar hadn't opened for trade yet, although the door was unlocked, and two cleaners were at work in different parts of the large room. George thought that the students they'd just left had done a good job in describing the layout. The dancefloor area, set to one side, was just as he'd imagined from their words. The whole place looked spacious now, but he could imagine that perception would disappear once it began to fill with people. Sitting, standing, dancing. Drinking and eating. Chatting, maybe even shouting to make themselves heard above the hubbub.

'Sorry, we're closed.' A voice sounded across the gap between the bar and the front door. A middle-aged, dark-haired woman was watching them from behind the bar.

'Police,' George replied.

He and Jimmy walked across.

'PC George Warrander. This is my boss, DS Jimmy Melsom. We're here about the incident on Saturday night. And you are?'

The woman's face fell. 'Angel Scarlotti. I'm the manager. Tragic. We do our best to keep that kind of thing out of here, so people feel safe. But it's just impossible to be a hundred per cent sure. How is she?'

George tried hard not to show what he was feeling. 'Still in a coma. We can but hope. We have a few questions for you.'

'Can I call a colleague across? He was behind the bar when it happened and was best placed to see what was going on.'

'Of course.'

Angel beckoned a heavily built man across. 'Bobby's my assistant manager. He wouldn't normally be here at this time in the morning. He's come in specially because of what happened. We were expecting a police visit.'

'Can we go somewhere more private?' Jimmy suggested. 'We've already got an idea of the layout. We can have another look a bit later if we need to.'

Angel led the way through a staff door to a small office.

'We just hope the young woman pulls through.' She looked at Jimmy hopefully, but George could see that he was ignoring Angel's hidden plea for information. Better to be cautious.

'How common is it, the use of these incapacitating drugs? From your point of view, I mean.'

'It's an absolute pain,' came the reply. 'I'm sure Bobby agrees. People want to feel safe when they're out. How can they enjoy themselves if they have to constantly be on their guard? I just don't understand it. It's a problem for all the bars around here, the ones that young people use. We try our best, but it never seems to kill the problem completely. In fact, Suki's has the best reputation in the area for safety. Bobby here has trained the security staff in the things to watch out for. So it came as a complete shock.'

25

George frowned. 'Do you think the victim was deliberately targeted? Is that what you're saying?'

Bobby spoke. His voice was a deep rumble. 'There were none of the usual signs of a random attack. We can often tell. There'll be a couple of lads who stick out a bit. Wandering around, their eyes always moving, weighing up the girls, looking for likely victims. We didn't see anyone like that Saturday night. They don't come in here often because they know they'll be spotted and given the heave-ho. We don't take any chances. Guys who behave like that, they're out. No arguments.'

'Our future depends on providing our customers with what they want,' Angel added. 'And that's a safe, relaxing place to enjoy themselves. That's why this incident has upset us so much. I just hope the situation isn't taking a turn for the worse. All the bars will suffer if that happens. People will stop coming out and the students will stay on campus.'

George turned to Bobby. 'Do you remember the group of students? The ones Holly was with?'

'Yeah. They're often in at weekends. Nice bunch. And she's one of the nicest. Really cheerful and pleasant. Generous too. They all seemed relaxed. Do you want to go back out into the bar area? I can show you where they were.'

The two detectives followed Angel and Bobby back into the main room. Bobby showed them where Holly's group had been sitting, then the direction she, Josie, Katie and Simon had used to move towards the dancefloor.

'Their route would have been a bit indirect,' Bobby said. 'There was a big group standing at the edge, watching. No trouble though, not from what I could see. But those four had to make their way around them.'

'Were there any guys who didn't seem to fit in?' Jimmy asked.

'Not really. So many of the young men who come in here have a similar look. It's a kind of gender norm, isn't it? Girls always try to look different from each other. Guys like to look almost the same. Weird, when you think about it.'

'So you can't remember a particular individual who stood out?'

'Not really. We had several hundred. It was busier than normal.'

'CCTV?'

'Of course. One camera at the entrance. One at the bar. Two covering the lounge area. One over the dancefloor.'

'Can we see?'

'In the office. Follow me. But I need to warn you that the dancefloor area was packed when the incident happened. We've already had a look.'

Jimmy and George followed the manager through to the security office where they watched closely as several sequences of Saturday night's recordings were played over, showing the moment when Holly collapsed, caught from different angles within the premises. Each sequence started in the same way, with shots of young people enjoying themselves. Chatting, moving, laughing, drinking, dancing. The DJ played a couple of Dua Lipa tracks and the dancefloor became very busy. Then there was a sudden shriek, and the atmosphere seemed to fracture. People stepped back from the middle of the dancefloor. Others moved towards the area, trying to see what was going on.

'I see what you mean,' Jimmy said. 'I'd like copies of all of this. We'll need to analyse it carefully. It may give us some leads. We've got CCTV experts and software that can extract individual figures and zoom in.' He took out a flash drive and copied the film sequences.

'You look as though you know what you're doing,' Angel said.

Jimmy grimaced. 'I was regularly given CCTV recordings to wade through back when I was a junior detective. Can't say I miss it.'

'Did your door staff notice anyone leaving in a hurry after the incident?' George asked.

'We thought of that too. But the answer's no. No one stood out. I've had a close look at the footage from the door camera and didn't spot anything suspicious. Maybe you will.'

'Thanks for all your help. We'll be in touch.'

* * *

Once they were back at base, Lydia listened carefully to what the two detectives had to say. She had a frown on her face.

'How did you get on, boss?' Jimmy asked.

'Oh, you know. Holly's parents still sounded crippled with worry. I want to go across to Basingstoke to see the home early tomorrow morning, if they agree. It'll give me a chance to see Holly's room.' She paused. 'The medics aren't optimistic. Apparently, the brain scans are worrying. If she does pull through, she might be brain damaged.' Lydia looked at her two juniors. 'We're thinking of classifying it as attempted murder. The powers-that-be will probably be happy with that. If she doesn't pull through, it becomes actual murder and WeSCU will get involved. But they're tied up with the young lad's body that you found in that terraced house, Jimmy. The chief super is happy to leave us handling this one at the moment. Even if the worst comes to the worst and Holly doesn't make it, she'll leave us in charge, initially anyway. She says that we have the necessary local knowledge. That's partly because of you, George, with your experience of the local club scene. By the way, how's your old boss, Rose Simons, getting on without you? Do you keep in touch?'

'It was her who encouraged me to make the move,' George replied. 'I know people think that I did it to get away from her, but it really wasn't that.'

'Not even a little bit?' Jimmy asked, trying not to grin.

'Well, I suppose there was a small element. She could be a bit hard to take at times. But she's a great cop. Very astute, underneath that brash exterior.'

'She's got another rookie to train up now,' Lydia added. 'Let's hope they're as understanding as you.'

* * *

Holly Evans had always coped well with her need for caution while growing up, not letting her heart weakness interfere with her enjoyment of life during her childhood and teenage years. She'd been able to participate regularly in a range of sporting activities, as long as she stayed within sensible limits of exertion, and was looking forward to a long and bright future. Whoever had jabbed her in the thigh with a synthetic drug might well have put paid to that.

Even though Holly's condition stabilised a little more that night, a decision was made the next morning to officially redefine her case as one of attempted murder. Lydia remained as the SIO but reported to Sophie Allen now. This meant that Jimmy Melsom's earlier observation had come true: the old 'dream team' had temporarily reformed, albeit in very different circumstances and in different roles. No wonder Jimmy was smiling a lot. His two earliest cases with Sophie Allen's unit had changed the way he felt about his job. He'd never told anyone at the time, but he'd been seriously considering quitting the police and travelling the world while he tried to identify a different future for himself. But his exposure to this most serious side of criminal investigations — murder — had changed his views and his life. He knew he owed so much to Barry, Lydia and his ex-boss, Sophie Allen. They'd shown him a different approach to work and life. On the surface he still had the same happy-go-lucky personality, but he'd developed a greater resilience and a deeper sense of shared responsibility during those early years. Qualities that were still with him, some six years later, now a detective sergeant in Lydia's squad.

'We need to identify everyone in the bar when Holly collapsed,' Lydia said. 'Not only who was there but where they were during the key moments.'

'A sort of floor plan but with people on it? I'm happy to work on that, boss.' George was keen to get stuck into something tangible.

'Fine. Get as much help from computer forensics as you need. We have to identify people. But before that, remember we need to visit Holly's home in Basingstoke to have a look at her room. Get your jacket, Jimmy. You're coming with me.'

* * *

The Evans family lived in the Kempshott area, on the south-west fringes of Basingstoke. It was close to the M3 motorway, so the two detectives arrived within an hour. A paved driveway ran alongside the well-maintained semi-detached house, leading to an attached garage with a deep-red door. A neatly trimmed lawn and a rose bed occupied the front garden area. It was one of the tidier house fronts in the street.

The door was opened almost as soon as Jimmy rang the bell.

'DS Jimmy Melsom, DI Lydia Pillay. Dorset Police,' Jimmy said to the woman at the door. He could see a resemblance to Holly.

'I'm Louise, Holly's aunt. I'm here trying to keep things together. They're in the back room. They're still really upset.'

Louise led them inside and down a narrow hallway. The rear room of the house had clearly been extended, with an open view through French windows to the small back garden, currently basking in the evening sunshine. Holly's parents were sitting on a couch, looking tired and drawn. *Carole and Mark*, Lydia thought. *That's if my memory isn't playing tricks.* She walked forward, extending her hand.

'No, don't get up. DI Lydia Pillay. This is my colleague, DS Jimmy Melsom.'

Despite Lydia's request, Holly's parents struggled to their feet.

'We need to move a bit more,' Holly's father said. 'It does no good sitting moping all the time. But we're finding it hard to think straight, both of us. Louise is my sister. She lives nearby.'

Carole, Holly's mother, looked as if she was about to faint, and it was no surprise when she sat back down, flopping into the seat heavily. She held her head in her hands and looked exhausted.

'We're here to offer our reassurances,' Lydia said. 'And to let you know that we'll do everything we can to get to the bottom of what happened. Holly's a lovely young woman, from all accounts, popular with all her friends. I'll be heading up the investigation, although we'll be liaising with WeSCU, the Wessex Serious Crimes Unit. Jimmy and I have worked alongside them a lot.'

Holly's father looked puzzled.

'Although we've announced to the press that it's an assault, we'll be running it as an attempted murder investigation at first. Everything done thoroughly with no cutting of corners. Only when we have all the evidence and someone in custody will the CPS make a decision as to the charges that will be brought against the perpetrator. I thought I'd let you know.' Lydia paused. 'Can we see Holly's room, please? We won't disturb anything, I promise. Anything we move, we'll put back.'

The aunt, Louise, led them upstairs, where they were shown into a small bedroom at the side of the house. It was decorated in a lemon colour and had a window overlooking the garage, with pale-yellow, floral curtains. They had a look through the drawers and cupboards but didn't expect to find anything useful. After all, Holly was well into her second year at university and had a room in a shared house with her close friends. Her more personal effects would be stored there, so any glimpse into her private life would tend to show up in Bournemouth rather than here in Basingstoke. And now obviously wasn't the best time to talk to her parents about their daughter's character. That could wait a day or two until Holly's state of health became clearer.

CHAPTER 5: STRONG EMOTIONS

Tuesday

Jackie Spring, WeSCU's newest recruit, arrived at the Bournemouth incident room after a two-and-a-half-hour drive from her home in Watchet, one that took her from the north coast of Somerset to the south coast of Dorset. Rae looked up as the middle-aged woman clattered into the room and dumped a bag of cream cakes onto a spare tabletop.

'You wicked person,' she said with a grimace.

Jackie laughed. 'I've been on the road since six. I just popped into Wareham on my way past, to that cake shop the chief super keeps going on about. She's right, you know. It's a real gem. And you don't have to eat any, boss. There'll be plenty of takers for the spare one if you forego the pleasure.'

'God, what a dilemma. There's me trying to control my waist size and there's you bringing in stuff like this.' Rae watched as first Jackie then Tommy grabbed a chocolate éclair and each started to lick the cream. 'Oh, to hell with it. My mental resilience isn't what it should be.'

'It's the kind of thing that gets us through the day, boss. A psychological boost, even if it's got a calorific drawback.'

'You're beginning to sound like the chief super. She's got an answer to everything.' Rae closed her eyes as she took a bite. 'Oh, heaven.' She pushed open the door to Barry's office. 'Boss, you need to be out here, right now. That naughty Jackie Spring has arrived with cream cakes. Is there a promotion in the offing?'

During the early coffee break that ensued, Barry and Rae updated Jackie on the investigation, that of the child's body in the old suitcase.

'That's just dreadful,' was Jackie's immediate response. 'Can you tell the ethnicity?'

'Probably white, European. It'll come out in the DNA profiling, I'm sure. That should be with us later today. We're assuming his name was Ian, based on the old note we found. But it's possible the note and the body aren't linked. Unlikely, though.'

Jackie finished her cake. 'So, what do you want me to do, boss?'

'Work with Tommy. Missing children, from way back. Fifteen to twenty years ago. Also, residents of the house from the same sort of timeframe. Who lived there? What did they do for a living? Rae will give you the low-down. And thanks for the cakes.' He turned to the rest of the team. 'Back to work, everyone.'

Rae drew Jackie to one side. 'There's another investigation going on, parallel to ours. A spiking incident in a club three nights ago. The victim's been in a coma since it happened. She's got some kind of heart issue. That's what makes these spiking attacks so bad. How do the people who do it know whether their victim is in good health or not? How do they know the possible effect? The local unit are handling it at present, but I wouldn't be surprised if we get drawn in. Have you got any experience of that kind of thing?'

Jackie shook her head. 'Not in Watchet. People get blotto on cider. Isn't drink-spiking more of a thing in big cities and university towns? I suppose the principle's the same, though. Get someone inebriated enough, then make a move on them.'

'This was a jabbing, with a hypodermic of some sort. One stage worse than drink-spiking, I guess. But don't spend any time on it at present. We've got this tragic lad's death to work on. I only told you so you're aware. As I said, we need a complete history of people who've lived in the house.'

Jackie moved across to Tommy to see how he was getting on. He was finding it slow-going. It was easy to find owners now that the Land Registry records had all been databased, but tracing rental tenants was a whole lot more difficult. Some only stayed a few months. Jackie knew that from her own personal history back in Watchet. She'd rented when she first arrived in the town but had fallen out with the landlord once she'd complained about the totally inadequate boiler and the appearance of mould on several walls and ceilings. She was one of the lucky ones. Money had come through from several sources and she'd been able to scrape together the deposit for a mortgage. If this place in Bournemouth was at all similar, it might have had dozens of different tenants during those few years that interested them.

Jackie began her own specific search. Rae had passed on a message from Lydia that the drug-addled killer she'd been interviewing, Pippa Chandler, had talked of being left the house in Crawley Terrace by her late Uncle Gus, who'd died just a few months ago, but it didn't look as though she'd ever lived there. Pippa claimed that she'd only bothered to visit a couple of times. With this in mind, Rae had asked Jackie to find out more about the uncle. The solicitors would be a good place to start. It meant that while Tommy was working forward from two decades earlier, she'd be working backward from the most recent owner. Hopefully they'd meet in the middle somewhere.

* * *

'I've got a list of the owners,' Tommy said at the afternoon briefing. 'I've gone back twenty-five years, probably further than needed. Anne Spedding owned it until then. She was the only owner-occupier. She was a nursing sister in the hospital but sold the property when she retired. I think she moved to a smaller place in Ringwood, but I haven't confirmed that yet. It was bought by a couple, Justin and Wendy Wilson, but they never lived in the place. It looks like they did some work on it and then rented it out. It got sold a few years later to Gus Gibson. He sometimes rented out rooms. He's Pippa Chandler's uncle, the one who left it to her in his will.'

Rae explained. 'This is the woman who's just been charged with the murder of her disabled landlord. Lydia's team have been dealing with that case. She stabbed and strangled Joshua Quick during an argument. Apparently, the house hasn't been lived in for several years and it's filthy. Whoever the last tenants were, they couldn't have cleaned it much, if at all.'

'Students?' Barry asked.

Rae shrugged. 'That's what we need to find out next. Who the people were who actually lived there. Any details from the post-mortem of the boy yet? We could do with a date, boss. Then we can tie it to a particular person.'

'Soon. That's what they tell me. They've still got dating experts poring over the remains. A horrible business. Remember there's no confirmation of the sex yet. The only reason we're thinking it's a boy is because of the name on the note — Ian.'

'Point taken.'

CHAPTER 6: NEW DRESS

Dorset has some attractive river systems. One of the major ones, the Stour, rises well north in the beautiful Stourhead Gardens in the neighbouring county of Wiltshire, then winds its way south-east, past the Dorset town of Blandford Forum. As it approaches the coast it turns more directly east, flowing well north of Bournemouth, then kinks southwards and ends up pouring its watery contents into Christchurch Harbour. The Stour forms a kind of natural barrier north of Bournemouth and makes for a very attractive rural setting, popular with retired people and families alike. Several villages exist near the river, although the creeping effect of urbanisation has long since joined them to create the single large area that makes for greater Bournemouth.

During the easterly part of its flow, the river follows a series of bends, and modern housing developments have sprouted up nearby, consisting largely of bungalows for retired people. But there are some older houses dotted around these estates, dating back to a time when the area was made up of small farming communities. In one of them lived Bruce Greenfield and his partner, Kim Brogan. Bruce, a reclusive man in his fifties, was a somewhat dour individual, slightly grey in the face. He seemed to lack any discernible personality, and the grey sheen to his face tended to reflect his character, or lack of it. He was currently sipping a mug of tea in his lounge, a gloomy room shaded from any direct sunlight by the tall, overgrown shrubs that crowded close to the window. He was studying the local newspaper. He didn't much like what he read in newspapers, particularly local ones. They seemed to be full of moaning whingers and spongers, people expecting something for nothing. He felt like complaining to Kim about it, but she was out shopping, something she did rather more often than she used to. Bruce hadn't considered the possibility that her frequent expeditions into town could be because he didn't really provide her with much in the way of cheerful companionship at home, and that his constant negativity was getting her down.

He turned to page two of the paper and came face to face with a headline about a child's long-dead body being found crammed into an old suitcase, along with a photo of the house at Crawley Terrace. His face paled noticeably, though no one else was in the house to observe it.

'Shit,' he muttered to himself. 'Shit. How could that have happened?'

He glanced nervously around, as if to check that he hadn't been overheard by anyone, despite having the house to himself. He re-read the story, more slowly and carefully this time, trying hard to hold back the feeling of mounting panic. What to do? When to do it? Who to contact? These questions whirled around in his head. He swallowed the remnants of his tea, now lukewarm. One thing was for sure. He had to do something. What had really been going on all those years ago? Gambling that the problem would disappear if ignored was no longer an option, not with the kind of forensic techniques now being used by the cops. He'd watched from afar as Dorset Police had reorganised their violent crime and murder units, avidly studying every regional newspaper for years. He'd even sat in the public gallery at some of the more significant court cases. It was clear that the current police squads were out-and-out professionals who would miss nothing. He'd need to stay one step ahead of them. And, if it came to it, he could always scarper. Cash everything in and maybe head abroad.

He heard the sound of a key turning in the front door lock. Kim, home from the shops. What to do about her? At one time he wouldn't have considered taking her with him if he had to do a runner. But now? He'd grown a bit too fond of her in his old age.

* * *

Kim dumped her shopping bags onto the hall carpet.

'I'm back,' she called.

Was that a grunted reply coming from the lounge? She walked through, to find Bruce straightening up from the chair he'd been sitting in.

'Fancy a cup of tea?' he asked. 'I could put the kettle on.'

She blinked. What was going on? He'd never offered to make her a tea before, not in the two years she'd been living in his house. He'd always made clear that that was her job, along with cooking, washing, grocery shopping and giving him regular Thai-style massages, as he called them. Were they Thai-inspired? She hadn't a clue. She just made it up as she went along, but those sessions obviously kept him sweet. Why the sudden change in outlook just now? Had he had some kind of brain malfunction? She tucked her blonde curls behind her ears.

'Great, babes. I'm parched. Gotta new dress, really sexy. Thought you'd like it. Need the loo kinda urgent. Do you want me to put it on now or wait 'til later?'

He frowned. 'Maybe later, after some food. What's for dinner?'

'I got us a lasagne. I'll stick it in the oven with some garlic bread, wait half an hour and hey presto! White wine, yeah?'

He frowned and shook his head. 'No, you silly cow. Not with lasagne. It needs to be red. You should know that.'

'Oh God, I wish I wasn't so stupid. I'll hop upstairs, shower and put the dinner on. Red wine with it. Then one of me Thai special massages. Okay, yeah?'

She wiggled her rump at him and laughed throatily, before heading briefly upstairs. A quick loo visit to relieve her bladder, then she entered the bedroom. She held the new dress up against her and looked in the mirror. Just the thing. Tight and clingy animal print that would show a lot of thigh, and even more cleavage. Bruce never complained, despite the expense. Easy to please, that had been her early judgement about her partner. Now she wasn't so sure. He was deeper than she'd realised, prone to dark moods. She suspected that thoughts swirled around in his head that she knew nothing about.

Kim had only moved in with him a couple of years earlier. She was already starting to wonder if she'd made the right decision. But what other options had been open to her? Left homeless when her husband had suddenly died, she'd found herself with unexpected debts and few options. Her informal agreement with Bruce had been something of a godsend, to be honest. She still went out occasionally with Doreen, her best friend, attending some kinky parties in plush hotels. Bruce thought she was on quiet weekend visits to rustic locations. In fact, she and Doreen were living the high life in Brighton, being wined and dined by wealthy businessmen. The appeal of that kind of life was fading though, especially since Doreen had started to drop out of the scene a few years previously. It was becoming too shallow and seedy, Doreen claimed. Kim wondered if there was more to Doreen's decision than that, but she never argued the point with her friend. You questioned Doreen's decisions and motives at your peril. She'd learned that the hard way early on in their friendship. And when Kim did disappear off for a weekend, Bruce never questioned her too closely on her return. No, Bruce had been a lucky find at just the right time, able to bring some stability back into her life. His offer for her to come and live with him had been a blessing in disguise. But now? Was he getting fed up with her? Or was it the exact opposite? Was this sudden change of attitude, signalled by the offer to make her a cup of tea, the start of something rather more permanent?

Kim sighed. Only time would tell. She sauntered down the stairs and found him carrying a tray through to the lounge. A teapot, for goodness' sake! Proper cups and saucers. A plate of biscuits. What was going on? What had come over him? Better not to ask, though. Not yet. She didn't want him flipping into one of his dark moods. Just go with the flow.

She picked up the newspaper and glanced at the page Bruce had been reading. God, how awful. A kiddie's body found mummified in an old suitcase. How weird was that? And in Crawley Terrace too. She knew that street. Bruce would know it too, only too well. She knew the street because her Gran had lived in the next road and Kim had often visited her as a child, even staying over sometimes. Her gran's home had been a refuge for her when growing up, used to escape the constant friction of her own home, with a domineering father and a mother who'd been all over the place in her approach to child-rearing. Kim had been devastated when her Gran died suddenly. There had been no other place to go. She'd put up with the tensions of living at home until she finished school at the age of sixteen, then she'd done a runner. It was only recently that she'd made some kind of peace with her parents, now well into their sixties. At least they were mellower now and seemed happier in themselves. Her father appeared to have lost most of his aggressive streak. Kim had even begun to wonder if she'd imagined it as a youngster. Had he simply wanted to keep her safe in an unsafe world? Had she, in fact, been too rebellious? Well, it was all water under the bridge now. One thing was for sure: neither of them liked Bruce. That was patently obvious.

* * *

Bruce had made a couple of phone calls to people he hadn't seen or spoken to for some time. Each short conversation followed a similar pattern. Had they seen the news about the body found in the house in Crawley Terrace? Did they know anything about it? Were they worried? Should he be concerned? What was anyone doing about it? Who was to blame?

This last question tended to be met with a short but awkward silence that told Bruce something. These people had obviously known about it, even if just from second-hand rumours. Even Chalky Busby, his closest pal in the old days, cleared his throat a lot during the few minutes of conversation. A dead giveaway. And Pippa Chandler? Bruce thought better of attempting to contact her. She was in custody for murder, according to a different newspaper story. That in itself was a real turn-up, though not a surprise, given her foul temper, violent disposition and liking for mind-altering drugs, even as a relative youngster. So she'd inherited that house? Left to her by old Gus Gibson. Who'd have guessed it? Bruce hadn't realised the two of them were uncle and niece. It explained a lot, though.

The key question, of course, was how much the cops knew. Or, more precisely, how much time and effort they were planning to put into finding out. It wasn't a reassuring thought. In recent years there'd been too many high-profile cases in the area, where various gangs had been taken down for fraud, intimidation and murder. It would need some careful planning if his old lot weren't to go the same way. And for more than a decade he'd conveniently forgotten about that kiddie. He felt like wringing someone's neck.

He picked up his phone once again, this time to look at flights to Spain. Maybe he'd reached the point when enough was enough and the sensible option was to scarper to warmer climes.

CHAPTER 7: EVIL

In the solitude of her cell the next morning, Pippa Chandler was starting to regret her decision to admit to the murder of Joshua Quick. Why had she owned up to it? She tried to recall the interview with the dark-skinned detective woman, but it was a hazy mess. She'd been coming down from a two-day drug bender and her brain had been all over the place, with dark and brooding fears flickering through her skull. Now, after some long-needed sleep, her thoughts were rather more lucid.

Or maybe it had been the right thing to do. The evidence had seemed overwhelming, that's what the brief had told her in a private conversation. Pleading guilty would reduce her sentence by a quarter, and that was certainly worth thinking about. If she could convince the judge that she'd been provoked by her partner's unwelcome and animalistic sexual needs, she stood a chance of getting an even lighter sentence. Even better if she blamed the drug use on him as well. Maybe say that Josh was the one who'd got her hooked? She'd just need to be imaginative in the lies she told. Counter all the accounts from friends, family and neighbours, who would say that Joshua could never harm a fly. She could respond by saying they were all outside the relationship, peering in. They couldn't know what he was like in the dead of night when the moon was out and the crack was flowing through his veins.

She almost laughed to herself. Joshua Quick taking drugs? Being violent? Not likely! But the judge wouldn't know that. If her plans all came together, she might get her sentence reduced to manslaughter and be out in six years.

She scratched her armpit. This cell was putrid. Something smelled rotten, like stale vomit. Maybe that was what it was. Whoever had been inside it before her had probably thrown up and it hadn't been cleaned properly. Fucking disgusting.

She heard the sound of footsteps approaching and one of the warders peered through the grille before unlocking the door.

'Someone to see you, Pippa. A couple of detectives. Come with me, please.'

* * *

Barry Marsh looked around at the sparse fittings and furnishings in the prison's interview room. It was always depressing, visiting a place like this. A discouraging room in a building devoid of hope. Inmates like zombies, many of them psychologically traumatised by being locked in their cells for much of each day. It wasn't as though he was a softie by any means, but surely some money put into rehabilitation and education programmes would be a good thing? Most of the inmates would be returned to the outside world at some point. Without the skills and knowledge to fit in with society, many of them would soon drift back into a life of crime, creating more stress for law-abiding people and more work for the police.

His thoughts were interrupted as the door opened and a warder led a stocky woman in a grey tracksuit into the room. The warder pointed at an empty chair situated across the table from where Barry and Jackie Spring were sitting, then stood by the door. So this was Pippa Chandler. Violent and manipulative, according to Lydia Pillay.

She sat down, eyeing the detectives suspiciously.

'What now?' she asked, as if her patience was being worn thin by constant interruptions to a busy, active and interesting day.

Barry looked up. 'Detective Chief Inspector Barry Marsh,' he said. 'This is DC Jackie Spring.'

Pippa looked at them warily. Barry got the distinct impression that she was deciding whether a show of good manners was worth it in the long run. She remained silent as she sat down. Lydia had been right. Pippa did have small, dark eyes. Eyes that looked as if they were always weighing up options, judging people. Her gaze flickered between him and Jackie.

'Your house in Crawley Terrace,' Barry said. 'Tell us about it.'

'Huh. Not much to tell,' grunted Pippa. 'S'been in the family a long time. My Uncle Gus had it for yonks. Now it's mine. Why d'you wanna know?'

'It's become a place of interest in a different investigation,' Barry replied. 'Our investigation, in fact. We're from WeSCU, the Wessex Serious Crimes Unit.'

Her reply was quick. Rather too quick, in fact. 'What's in it for me?'

She paused, her eyes now hooded and wary, as if seeking opportunities to exploit. 'What I mean is, is some kind of deal on offer?'

Barry was prepared for this. 'We can't change the course of the investigation in your own case, Pippa. All we can do is let the court know that you've helped us with a different one.'

'Yeah, but will you? I could tell you stuff, then you could do the dirty on me.' Her eyes narrowed.

'You'll just have to trust us.'

She watched him for almost a minute. 'Okay. What do you want to know?'

'Who left it to you and why? Who lived there and when?'

She snapped back at him. 'I already said. It was my Uncle Gus.'

'How was he related to you?'

'My mum's brother. They hated the sight of each other, but I got on with him okay. He gave me and my pals sweets when we was small. Then booze when we were a bit older. Then pills that he told us were sweets. They weren't.' She sniggered and looked at him through her lowered eyelids. There was an undercurrent here, something salacious.

'What was his full name?'

'Gus Gibson. Dunno if he had a middle name.'

'You got to know him quite well?'

She shrugged. 'As well as anybody. Better than most.'

'What was he like?'

She laughed throatily. 'Dirty-minded guy. Always thinking of sex. He'd fuck anything in a skirt, good-looking or not. Old, young, middling. He had me a couple of times, when I was out of my head on shit of some kind. That's when I was a youngster. Not lately. Even I have standards.'

Barry realised that she was watching them, gauging their reactions. Was it true, what she'd just told them?

'If children were being abused, we'll need to report it, Pippa. Even if he's dead, what you say will need checking out. Were others involved?'

'That's all I'm saying about it. That's not what you're here for, is it? It's a present for you.'

'Okay. It'll need to be investigated, so someone else might well be in to see you. Let's go back to the reason for us being here. How come you got to inherit the house?'

'He left it to me. For favours rendered.'

'Could you explain?'

Pippa shrugged. 'I did stuff for him. Collected stuff. Delivered stuff. Passed messages on. That kind of thing. No one else in the family would. There weren't many left, though. They'd all snuffed it. Cancer, heart attacks, diabetes, overdoses. You name it, they died from it. I might have a couple of cousins still alive, but the rest are all gone. Maybe he was grateful for what I did. Fuck knows I've never had a favour from anyone else in the family. It was about time.'

45

'Was anyone else living there with your uncle? In the last few years, I mean?'

She shook her head. 'Don't think so. No one could stand him, that's my guess. He smelled something awful. God knows how often he had a bath. Once a year, if that. Rancid bastard, even when he was younger. And the place was rancid too.'

'So you don't think he ever rented the house out? He lived there all the time?'

'S'what I remember. But he took in lodgers. Some right weirdos. They'd have to be to cope with living in that place, with him. I can't remember any names though, if that's what you're after. It was ages ago, and I was usually a bit blitzed when I was over there.'

Barry frowned. 'Okay. The place was a bit of a mess when I was there a couple of days ago, Pippa.'

'Yeah, well, his solicitors wondered about cleaning it up a bit, if it was goin' for sale. It was right scummy. They was goin' to dip into a pot of money he'd left. Not that he'd left much. They told me the place would sell for more if it was cleaned up, but I hadn't decided.' She paused, and her eyes once more flickered between the two detectives. 'Why do you want to know about the place? What's happened?'

'We found a body. A child about ten or eleven, maybe younger. It's been there a long time.'

Pippa's eyes widened and she screwed up her nose. 'Fuck. That's a turn-up. A youngster? Weird.' She shrugged slightly. 'Gus used kids as runners.'

'What do you mean?'

'You know, fetching stuff, carrying stuff around the town. The kind of things I did for him when I was a kid. But I wasn't around all the time. My mum didn't trust him, see. She knew what he was like. I didn't tell her I was round there.'

'Did you ever see someone about that age when you were there?'

Pippa gazed at him a moment. 'Nah. I was out of my head too much.'

'Ian. That was the name, we think.'

She shook her head. 'Don't remember nuffin' about an Ian.' Her eyes gave nothing away.

'Anything else you can tell us?'

Her gaze once again moved over the detectives, but she chose not to elaborate further, merely shaking her head.

'If you think of anything, get a message to us.'

'Well, that's gonna be tough, ain't it? Wiv me in here?'

'The prison governor has our details. It won't be hard.'

She stroked her lip, stood up and made for the door. Her closing comment was an over-the-shoulder remark to Jackie as a warder led her out of the interview room.

'You didn't say much. Cat got your tongue? Or scared to speak up in front of your boss?' Pippa sneered.

'Believe that if you want to, Pippa,' Jackie replied. 'Nothing you think or say bothers me, not really.'

'Ooh, get you, Miss Snooty.'

With that, she was led away by the warder.

'What did you think, Jackie?' Barry asked as they made their way out of the prison.

'Really hard to say, boss. She's probably a habitual liar. It could have all been true or a complete pack of lies. If you pushed me, I'd say she gave us a mixture of the two, but I couldn't say which bit was which. She's devious. She could have even killed that boy. She'd have been, what, about eighteen at the time?'

'And, by her own admission, sometimes out of her head on drugs and drink,' Barry replied. 'I agree with you, and with what Lydia told us. She's devious and manipulative. The word evil springs to mind.' He paused. 'My guess is that she does know something about the boy. Something about her manner changed during that bit of our conversation. Very slight, though. I may have imagined it.'

'I don't think you did. I didn't like her one bit. Nasty. I didn't spot anything about her that made me feel sympathetic to her situation. No obvious redeeming features. How do you even start to get through to someone like that? Make her realise that she's ruining her own life by the choices she keeps making?'

Barry shrugged. 'It's too late now, anyway. The murder of this Joshua Quick character is cut and dried, according to Lydia and Jimmy. Pippa might be trying to dream up extenuating circumstances, but it isn't going to work, not in any significant way. I don't think she can hide her true nature for long. Think of that remark she made to you at the end. What was the point of it? Did it help her relationship with us, was it to her benefit? Of course not. The same thing's likely to happen in her court case. Sooner or later her nasty side will come out under questioning, and she'll turn any judge or jury against her. I've seen it all before, too many times.'

CHAPTER 8: SICK

DI Lydia Pillay was examining a large, enhanced image extracted as a still from the CCTV footage generated by a camera situated to one side of the dance area at Suki's Bar. It showed the young victim, Holly Evans, easily identified in her sapphire-blue strappy dress, as she pushed through a group of young men standing on the edge of the dancefloor.

'If we assume it was someone from this group who jabbed her, then we need to identify them and talk to all six. But not in a group. We'll see them separately. How are we getting on with the identification?'

Jimmy Melsom pointed to the tallest figure among the cluster of young men. 'Wayne Silverman,' he said. 'We think he's the dominant personality in the group, but that's only a guess, from watching the CCTV footage. Economics student.'

Lydia took another look at the man. He was tall, she thought, maybe around six foot two or so? Fair hair falling in an unruly mop over his forehead.

Jimmy continued. 'He's on the right-hand edge of the group. Holly doesn't really get close to him as she pushes past. You can see she's much closer to these two. We think they'd been talking to each other, but she moved between them, causing them to step back.'

He pointed to two young men, one either side of the slim figure in the blue dress.

'The one to Holly's left is Dan Morrow. Fair hair and pale skin, grey chinos and a striped top. We don't yet know the other one, or any of the others in the group. But we're making progress.'

Lydia looked more closely at the man standing to Holly's right. Short brown hair, pale-blue denim trousers and a mid-blue T-shirt. He, too, looked tanned.

'How does this drink-spiking business work?' she said. 'What's the usual order of events?'

George explained. 'The perpetrator hangs around, waiting for it to take effect. Offers to act as a friendly taxi service to get the drugged woman home. Assures all her friends that she'll be perfectly safe. Everyone thinks she's just a bit drunk.'

'I can follow that, if he's completely unknown in the place. But these guys were known to the staff, weren't they? He'd be identified, surely? If so, what was the motive? Rape? Once he got her out of the club and had her somewhere quiet?'

'Maybe one or two of the others were in on the plan,' George mused.

'Hmm. And was she targeted or was she just in the wrong place at the wrong time? Too many questions. For now, just get that group identified and speak to them all. We need answers, and quickly. Otherwise, I'll have Sophie Allen breathing down my neck, and I'm trying to run an independent unit here.'

* * *

Wayne Silverman seemed happy to answer the detectives' questions when they visited him in his room in the student accommodation block at lunchtime.

'Yeah, God, I saw something happened, but other people had more first-aid skills than me, so I let them get on with it. Really bad, what happened to her.'

Jimmy watched him carefully. 'We're treating it as attempted murder.'

Silverman turned visibly pale and put his head in his hands. 'What? But why? Didn't she just collapse?'

'Someone jabbed her with a needle just beforehand.'

'What? One of these date-rape drugs? Is that what you're saying?'

'Something like that. You can see why we're pushing for information.'

The man ran his fingers through his hair. 'God, that's a shock. But I really didn't know her. I'll try my best to answer all your questions, but I can't see how I can help you.'

'Just a minute or two before she collapsed, she walked through the middle of your group of friends. You were standing on the edge of the dancefloor. We need to identify everyone you were with.'

George pushed some books aside and laid a copy of the photo on the desk surface.

Jimmy spoke. 'This is the best CCTV image we have. It shows you and your friends, with Holly walking through the middle of you all. We want the names of everyone in the group. You can see we've labelled all the figures with letters. Let's start over here on the left.' He tapped the photo with a finger. 'Who's this?'

'Leon Pawlowski.'

'Is he a student?'

Wayne nodded. 'Computing. Second year.'

'Is he in halls or renting privately?'

'Neither. He still lives at home. Ringwood, I think.'

George was busy making notes.

'Person B,' Jimmy said when George finished, moving his finger.

'That's Alex Winyard. Psychology, possibly? He's got a room the level below mine, here in this block. He's in his final year.'

Jimmy moved his finger again.

'Dan Morrow.' Wayne was frowning. 'He wouldn't do something like this. He's a really nice guy and very popular with the girls. Anyway, he's got a girlfriend. She joined us later.'

'Details?' Jimmy said.

'Sports Therapy, I think. He's nuts about anything to do with sport. A real fitness freak.'

'Where does he live?'

'He shares a flat with his girlfriend. She's loaded. Rich family.'

'Okay. Next one?'

'D? I don't really know him. He's not a regular in our group. He came along with one of the others. I think his name's Curtis, but I can't be sure.'

'Is he a student?'

Wayne shrugged. 'I don't know. Maybe one of the others knows more.'

'It looks as though he was talking to Dan Morrow,' George said. 'Did he come with him?'

A frown. 'I don't think so. He said something about tennis. That got Dan's interest. But he might have come with one of the others. I can't remember who, though.' The frown deepened. 'You know, he might not have come with anyone. It's possible he latched onto us once we were inside Suki's.'

Jimmy took over. 'Have you ever seen him before? Either in Suki's or some other place?'

'Yeah, well, he did seem a bit familiar, so I've obviously seen him somewhere. Maybe in another club, maybe on campus. Sorry I can't be more definite.'

Jimmy moved his finger. 'Person E?'

'That's Ollie Morgan. Welsh. Great guy. You can see we're talking. Doing Psychology, like Alex. I remember now. Alex is definitely doing Psychology. That's how they know each other. He's only in his second year, though. They're on some student committee together, one for Psychology students.'

'In halls?'

'I don't think so. Ollie house-shares, I think. Don't know where, though.'

'How did you all meet up that evening?'

'Dan and I had a pint in a pub a bit earlier. It's round the corner from Suki's. Ollie met us there just as we were leaving. The three of us walked over to Suki's.'

'Does that mean Leon and Alex came together a bit later?'

Wayne scratched his head. 'I think so. That would make sense. They're pally. But it was only a few minutes after us. I think we were still queuing at the bar when they arrived.' He paused. 'That might've been when the other guy arrived. I kind of assumed he was with Leon and Alex.'

'What else do you remember from that night?' Jimmy asked.

Wayne shook his head. 'I can't help much. It was a good atmosphere in Suki's. Everyone was happy, you know? It was a bit of a shock when that girl collapsed. The place went a bit mental. No one knew what to do. Then the medics arrived.'

'Can you describe what happened? Did you have a good view of her?'

'Sort of. There was someone in front of me, but I could see over his head. I was looking at her, if I'm being honest. She looked stunning in the dress she was wearing. One moment she was dancing, then she lurched a bit. It looked as if she was trying to stay upright but was losing control of her legs. She just slumped down on the floor as if she was sitting down. Then she slipped over sideways. There was obviously something wrong. Then her friends converged around her and shouted for help.'

'Did you stay together as a group after that? All six of you?'

Wayne rubbed his forehead. 'Not really. Dan and I hung around to see if we could help. Dan knows a bit of first aid from his course. But there were a couple of people there who knew what they were doing, so we didn't really get involved. Leon joined us a bit later and we left. Went back to the previous pub 'cos everything had stopped at Suki's.'

'You don't know what the others did?'

A shake of the head. 'No. Are you serious about it being attempted murder?'

'Yes. We've reason to believe she was deliberately targeted.'

'That's pretty shit. I hope you catch whoever did it. It's sick.'

The two detectives visited Alex Winyard's room before returning to their car but there was no answer. They decided to split up for the next hour or two.

CHAPTER 9: QUESTIONS

Leon Pawlowski didn't look like a typical computer geek, with a diet of burgers, crisps and coke, and rare trips out into the fresh air. He had a clear complexion, wavy fair hair, and seemed happy to chat. *I shouldn't take these stereotypes seriously*, George thought to himself. Wayne Silverman had said that Leon lived at home still, despite being in the second year of his degree. Maybe that was the reason for his clean-cut appearance. Good food prepared by his parents. They probably did his laundry too. George wondered if he was being too judgemental.

'Do you have a few minutes, Mr Pawlowski?' he asked. 'We're chasing up everyone who was in Suki's Bar a few days ago when the young woman student collapsed.'

'I heard her drink was spiked,' came the reply from Leon. 'Totally awful. How is she?'

'Not good news, I'm afraid. She had a turn for the worse last night. She's hanging on by a thread. It'll probably be on the local news tonight.'

'God. That's the pits. Some of the others said she was a nice-looking girl. I didn't know her, though.'

'I just want your recollections of what happened that night.'

'To be honest, I didn't see much. I was chatting with Alex when it happened.'

'When what happened?'

Leon looked puzzled. 'When she fell over.'

'What about a minute or two earlier? She walked through the middle of your group so she could get to the dancefloor. Did you notice her then? Others have told us that she looked quite striking.'

The student shook his head. 'No, didn't spot her at all. I'm not a very observant person, to be honest. I sometimes miss stuff that's going on right next to me.'

'What were you talking to Alex about?'

Leon shrugged. 'Sorry. Can't remember. Something pretty stupid, I expect. Alex is into one-liner jokes and uses me as a test dummy. He's trying to put together an act for a stand-up comedy night.'

'Any good?'

Leon looked at the detective with renewed interest. 'Surprisingly, yeah. Though I think he should go for longer stuff. You know, monologues and personal stories. Maybe an occasional one-liner is okay, but they get a bit boring after a while. And Alex sometimes dreams up bizarre situations.'

'Who else was around you, in your group?'

A frown crossed his face. 'The usual crowd. Wayne, Ollie and Dan. Me and Alex, of course.'

'There seems to be a sixth person with you.' George pulled the photo out and pointed to the other figure.

'Don't really know him. He's been around a few times recently, but I don't know much about him. He talked to Dan, I think. His name might be Chris or Curtis. Something like that.'

'Have you chatted to him at all?'

Leon shrugged. 'Not really. Just to say hi. Nothing more.'

'Have you talked to any of the others about him? Have they said anything?'

A shake of the head. 'Not really. Dan might know more. He was talking to the guy that evening.'

'Okay, thanks. Anything else you can think of that might be helpful?'

'Don't think so.'

'Let me know if anything does occur to you.'

'If it was only spiking, why is she so unwell? Don't people get over that kind of stuff?'

'Usually. But not always. We all have different body types and metabolisms, Leon, so we react to drugs in different ways. It's unpredictable. I'm not saying any more.'

* * *

George's boss, Jimmy Melsom, was visiting a terraced house near the campus, one divided into four student flats. He found the room he was looking for.

'Ollie Morgan?' he asked, as the door was opened by a dishevelled-looking young man wearing a creased shirt that was in dire need of ironing. Jimmy thought he was swarthy-looking, rather like a buccaneer of old.

The student nodded, then yawned. Had he only just got out of bed or was it due to several hours of studying at a desk?

'Sorry,' he said, rubbing his chin. 'Slept late. Stayed up working on an essay last night.'

'I'm DS Jimmy Melsom. Can I come in? You witnessed an incident in Suki's Bar a few nights ago and I'd like to hear your take on things.'

Ollie stood back and waved his hand in a vague manner, looking puzzled.

'I didn't see much,' he said, following Jimmy into the room.

Jimmy had expected to see a dishevelled mess of books, clothes and student paraphernalia in the small room, but it was surprisingly tidy. *Mustn't prejudge*, he thought to himself. *Bad habit.*

'You're talking about that girl who collapsed?' Ollie asked.

'That's right. She's in a really bad way.'

'Oh. God. That's tragic. Bloody awful.'

'She walked through the middle of your group of friends as she reached the dancefloor. She collapsed a couple of minutes later. Did you notice her?'

Ollie rubbed his chin. 'Yeah, I did. She was a bit of a looker, and she caught my eye as she came towards us. I think she had another girl with her. A friend, I guess. They were giggling about something.'

'Your group was blocking her route.'

'We weren't actually blocking her, not deliberately, anyway. We were just chatting and sort of watching who was dancing. I think we moved aside to let her through.' He looked puzzled and worried.

'Had you seen her before?'

'I don't know. Well, I don't remember her. But she stood out a bit that night.' He paused and put a hand to his head, somewhat melodramatically. 'I didn't mean that the way it came out. I mean she looked stunning, not that she fell over. Why are the police involved? Didn't she just collapse? Or was there something else?'

'She was probably drugged against her will. Spiked, we think. Would you know anything about that?'

Ollie's face darkened. 'Of course not. I think that kind of thing's the pits. No one should have that done to them. Did she have a bad reaction to the spiking drug?'

Jimmy nodded. 'Afraid so. So this has become a serious investigation. Your group was the last she passed before getting onto the dancefloor.'

'Yeah, but it wouldn't be any of us. I know these guys. They're all good people. They just wouldn't. I know it.'

Jimmy laid the photo extracted from the CCTV system on the desk. 'Tell me who all these people are, please.'

'Are we suspects or something?'

'Look, Mr Morgan, we have to account for everyone there and check them. You can understand that, surely? It's a process we have to follow. That poor girl was deliberately targeted, and we intend to investigate the circumstances thoroughly. It's not a guessing game. She deserves justice. Don't you agree?'

'Of course I do. Okay, I'll tell you who these guys are. But you're wasting your time. It wasn't any of us.' He pointed to the figures in turn. 'Leon Pawlowski, Alex Winyard, Dan Morrow, me, then Wayne Silverman.'

'Who's the guy in the middle standing right next to Holly as she walks through?'

'I really don't know. Some guy who got talking to Dan at the bar, I guess. Maybe he followed us across. He was a bit of a pain, to be honest.'

'In what way?'

'He didn't pay for any drinks. That was after Dan bought him one. Dan's too good-natured to make a thing about it, but I noticed.'

'Do you remember his name?'

'Craig. Curtis. Something like that. I wasn't interested in his name, to be honest. I don't like guys like him. People who don't play fair with the cash.'

'Have you seen him before?'

'Think so. Maybe the previous weekend? In a different bar, though. He hooked up with Dan then, too. Well, for a while. Then he skedaddled. A bit of a loser, I thought.'

'Anything else about him that you remember? Whether he's a student? Where he lives? What his interests are?'

'No.' Ollie's reply was short and sharp. This was intriguing.

'Has he done something to upset you? Your dislike comes across loud and clear.'

Ollie glowered. 'I just don't like people who don't pay their fair share. That's all it is. If guys take drinks from others, they should do their bit in return.'

Jimmy waited, feeling instinctively that there was more.

'There's something about him I don't like,' Ollie finally said. 'I don't know what it is, not clearly. I just feel I can't trust him.' He clammed up.

'You must have a reason for feeling like that,' Jimmy suggested.

'Yeah, I suppose. I saw him in a shop once, down in the town centre. I'm sure he was lifting stuff. That kind of thing makes me uneasy. My parents run a corner shop back in Cardiff. They work their socks off. So do I when I help them in the holidays. Shoplifting's getting worse and no one seems to do anything about it. It really worries them. They don't know if they can keep the shop going in the long run. It's not right. The local cops should do more. It makes me angry, even more than them. My mum just shrugs her shoulders and says it's part of some people's nature. But worrying about it is really having an effect on my dad's health.'

Jimmy merely nodded in agreement. He really didn't want to comment, particularly on Ollie's criticism of the police. He knew full well that most cops did what they could in the time available and with the resources they had to hand. If people wanted a more effective crime and justice system, they'd need to show a willingness to pay more for it, and that wasn't forthcoming in any recent poll.

CHAPTER 10: PICKING ON US

Jimmy had expected Dan Morrow to be a cross between a surfer dude and a football star — sleek, tanned and muscular — although it had been difficult to make out any details from the photo. The young man wasn't like that at all. He was thin and had fair skin, as if he didn't get enough sun. His pale ginger hair corkscrewed out from his head.

Dan stared suspiciously at the detective standing in the doorway. 'Yeah, I know why you're here. Someone's just messaged me. It's about the girl, isn't it? She's still in a coma. Is that right?'

Jimmy nodded. 'Can I come in?'

'Well, you're here now. I can't really keep you out, can I?'

The flat seemed surprisingly untidy, with books, clothes and sports magazines piled up on every available surface.

'Why would you want to keep me out, Mr Morrow?'

The young man shrugged. 'Cops always seem to have it in for me.'

'Your friends have all been co-operative,' Jimmy said. 'They've been very open. They seem to want to help us get to the bottom of the events at Suki's. Do you feel differently, then?'

'No. But you cops shouldn't be picking on us. There were loads of people there that night.'

'And we'll be speaking to all of them. Maybe this might explain why we're talking to your group first.' Jimmy took the photo out of his pocket and placed it on the desktop. 'This is a still from the bar's CCTV. There's the young woman who collapsed, making her way to the dance area. Moving right through your group. Directly next to you, in fact.'

'So what? It was busy in there. Lots of people passed close by. She wasn't the only one.'

'She was spiked, Mr Morrow. Someone jabbed her with a needle, and she collapsed soon after. Her name is Holly. She's still in a coma and her prognosis is not good. Maybe you don't fully realise how serious that makes it. I have a duty to her and her family to find out who did it. If we have to tread on toes to get the information we need, then so be it. But I don't really understand why it should cause resentment. Do you have something to hide?'

'Of course not,' Dan blustered.

'Well, I suggest you get rid of the petulant attitude. It comes as a bit of a surprise. Some of your friends describe you as a really nice guy, so why the backchat?'

Dan looked close to tears. 'It's not relevant and it's not connected to this in any way.'

'Well, in that case, can I suggest we start again?' Jimmy paused for a few seconds. 'Can I have your help in an investigation I'm on, Mr Morrow? Into the assault of a young woman who was spiked with a drug at Suki's Bar a couple of nights ago?' He pointed at the photo. 'Who are these people?'

Dan took a deep breath, then spoke more calmly. 'Leon on the left. Alex, then me. The girl. Is that her, the one who collapsed? I didn't realise she passed so close. Curtis. Then Ollie and Wayne.' He was frowning.

'This Curtis,' Jimmy said, pointing at the figure in the photo. 'Is he a regular member of your group?'

'No. I got to know him playing snooker in one of the local clubs. The other guys prefer pool in a pub.'

'Is he a student?'

'I don't think so, but I can't be sure. He doesn't say much about himself. He's only an acquaintance, not a friend. If we bump into each other, we chat for a while. But I don't go out of my way to find him. He's not a member of the group, even though you might think so from the photo.'

'What did you talk about that night?'

Dan shrugged. 'I can't remember. Nothing important.'

'Did you or he get annoyed when Holly pushed between you?'

'Of course not. It was crowded. That's what it's always like. You get used to it. God, if you got angry whenever anyone got too close, you'd be in a constant rage.' He suddenly stopped speaking and frowned.

'What is it?' Jimmy asked.

'Him. Curtis. I think he said, "She's hot." He watched her walk away. She was really stunning, to be honest.'

'She's still in hospital, Dan. She collapsed three minutes after passing you both by. She may never recover.'

Dan seemed to take stock for a few seconds, furrowing his brow. 'Well, it wasn't me. I can't vouch for the other guy, Curtis. I don't think he'd do something like that, but I don't know him well enough to be sure.'

'Do you know his surname?'

Dan shook his head. 'No.'

'Where he lives?'

Again, a shake of the head. 'I don't even have his mobile number, before you ask. He doesn't give much away.'

'Someone said your girlfriend arrived later in the evening. Is that right?'

Dan's face darkened. 'Yeah. Well, she's my ex-girlfriend now. We had a row yesterday and she told me we were over.'

'Is that the reason for you feeling a bit stressed?'

'Yeah. I've been given my marching orders. That's the only reason you've found me here this morning. I'm getting all my stuff. Dunno where I can go next. Maybe one of the others will let me kip down on their floor until I get things sorted.'

Jimmy looked around. It was a pleasant and roomy flat from what he could see. Well-furnished too.

'Where's your ex-girlfriend now?'

'In town somewhere. She gave me two hours this morning to clear my stuff out.'

Dan looked more than a little lost. Jimmy realised that he'd caught the young man at a vulnerable time.

'What's her name?'

'Tanya. Tanya Hancock.' His eyes dropped and he looked around, almost despairingly. 'I've been living here for nearly a year. It's her flat.'

'It is a nice place,' Jimmy said. 'But I'm sure you'll bounce back. What brought things to a head, if you don't mind me asking?'

'Some other bloke, I think. But she won't tell me who.' He looked forlorn, as if all the self-confidence had been knocked out of him.

Jimmy decided not to share his thoughts on probable reasons as to why she wouldn't tell him her new beau's name. That either Tanya was worried that Dan would seek out her new boyfriend and look for some kind of revenge, or that her new boyfriend was someone Dan knew.

'I know it won't help in the short term, but you'll get over it in time. It happens to the best of us, Dan. Contact me if you remember anything,' Jimmy said as he left.

'Is that likely?' came the reply. 'I can't think straight at the moment.'

* * *

Jimmy and George met up later that morning, outside the residential block where Alex Winyard lived. Maybe he'd be back by now. They entered and made their way to his room and George knocked on his door. This time there was the unmistakable sound of movement inside and the door opened.

'Alex Winyard?' George asked, holding out his warrant card for inspection. 'I'm DC George Warrander. This is DS Jimmy Melsom. Can we come in and speak to you, please?'

Alex was tall, gangly even. He wore black-framed spectacles that gave him a studious look. He wasn't wearing them in the CCTV sequence from the night of the attack on Holly. George thought that he looked older and more mature than his friends. Not really a surprise, given the fact that he was in his final year. And if he was on a sandwich degree, he'd have spent a year out on a placement. That might make him at least two years older than any of the others.

'Of course.' Alex pulled the door fully open and ushered the two detectives inside. 'I expect this is about the incident at Suki's on Saturday night. Wayne called me about it and told me to expect you.'

George glanced around. The room was cleaner and tidier than some of the others they'd visited. Did that reflect the extra maturity Alex had? Or was he just more particular about his living conditions?

Jimmy started the questioning. He took out the still image from the CCTV extract and laid it on the desk in front of them.

'This is why we're speaking to everyone in your group of friends. Holly had to push through you all to get to the area where people dance. The six of you are standing right in the middle of the access route, blocking it. How did that happen?'

Alex shrugged. 'I don't know. It wasn't deliberate, if that's what you mean. The place was packed. We just got our drinks and moved away from the bar. All the tables were full and a lot of people were standing talking. We just seemed to end up there. I guess I just followed the others. It was probably Wayne who led the way.'

That made sense, Jimmy thought. He was on the right-hand end, furthest from the bar, and that would suggest he'd moved away first.

'What were you talking about?'

Alex shook his head slightly, as if trying to clear his thoughts. 'I'd just finished talking to Ollie about my placement year and how it helped to sharpen my understanding of the course I'm on. He moved on to chat with Wayne about something. I wanted to check in with Dan.'

'About what?'

Alex seemed taken aback by this question. 'Is it important?'

'It might be. You have to let me be the judge of that.'

'If you must know, I'd heard some rumours that Dan's girlfriend had been seen out with someone else. I didn't tell him that, but I wanted to find out if he was okay.'

'And was he?'

'Yeah. I kept it very general. You know, how were things? How was his girlfriend? He was obviously oblivious to the gossip.'

'That makes sense. And it reflects well on you, Alex, that you should be concerned about your friends. Now, take a look at the photo. Tell me who's who.'

The man identified his friends quickly but hesitated about the stranger in their midst. 'Curtis? I can't be sure. He was chatting about tennis with Dan.'

'Did Holly say anything as she passed by? Did she have to ask any of your group to move?'

Alex shook his head. 'Dan spotted her coming. He moved out of her way. The other guy didn't budge. I remember that.'

'So you were watching quite closely?'

Alex frowned again. 'She was quite memorable. Really lovely. Sort of sweet looking. Someone else was behind her — a friend, I guess. They were moving to the dancefloor beside us, as you've already said.'

'What happened then?'

'We continued chatting. Then I heard a rumpus and people moved. Someone had collapsed but I couldn't see who. It was a few minutes before I realised. Staff from the bar got there quite quickly, so I stayed back. Nothing much I could do to help, to be honest.'

'Is there anything else you remember? Anything that might help us?'

Alex shook his head. 'Not really. I wish I could.'

'Get in contact quickly if anything does occur to you.' Jimmy handed over a contact card and the two detectives left.

'What did you think, George?' he asked as they walked out towards the car.

'Very helpful. Very factual. But also very controlled. I think he was ready for us.'

'He told us that Wayne Silverman had already called him.'

'I didn't just mean that. His whole attitude was careful. I wonder if he's always like that.'

'Interesting point. And we need to follow up on Dan Morrow. He said to me that cops always seem to have it in for him. I wonder if he's been in trouble before.'

CHAPTER 11: JUSTICE FOR JAN

Sophie Allen and Barry Marsh were sharing a coffee with Benny Goodall, Dorset's senior forensic pathologist.

'Things are taking longer than usual? Much longer?' Sophie sounded disappointed.

'Of course. Bodies that are in such a desiccated state don't crop up very often, Sophie. And all the literature is based on adults, not malnourished children. I need to do things step by step.'

'Well, at least can you tell us whether he was malnourished?'

'Probably. Teeth in a poor state. Some of the bones not any better. We got that from X-rays. They showed low density.'

'Lack of calcium, then?'

'Looks like it. I'm already worried that I've said too much.'

'Too much? You've hardly said anything at all.' Sophie's tone of voice showed her sense of frustration.

Benny screwed up his face. 'I can see you're irritated. But we can only proceed at the speed at which information becomes available to us. And you do need to be careful about jumping to conclusions on this one, Sophie. I don't mean you specifically. I mean your team.'

'What on earth do you mean?' Sophie's voice was raised.

'You're assuming the body's that of a boy. It isn't. It's a girl. I did sneak a body scan last night. I called in a few favours and got access at three this morning.'

'For goodness' sake.' She looked at Barry. 'How did this happen?'

Barry looked horror-struck. 'The name on the letter. Ian. And the clothes were boys'. Cropped hair too.'

'Too easy an assumption, I guess. And no wonder you look tired, Benny. Sorry for shouting at you like that. I should have known better. You've never let me down.'

'And I hope I never will.' He took a sip of coffee.

Barry took over. 'So did the body scan show anything else useful?'

'I'll have more details within a couple of hours. I guessed you'd have wanted it done for the extra information it might give us, particularly on the skin residue. You mentioned a written note that had been found and the possibility of burn marks on the skin. They might show up in some way. I also wanted to have a check on the internal organs, looking for damage. Graham Lampard's emailing me with the results. He's the senior radiology consultant and spotted a sudden cancellation for last night.' He paused and looked at Sophie. 'He's got a weakness for fine wines from Alsace.'

'Is that a hint, Benny?' Sophie replied.

'Well, he came in himself. Unheard of, to be honest, at that time of night.'

'Okay. I'll see what I can do.'

'He wants to go on the next birdwatching trip to Arne.'

Sophie was looking bemused. 'So?'

'Martin's the current club secretary. Graham missed the cut-off date for signing up. It's the trip with the Osprey expert.'

Sophie rolled her eyes. 'And you want me to bully my husband into adding him to the list? You don't expect much, do you? You know Martin's prickly about these things. You are his best friend, after all. Why didn't you ask him?'

Benny looked exasperated. 'It has to involve you, Sophie. Graham's done a favour for you, not me or Martin.'

'Okay, okay,' she snapped. 'I'll do it. Though I don't know what inducement I can use.' She paused and looked Benny in the eye. 'Don't say it. I know what you're thinking but just don't mention it. Or any other kind of inducement that might pop up in that peculiar brain of yours. Bloody hell. The things I have to do.' She switched her gaze to WeSCU's bemused-looking number two. 'Forget this conversation, Barry. You never heard it.'

* * *

'That's the burn marks confirmed,' Sophie said to the rest of the WeSCU team as they gathered for a late-morning briefing. She was flicking through the pages of a thin summary report from the scan.

'So that note was right,' Barry said. 'The boy, as we thought then, was being tortured. Any information on how she died?'

'Broken leg, fractured arm. Several severe head injuries that were probably fatal.'

'That's awful,' Jackie said. 'Who would do that to a child?'

'We shouldn't jump to conclusions,' was Barry's reply. 'Those injuries are also consistent with a fall down the stairs.'

'Tommy and I took a look at that house yesterday,' Rae said. 'The stairs are narrow and steep, and there isn't a proper handrail. I felt quite vulnerable coming down them. It was like coming down a ravine, to be honest. So we shouldn't rule it out.'

Barry picked up the original flimsy letter, protected inside a transparent plastic evidence sleeve and peered at it closely.

'It certainly looks like an I at the front of the name, but it could just as well be a J. Jan rather than Ian. What do you think?'

He passed the sleeve to Rae, who examined it closely from all angles.

'It might explain a lot, boss, like why we've got nowhere in our initial checks. We've been focussing on a missing boy from all those years ago. But if it's a girl? Well. A couple of places that said they had no record of boys going missing did say they had a couple of girls.' Rae took a final look at the letter before passing it on to Tommy. 'It's so faded anyway that it's difficult to be sure.'

'It's got to be one of the two, hasn't it? Ian or Jan.' Tommy was using a magnifying glass to inspect the badly faded lettering. He passed both to Jackie.

She screwed up her face in concentration. 'The problem is, the paper is dried and speckled with spots of mould. You know, I think it is a J now I've been prompted. So we start again, this time looking for a girl? Janet or Janice?'

Barry turned back to Sophie. 'Anything else of interest?'

She flicked through the pages again before handing them across to Barry. 'It mainly confirms what Benny had already told us from the X-rays. Probably poorly nourished. Slightly built, though that could be just an inherited trait. It's impossible to be sure how old she was from any of this. So we need to get in contact with schools and the social work department and trace records of any missing children from about fifteen to twenty years ago. Grinding work, I know. But it has to be done. Someone must have been responsible for her — and whoever it was, they were negligent in the extreme. The only thing we thought we knew about her was the name. But even that's wrong.'

She looked at Barry and Rae. 'You both know the ropes for something like this.'

Barry looked up from the notes. 'Yes. We've already discussed it. We'll use the same methodology as that case in Dorchester.'

'We all feel the same way about this kind of case,' Sophie went on. 'It's a horrible thing for the brain to deal with. You'll probably feel a mix of emotions at first, but we owe that child justice for what happened to her. From now on, we refer to her as Jan. She's a real person in our lives. She isn't just a dried-up body found in an old house. Jan was a girl with her whole future ahead of her, a future that was wiped out by people who should have been caring for her. Use that thought to drive you on when you feel down. Justice for Jan. Put that as the heading on the incident board, Rae. All of you, look at it every day. Barry, Rae and I have been through this before. We know how hard this investigation will be, not just in terms of time and effort but in terms of our emotional response. But keep those watchwords in mind when times get tough and you need a bit of motivation. *Justice for Jan.*'

* * *

DC Tommy Carter was the youngest member of the WeSCU team, even though he wasn't the most recent recruit. Jackie Spring had only joined the unit a few months earlier, but she was a latecomer to policing, having joined after several years as a volunteer special constable in Somerset and a twenty-year career in the county library service. Tommy got on well with the vivacious Jackie, but he did feel that she mothered him rather too much. She was doing it now.

'How should we break this up between us, Tommy? Any ideas?'

He was about to speak and say something along the lines of *I really don't mind*, when Rae approached.

'The local social work and family support teams first, I think. There's a support team who cover Bournemouth and others in Poole and Christchurch. We may have to widen to other Dorset locations if we find nothing. Bournemouth is a bit of a magnet for youngsters who run away from home. Not that we know whether that happened in this case.'

'Sounds good,' Jackie replied.

Rae continued. 'We also need to check local police records. Missing children have always been a high priority. It should still be an open file if she was reported, an unresolved case. Tommy, you've got the local police contacts, so you take that part, but check the records first before approaching any of the local cops. They're busy on that spiking case, or out on the door-to-doors. That leaves Jackie with social services. Barry's convinced that there'll be a record somewhere. I'll start thinking about her schooling. The problems will crop up if she wasn't local. Let's just hope that wasn't the case.'

The three junior detectives got to work, making phone calls, checking old computer records and trying to unlock people's memories. There were no police records of missing girls named Jan, not from any of the years that might correspond to her death. Tommy had wondered if this might be the case. After all, missing children were always a high priority, particularly if they had not yet reached their teens. A child's continued presence on such a list would have been flagged up for a recheck several times. Tommy spoke to several current and former serving officers, but he could almost hear the sound of scratching heads over the phone. He then transferred his enquiries to the neighbouring police forces of Hampshire and Wiltshire, but with the same negative result. He looked at his list despondently when he'd finished the checks. All the names had been contacted, and all had crosses beside them. He'd got nowhere.

Rae had made little progress either. Schools would have logged such a disappearance, and the name would have appeared on council lists. Rae wondered if there might have been an opportunity for someone to slip through the net as they transitioned from primary to secondary school. She obtained a set of transfer records for the Bournemouth area and spent an hour ploughing through them, looking for any note of a missing child by the name of Janet or Janice, but to no avail. So, if she was local, she'd either made the transition or somehow been missed off the records, or her disappearance had not been picked up. Could problems in record-keeping and storage have occurred as a result of the seemingly large number of council reorganisations that had taken place over the years? In theory, such changes shouldn't have caused an issue, but was that the case in practice? Rae realised that these thoughts were, in reality, a distraction. Jan hadn't been identified as having gone missing, but maybe she'd avoided that somehow. How would it be possible to fail to pick up the fact that a child hadn't appeared at their designated senior school? Maybe news of a decision by parents or guardians to move somewhere else or to shift the child into private education? Rae felt in her bones that there was a greater likelihood of a child going missing during that transfer window. The age was right.

She went to see Tommy and Jackie. Nothing from them, either. Jackie reported that the local family support unit had records stretching back more than sixteen years, but that there was no record of a Jan of the right age going missing during the period in which they were interested.

'What now, boss?' Tommy asked.

'I hate to say this, but we have to be sure. So we contact each school. Primaries are our best bet. We're looking for a slightly built girl, Janet or Janice, maybe with a troubled background and unreliable or non-existent family support. We speak to the headteacher and explain our problem. Primary schools often have staff who've been in the place for ages. Usually a teacher, but it may be a classroom assistant, canteen staff or even a caretaker. Let's make a list and try to get through the bulk of it by late afternoon before school staff all go home for the day. There are three of us, after all. We probably won't get any immediate answers anyway. People often need a couple of days to get their memories working for the kind of timeframe we're looking at.'

CHAPTER 12: HISTORY

Wednesday

Lydia Pillay always experienced a mix of emotions when one of her investigations overlapped with Sophie Allen's unit. She admired the older woman. The WeSCU leader was an almost-perfect role model for ambitious women detectives. Coming from a single-parent background, fiercely ambitious yet successfully juggling her career with raising a family, overcoming misogyny in her earlier working years, she still managed to retain a somewhat offbeat sense of humour. The problem for Lydia was that she also experienced a mix of other feelings. One was an undoubted sense of sexual attraction that was an absolute no-go area, even though she wondered if this particular feeling might be somewhat reciprocated. But it was partly mixed up with a strange kind of mother–daughter sentiment that confused matters. Lydia was occasionally invited along to social events involving the Allen family, often with overnight stays in their Wareham home. She'd even formed a close friendship with Hannah, Sophie and Martin's elder daughter. All these things could be viewed as positives, reasons for her to feel happy about coming back into the orbit of such an inspirational figure. But there was a big problem, the same one that had caused her to suddenly leave Sophie's unit early on, little more than a year after she'd joined. Her suspicion that Sophie may have carried out a serious assault on Charlie Duff, the psychopath who'd murdered her father, the night before Duff was arrested. A mysterious woman who'd never been identified had lured him to a bondage club, talked him into taking her home, strapped him to a bed and tortured him. The torture had included severing the nerves in his wrists, causing him to lose the control of his hands for the rest of his life.

Lydia had always wondered if that woman had been her then boss, in disguise. Goodness knows, Sophie had every reason to hate the man who'd killed her father for no real reason, condemning her and her mother to years of struggle and hardship. Duff had also murdered at least five other people who'd strayed into his twisted path through life, often through no fault of their own. Didn't he deserve to experience for himself the kind of life-changing misery that he'd inflicted on so many others? But Lydia's suspicions about Sophie had lingered in her mind for so long that she'd made the decision to force a clean break by leaving the unit. Then, after a gap of two years, she'd returned to Dorset to start a job as a newly promoted DS in Bournemouth, and she'd taken to it like a duck to water, gaining plaudits from all and sundry. She'd also come into contact with a certain Jennie Brown at a social event in the town, a tall brunette with a ponytail who'd seemed somehow familiar. They'd struck up a friendship and occasionally met for a meal or a few drinks. And Lydia had slowly and almost imperceptibly probed into Jennie's background and her own link to the Charlie Duff case.

Lydia wasn't a highly rated detective for no reason. She listened carefully to what people had to say, she thought deeply about the things that had been left unsaid, and she made connections between odd snippets of information. She searched out the case notes on the Charlie Duff investigation. She pondered on the minimal clues that had been recorded about the torture of Duff. As people had said at the time, why worry about the nature of his arrest, even its immediate prequel, when it bags a psychopathic mass-murderer?

At the time, Lydia had thought that Sophie had been the woman who had carried out the act of torture. She could now see that she'd been mistaken in that simplistic suspicion. After all, the logistics of the sequence of events didn't fit. But now she knew that Jennie Brown's father had also been one of Duff's victims, killed by him soon after Jennie herself had been adopted as a baby. And Lydia started thinking, probing a little more deeply.

Jennie's backstory bore so many similarities to that of Sophie Allen. What if the two women had met unofficially, outside of the investigation? What if they had shared their histories? And what if they'd planned and carried out the Duff operation together? Jennie had admitted that she'd half completed a medical degree before switching to Economics. That would have given her the necessary knowledge of wrist nerve locations and, presumably, some skills with a scalpel. Sophie could have easily done the planning, helped to ensure that Duff's flat was free of any clues, and then acted as the getaway driver. Jennie had told Lydia about her erstwhile interest in the world of S&M. It all fitted together. It was perfect.

Lydia then hit the usual brick wall. There was no actual evidence. It was all conjecture. And, anyway, would she want to probe into the assault when it had led to Duff's arrest and successful prosecution? All the evidence at the time suggested that he'd been ready to flee the country, having guessed that his time was up. The night-time activities of the mysterious woman, cruel as they were, had ensured he was caught. Those perspectives on what happened to Duff could be no different now, six years or more later.

No, she'd keep things to herself, certainly for a while longer. Sophie Allen did so much good, both in her working life and outside it. And Jennie Brown had become a good friend, steady and reliable. It would ruin so many good things if she pursued the matter. It had next to no chance of success, and what would be gained? Nothing. Better to let sleeping dogs lie. Better to let her slight feelings of tension in Sophie Allen's presence continue to run their course. But also, better to keep professional contact with Sophie to a minimum and deal with Barry and Rae instead, wherever possible.

She lifted the phone on her desk and called Barry.

'Hi, Barry. How are things going with the child's body in the suitcase?'

She listened to his measured reply. His careful and considered approach to an investigation hadn't changed much over the years.

'I'm calling to find out how you got on with Pippa Chandler. You and one of your team visited her yesterday, didn't you? Did you pick up on anything?'

'She claimed that her uncle sexually abused children, including her. Gus Gibson. That's the name. It'll need following up. She claims she never came across the boy, Ian. But we're not convinced. She also said that Gibson wasn't into boys, as she put it. He'd go for anything in a skirt, though. But we now know the child was a girl. Probably a Janice or Jan. Pippa was looking for some kind of deal, Lydia. I told her there wasn't a lot I could do, but that being co-operative towards us might have a bearing on the length of sentence she gets. My guess is that she's thinking things through, weighing up her options. Not that there are many, from what you say.'

'It's cut and dried. There's no way out for her over the Joshua Quick murder. She knows that. But she's devious, Barry. Just remember that. Don't trust anything she says.'

'No, we realised that. I took Jackie Spring along with me. Part of her training programme. She found it all intriguing but also very disturbing. I don't suppose she's met anyone that manipulative before.'

'Not many people do. It's not common in everyday life, is it? And thank goodness for that. Maybe we need to talk about more pleasant things. How's Gwen?'

'Fine. We're just planning an autumn break somewhere.'

'Jetting off to the sun?'

'Probably not. We did that for our honeymoon, back in the spring. Somewhere quiet in Britain, probably. Gwen wants to show me around parts of Wales at some point. Maybe this is the time. So much depends on the weather if you stay here, though. And that's potluck.'

'God, yes. I did a holiday with Anna earlier this year in Norfolk. It drizzled with rain almost every day. North Sea weather. We abandoned our great plans for walking most days and spent far too much time in various pubs. I put on several pounds. Also spent too much hard-earned money in the shops. It cemented our relationship, though. That kind of experience tends to be either make or break.'

'I heard you were in a more settled relationship. Good for you. Is this the one?'

'Early days yet, Barry. But maybe. Actually, I'm being far too cautious in saying that. I bloody hope so. I love her to bits.'

'Glad to hear it. And I'll keep my fingers crossed for you.'

CHAPTER 13: A NAME FROM THE PAST

Rae and Tommy were back in the area of Crawley Terrace, walking the roads in the immediate vicinity. The streets had the feel of so many similar Victorian terraced areas in towns and cities across England, all built on a basic grid pattern with front doors that opened directly onto the street, and back alleys that would have given access to dust-filled outhouses in which coal could be stored in that long-gone, smoke-filled era. The back gardens would have probably been used to grow vegetables back then, but there were few vegetable patches now. Most of the rear areas had patchy lawns or flagstone patios, often with some kind of barbecuing device to hand. Timber decking seemed to have become a recent favourite too.

Many corner plots would have been occupied by a shop or pub, but these had all but disappeared. One pub, curiously named the Watermelon Arms, remained, on a corner only a few hundred yards away from the house owned for so many years by Gus Gibson, and now passed on to his niece, the psychologically disturbed Pippa Chandler. From the look of the place, Rae wondered if it had a strong Caribbean influence. She walked closer to take a look. She was right. Menus in the window showed options such as jerk chicken and curried goat.

Rae decided that a visit to sample the food might be in order a little later. Jamaican food was a must when it was on offer.

The corner of Crawley Terrace and Lincoln Street looked as if it had once housed a shop, possibly with a flat above, but the premises had been converted into a purely residential property. It was only three doors away from the house that had held little Jan's body for so many years. The immediate neighbours had all proved to be newcomers, with some of the properties converted into student flats, but Rae thought there might still be a chance that a few people could be residents of old. With luck, some might have lived there at the key time, twenty years previously or thereabouts. Pubs and old-fashioned corner shops were often hotbeds of gossip in which comments about local down-and-outs spread like wildfire. Surely the strange happenings at number sixty-eight wouldn't have escaped attention? The residents of neighbouring houses in such close-knit communities would be aware of comings and goings, and would inevitably talk about them. And what better place to do so than in the local corner shop or pub?

Tommy knocked on the door of the corner property and waited. It was opened by a neatly dressed middle-aged woman.

'DC Tommy Carter and DS Rae Gregson,' he explained. 'We're doing background checks in the area. It's to do with the discovery three doors down at number sixty-eight. We wondered if your house used to be a shop. Do you know?'

The woman put a hand to her mouth for a few seconds before answering. 'I've already had police here doing a door-to-door. They didn't ask that.'

'No, they wouldn't. We're detectives investigating events from many years ago. So, was it a shop? It has that look, we thought.'

'Umm, I believe so. We've only been here for six years but someone converted it about ten years ago, I think. Maybe a corner shop of some type?'

'That's what we thought. Do you know anything about its history?'

The woman frowned and shook her head. 'No. As I said, we're relative newcomers to the area, moving down from Birmingham. But Romy Mathieson next door has been here for most of her life. She'd remember if anyone does. She must be in her seventies, I'd have thought.'

If Rae and Tommy held any age-based prejudices that people in their late seventies would be well down the slippery slope to mental deterioration, their views were challenged by the vibrantly active personality that greeted them at the door of number seventy-two. She was slim, small-boned, with intensely copper-coloured hair and a decidedly mischievous glint in her eye. She was wearing slim-fit jeans and a figure-hugging animal-print top.

'Good morning. I'm Romy Mathieson. You look like police officers to my eye. Am I right?'

'You certainly are,' Rae replied, taken by surprise. 'Do we stand out that much? I'm DS Rae Gregson. This is DC Tommy Carter.'

Romy giggled. 'No, you're not really that obvious. I caught sight of you chatting to Helen at the corner house and thought you were probably detectives. I had the idea of stirring you up a bit. Anyway, we've met before, though it was a few years ago and it was very brief. I'm an occasional member of Flick Cochrane's walking group, the Dorset Chatty Ramblers. We seem to have been caught up in a couple of your previous investigations. Suspicious deaths, I think. One on the coast path near Dancing Ledge and another at Arne.'

Rae tried hard to clear the memory fog from her brain and hoped that she didn't come across as totally stupid. She smiled briefly. 'Yes. Although I think it was my boss who may have seen you.'

'Was that the ginger-haired guy or the somewhat glamorous middle-aged blonde?'

Rae felt wrong-footed again. 'Umm, could have been either, I expect. I'm afraid my memory is less clear than yours.'

'Well, that's to be expected, isn't it? They're the only times I've been involved with that kind of thing, murder sort of stuff. It'll be a daily occurrence for you. It's your job, isn't it? You called to collect a written statement each time. I was just corroborating what Flick would have told you. She was the main witness. No, I'm wrong. The second time was Pauline Stopley. She led the walks when Flick was in hospital.' A brief pause. 'I expect you're here about that poor kiddie's body in the house two doors down. Do you want to come in? I'd prefer not to talk about it on my doorstep.'

Romy led the two detectives into her house and through to a small sitting room. She spotted Rae looking around. 'It's small but it suits me fine. And there's a really supportive local community feel around here. Well, with most of the residents. There are always a few nutcases and selfish people, aren't there? Like those in number sixty-eight.' She shook her head as if to emphasise the point. 'Weird. Really not nice, most of them. Odd comings and goings.' The grim expression on her face remained, as if she was struggling with unpleasant memories.

'Helen said you'd lived here for a long time and might remember back to the time the child was around. We think she died about eighteen years ago. Maybe longer.'

Romy nodded. 'Yes. I've been here for nearly twenty-five years. And I try to keep abreast of things that are going on. Someone called Gus Gibson owned the house for most that time. Well, until he died a few months ago. Sometimes he took in lodgers. I didn't like him, to be honest. Nasty individual. Always leering at me.' She shuddered. 'Strange people coming and going, mainly at odd hours.'

'Have you any memories of the child? We think the name might have been Jan, if that helps.'

Romy was frowning in concentration. 'Not really. But my memories of back then are all a bit vague. I have recollections of a child hanging about at unusual times, but I can't recall any details, though I remember being a bit concerned. I thought it was a boy's body that had been found?'

Rae shook her head. 'The local press, jumping the gun as usual. What you've said about the house is very useful to know, Romy. Were there other visitors you remember?'

'Not specifically. Most of them arrived late at night. Maybe pub closing time. They were all a bit scruffy. I know that's bad of me to say it. I don't have a problem with people who dress in an untidy way. But some of these were seriously grubby. Men swearing. Women with their busts hanging out of their tops. All of them either staggering about or slinking by, keeping to the shadows. Am I being a bit too dramatic? I wonder if my memory is at fault and I'm exaggerating things without realising it. It was a long time ago. That man Gibson got a bit better over the years. Only a bit, though.'

'Did you ever find out any more about the child?'

Romy looked worried and upset. 'I feel so guilty about what happened to her. I only spoke to her a couple of times, but she didn't answer. Looked scared. Then she stopped appearing. I thought that she might have moved away, and I didn't follow it up. I feel so bad about it now, with the body being discovered.' She paused. 'Actually, I did speak to someone about it. There was a man around a few times. I was told he was a detective, investigating drugs. I told him about the girl and that I was a bit concerned. Never heard anything, though.'

Rae was both intrigued and worried. As far as she knew, there was no police record about number sixty-eight being a place of concern. So why was it being investigated, and who by? 'Can you remember anything about him, this detective?'

'Not really. It was a long time ago. All I remember was that he was tall and wore black. Black trousers and a black leather jacket. A short, zipped one. Oh, and he was a bit sal-low-looking. I didn't feel that I could trust him. Not entirely, not like you two.'

'No name, then?'

Romy shook her head. 'Sorry. Too long ago.'

'But he was definitely police?'

'Yes, I'm sure of it.'

* * *

'Christ.' Rae was raging inside as the two detectives drove back to the incident room.

'I thought we were going to visit that pub we looked at, boss,' Tommy said, finally summoning up enough courage to speak. He'd rarely seen his superior officer so obviously upset.

'Bloody hell,' was all the response he got.

He chose to remain silent. She didn't appear to have even heard his comment about the pub.

Barry looked up as the two detectives entered the incident room. He glanced at Rae's face. 'What's up?' he asked straight away.

'Phil McCluskie,' she replied. 'Fucking Phil McCluskie. He was there, outside that house, around the time the girl disappeared. He must have been investigating the drugs or something.' She paused, as if calming herself. 'Would he have still been a DS then? Was that before he was busted back down to DC?'

'I think so. Wasn't it the chief super who initiated the action against him, soon after she first arrived? Isn't that what she told us a few years ago? What is this, Rae?'

'We have a witness who saw him. She reported her concerns about the child, Jan, to him. And the house. And he obviously did nothing. The bastard. He's landed us right in the shit.'

Tommy looked bemused. 'Who is this man? I've never come across him.'

Rae spoke bitterly. 'He's dead, Tommy. And bloody well deservedly so, in my opinion. You remember Stu Blackman, the bent cop we dealt with a couple of years ago? Well, McCluskie was his even more evil buddy. Nasty, slimy, clever and devious. And he always wore black.' She looked at Barry. 'We're gonna have to tell the chief super, boss. He was obviously up to something and didn't record it anywhere, not officially. No wonder we've had to start from scratch. Christ.'

Barry pulled his fingers through his hair. 'She'll be in soon. We'll catch her when she arrives.'

* * *

Sophie listened carefully to what Rae had to say, then stood up and gazed out of the window.

'It doesn't surprise me. He'll have been investigating something and manipulating it for his own gain at the same time. Didn't you say there were women hanging around the place back then, probably looking for money to get drugs? That's what will have got his attention. He couldn't resist someone flashing a bit of leg or cleavage at him.'

'Wasn't he investigated thoroughly when he was demoted? Didn't anything crop up then?' Barry asked.

Sophie shrugged. 'I know I instigated the action against him, but I wasn't senior enough to run the review into his conduct. I hadn't been in Dorset long. It would have been Neil Dunnett. He arrived about the same time as me. He was the chief super in charge of internal affairs and staffing.'

Rae exhaled sharply. 'Bloody hell. It just gets worse, doesn't it? That man was incapable of any original thinking at all. I remember that from my time in Wiltshire, working under his so-called direction.' She snorted after she'd uttered the last few words.

'McCluskie would have wrapped him around his finger,' Sophie said. 'He'd have spotted Dunnett's narcissistic streak right away and used it to his own advantage. Well, they're two figures from the past, both long gone.'

'But they've come back to haunt us, boss. Even after all these years. If they'd done their jobs right, this might have all been investigated years ago,' Rae added. 'McCluskie should have followed up on my witness telling him about her concern for the kiddie. And Dunnett should have probed deeper into McCluskie's past. Maybe he'd have uncovered all this.'

'How likely would that have been, Rae? You knew him better than anyone. He didn't have the skillset.'

Barry broke in. 'I hate to break up your cosy bout of nostalgic moaning, but it isn't getting us anywhere. There must be a record somewhere that details what investigation McCluskie was on. We need to find it. Maybe deep in the archives at HQ. Didn't you used to know someone who looked after all those old records?'

He was looking at Sophie. She was chewing her lip.

'Charlie Barrett,' she said. 'Old school, but a really decent guy. He was also the custody officer here for a while before he moved to Blandford. Knew everything and everybody.'

Her two juniors looked at her but didn't speak.

'It has to be me, doesn't it?' she said. 'That's what those plaintive looks are saying.'

Barry tried to be diplomatic. 'I don't think any of us know him, to be honest. Anyway, you can charm information out of anybody. You know it.' He paused. 'Ma'am.'

'Okay, okay, I'll see what I can do. And that's the first time you've called me ma'am in months, Barry. You must be feeling desperate.'

CHAPTER 14: MURKY POT

Charlie Barrett was a dapper man, slightly built and of middling height. Sophie had always thought that he'd have been popular in his heyday, especially with female police officers. He'd always shown a great deal of empathy towards cops who'd been struggling with life's issues, offering a shoulder to cry on. He'd even shown compassion towards some of the criminals he'd come into contact with during his time as a custody officer. 'There but for the grace of God' had been one of his regular comments. His understanding of the way youngsters were slowly corrupted into a life of crime by the circumstances in which they'd grown up had sometimes earned him the disapproval of his colleagues. But even they had to admit that he drew the line at violent crime. Once a suspect had been shown to have crossed the line into assault and serious intimidation, he'd withdraw his sympathy.

He also had a winning personality, coupled with mischievously twinkling eyes. He still had an impish look about him, even now, some five years into his retirement. He was at the door, smiling, as Sophie climbed out of her car in his driveway.

'Hi, Charlie,' she called. 'Good to see you.'

'Well, how could I resist a visit from the duchess of detectives?' he replied. 'Your call sounded full of intrigue. I want to hear more.'

She laughed. 'Coffee on the go?'

'Do you doubt me? I'm not doolally yet, I'll have you know. I do remember our chats about coffee blends.'

He watched as she pulled her crutches from the car and made her way over towards him. 'They give you a certain *je ne sais quoi*,' he commented. 'Stylish.'

'Cheeky,' she replied, as they made their way inside. She looked around. 'Nice.'

Charlie's new partner peered around the kitchen door. 'Hello,' she said. 'I'm Angela. I'd come out to greet you properly, but my hands are covered with flour. It's my baking day. Every Wednesday.'

'Come rain or shine,' Charlie added, rolling his eyes. 'Great cakes, though. Shall we go into the lounge? Then you can explain more. I could tell you were keeping things back when you called.'

Once they were comfortably seated, with a mug of coffee sitting beside each of them, Sophie explained her suspicions.

'I told you it was about Phil McCluskie, back when you were both in Bournemouth together, but not the context.' She took a sip of coffee. 'His name's cropped up as a possible person of interest in the latest investigation. The body of the child in Crawley Terrace. The thing is, nothing shows up in any of the official records of cases that were ongoing then. There was some drug trading at a fairly low level. People being drunk and disorderly. Minor scuffles. A pub with a dubious reputation. A couple of call girls operating somewhere in the area, maybe even in the pub. But nothing shows that McCluskie was involved. So why has his name cropped up? A witness describes a cop being around at the time and the description matches. Was he up to his usual tricks?'

'When you phoned, I guessed it would be something like that. I was thinking about it when I took the dog for a walk earlier. The thing is, with McCluskie, he was devious but he was clever with it. He knew how to cover his tracks. I kind of guessed at the time that he was always on the lookout for some kind of gain for himself. He lived a strange kind of life. That was when he was still married. My Pauline felt kind of sorry for his wife. I think her name was Moira.'

'I didn't want to bring up old memories for you, Charlie. I was trying to avoid it.'

Charlie raised his hand. 'It's not a problem. Pauline's cancer was awful at the time but I got over it. And Angela's such a great person to be with. Very different, though. In a way I feel lucky to have had two such lovely women in my life. Along with my daughters, of course. I've got to bring Pauline into it though, because Moira used to confide in her. She didn't tell me everything. Pauline wasn't like that. But she found it hard to get her head around Phil's behaviour and his reasons for being like he was. Can it be explained, when someone like him behaves the way he did? I don't know. He was what he was. The one thing I will say in his favour was that he wasn't bent in the usual way, not in my mind. I was never aware of him taking money from any of the gangs that operated in the region. I don't think he was corrupt like some bad-apple cops. But I could be wrong. He was a clever bastard. I always thought Phil was in it for the women and the booze, and nothing more. Maybe I was mistaken.'

'So could he have been involved in something going on in Crawley Terrace? Have we made a wrong assumption here? It's not as though we have a definite, identifiable sighting.'

'There was an operation going on that centred around the pub, the Lincoln Arms, as it was then. I think it's run by a Jamaican woman now. Meant to be really good. But it was a real dive, back in the day. You name the pie, and their fingers were in it. I'm sure Phil was involved in that operation. The flat upstairs was being used as a knocking shop. That kind of thing would have attracted him, for sure.'

'So why isn't his name on any of the records?'

'Stu Blackman's uncle was still a superintendent then. Nasty piece of work. Even more devious than McCluskie. And Stu had become best pals with McCluskie. Does that help to explain things? The rest of us had to be really careful around the three of them. The older Blackman bore big grudges against anyone who crossed him. It wasn't a good idea to ask too many questions, not back then. So it was easy for both of them, Phil and Stu, to cover things up. Stu used his uncle to get himself promotion, as I'm sure you know.'

Sophie nodded. 'It puzzled me for a while when I first arrived here. Why they were both in place. I never met the uncle. So would there be records anywhere that might shed a light on McCluskie's involvement in the goings-on at Crawley Terrace?'

'Bournemouth nick has a small storeroom, down in the basement area. Lots of old stuff there. If you wangle me access, I'd be happy to have a look for you. I know the kind of thing I'm after.'

'It's a deal, Charlie. I'll tip them off about it now. And there's a meal in it for you and Angela. You're still a curry enthusiast, aren't you?'

He nodded vigorously. 'Oh, yes. That's how we met, a local curry club. If anything, she likes them even more than me. We exchanged a few recipes and hit it off.'

'I thought I could detect a spicy aroma in the air. I'm feeling envious. Martin isn't keen. With him it's Italian food. Maybe I could bring Barry Marsh along. He loves curry.'

* * *

Charlie was never one to let the grass grow under his feet. He had nothing else of any importance to do, so he set off some two hours after Sophie had left, having received a message from her that she'd arranged access to the storeroom.

Bournemouth Central nick hadn't changed much in the few years since he'd retired. The same tired décor and antiseptic smells. He was even recognised by some old-time colleagues as he logged in at reception.

'What are you up to then, Charlie?' the ex-colleague manning the desk remarked.

He tapped his nose. 'Never you mind. But it's good to be back. Well, in a limited way. Can I have the key to the downstairs storeroom, please?'

'We'll need a signature,' came the somewhat stern reply.

'I wouldn't expect anything less. My clearance came through alright, then?'

'Friends in high places, eh? What it must be like to have your level of influence in the upper echelons of Dorset's finest. I should be envious. But, strangely, I'm not.'

Charlie took the proffered key and made his way downstairs to the storage area. The old records office smelled of mildew and dust as he made his way to the shelf he was seeking. There it was, the box he needed, detailing enquiries into assorted nefarious activities in the area around Crawley Terrace and the Lincoln Arms, extending across a three-year period almost two decades earlier. He pulled out the folders and took them across to a small table in the corner of the room, then settled down to start reading, scanning through the documents, looking for pages that might be relevant.

It took an hour to find something relevant and another half-hour to find more. The Lincoln Arms had been visited several times because of persistent reports of drug-dealing and rumours of several of its upstairs rooms being used as a base by sex workers. DS Phil McCluskie had been present at several of those visits. Now to find out if his signature or initials were on any of the statements taken. Time flew by as Charlie settled into his task. Just like old times.

* * *

It was early evening, and Sophie was clearing her desk ready to go home when her mobile phone rang. She glanced at the display. Charlie Barrett. She frowned. This was sooner than she'd expected. Did it mean he'd not managed to find anything? She put the phone to her ear.

'Charlie.'

'Ma'am,' came the reply. 'It could be worse than you thought. I've just had time to scratch the surface, really. McCluskie was there and involved in something. I've found some stuff that relates to him, though I haven't examined it closely yet. Do you want to drop by and collect it? I can't take it out without someone senior signing for it. It might be just what you're looking for.'

Sophie ran her fingers through her hair. 'With you in half an hour or so. And Charlie? Thanks.'

She had the distinct feeling that the lid was about to come off a very murky pot. Better be prepared.

CHAPTER 15: SUGAR DADDY

The Bournemouth team were just settling down for an afternoon briefing.

'Do we think we've identified everyone who was in the bar that night?' Lydia asked.

Jimmy nodded. 'Pretty much. It's taken a lot of manpower to speak to them all, but the CCTV was really useful. There are a couple of people we're still trying to trace but we'll get there. We've been working on this ground plan they gave us.'

He spread a large A3-sized sheet of paper in front of them, a floorplan of Suki's. It was covered in circles, each one containing a name in pencil.

'We've added everyone's position at the time Holly collapsed. You can see she's just stepped onto the dancefloor area. Everyone who's named has been contacted and asked to confirm roughly where they were in relation to the bar and the dancefloor. Except for the sixth man in the group she passed through. Curtis. We haven't traced him. There are still a small number of people near the entrance and a couple at the bar who we haven't traced either, but we don't think they're of prime importance. The CCTV shows they'd just arrived or didn't move from their positions. We've plotted Holly's movements with this dotted line here.'

'This is great,' Lydia said. 'Well done, the both of you.'

Her eyes tracked across the plan, inspecting the names and positions of the people in Suki's that night. She looked again at several stills extracted from the bar's CCTV recordings. She scanned the final image, checking it against the pencilled chart, pushed it away, but then pulled it back along with one of the earlier photos.

'This is the one just as she collapsed?'

Jimmy looked at the labelled heading on the photo. 'Yes, that's right. Why?'

'There's a shadow here, caught by one of the flashing lights from the lighting rig. Do you see it?' She used her pen to point to a slightly darker patch on the floor, near the far corner of the dance area. 'Is someone behind that pillar, out of sight?'

The other two detectives leaned forward for a closer look.

'Might be,' Jimmy said. 'It could easily be some kind of dark patch on the carpet, though.'

'Look at the one taken a minute earlier,' was Lydia's response.

The earlier one showed no such mark. Was it just an effect caused by the strobe lights, or was someone standing behind the pillar in the later shot, hidden from view of the security camera?

'Maybe we need another look at the CCTV sequence from that specific camera,' Lydia suggested. 'Try to zoom in on that patch, if only to rule it out as something suspicious.'

'Well spotted, boss,' was Jimmy's comment. 'We'll get it expanded and enhanced.'

George spoke. 'That corner is the closest part of the dancefloor to the toilet corridor.'

'And?' Lydia said.

'The corridor connects to the delivery entrance at the back of the premises. It's kept closed at night, but it functions as a fire escape with a push-bar mechanism.'

'There was no sign of it having been opened that evening,' Jimmy reminded him. 'The staff said they did a quick check soon after Holly collapsed. It was closed, with the mechanism fully engaged. Someone going out that way couldn't secure it after themselves.'

'Unless there were two of them,' George said. 'Someone stayed inside to shut the door. No one had any type of syringe or needle when they were searched, and nothing was found dumped anywhere.'

'I don't like it,' Lydia said. 'I'm getting the feeling that it might have been pre-planned, not the random attack we first assumed. Everyone acted quickly and efficiently that night. Her friends and the staff. Yet nothing was flagged, not on the security cameras or by the staff. All the punters are vouching for each other, other than your Curtis guy. But he was checked that night, wasn't he? It's a bit surprising, really. The girl's near death's door, after all. You'd think someone would break ranks and spill the beans.'

George was looking puzzled. 'But if her coma was accidental, would they? Whoever did it wasn't to know about her heart condition. They'd be scared, hoping that if they stay quiet it'll all blow over.'

Lydia explained. 'Holly was on medication for her heart condition. That surely means people would have known about it. I don't think she hid it from anyone. So that information could have been widely known, wider than her immediate friends. Look, I know the most likely explanation is that it was done by a stranger who didn't know. But we have to consider all possibilities. From what you've said, Suki's doesn't have a problem with spiking because of its tight security. It hasn't had an incident for a long time. Yet the night it happens, someone with a weak heart is the victim. Probably coincidence, but it needs thinking about. George, find out what you can about Holly's private life, but don't go near the family at this stage. They're already on edge. We need to know if there was anything in her background that might have created friction with someone nasty. She's been presented to us as a cross between an angel and Disney's version of Snow White. Come on, is that realistic in this day and age?'

* * *

George was, once again, trawling through social media pages, trying to probe below the surface, looking for things that Holly might want to keep hidden from friends and family. Sex? Drugs? Thrills of some kind? He really didn't know what he was looking for. Who was her closest friend? Josie had said that Holly was her bestie, but was it reciprocal? The other young woman who'd seemed close to her was the red-head, Daisy. Maybe it was worth having a look at their social media accounts too. He also thought it might be worthwhile trawling around some of the other Bournemouth pubs and clubs favoured by students and young people, showing Holly's photo and asking if she'd been a regular.

He visited the campus again and managed to catch Josie as she came out of her room. She frowned as she saw him.

'I'm on my way to a lecture. Can't it wait?'

'I'll walk with you, if that's okay. I'm trying to build up a picture of Holly's life. Her interests too. You obviously know her well, probably better than most. Does she have any worries, concerns? Things she might be reluctant to talk about?'

Josie stopped walking and turned to face him. 'What do you mean?'

George realised that he needed to choose his words carefully. 'Exactly what I said. Are you aware of any pressures she's under? I don't mean academic ones. Pressures in her personal life?'

Josie raised a hand to her face and started to bite one of her fingernails.

'I don't really know. Sometimes she looks a bit stressed but won't tell me what the problem is. "It'll sort itself out."

That's all she'll say. I get the impression that it might be caused by someone in her family.'

They started walking again.

'Why do you think that?' George asked.

'A month or so back she was working on a bit of paper, scribbling on it. It was a sort of spider diagram, with names. She screwed it up and threw it in the bin when I came into her room. Something was upsetting her.'

'Any idea what it was?'

'I asked her, but she wouldn't say anything. I think it might have been some of her relations. I caught sight of the phrase *Aunts and Uncles*. The thing is, I didn't know she had any. She'd always told me that her dad was an only child, and her mum had no contact with anyone from her family. That was when we were talking about cousins. I've got loads, you see.' Josie looked at her watch, a frown on her face. 'Look, I've got to get a move on or I'll be late.'

'Contact me if you think of anything else. You've got my number.'

George went in search of Holly's other close friend, Daisy, but to no avail. She didn't seem to be anywhere on campus.

It was late afternoon. He headed off in the direction of the bars clustered around the Triangle area, some of them slightly seedier than the newly developed clubs and cafés near the cinema complex and the lower gardens. George remembered his time as a student here. These places were a bit racier, a bit edgier. Worth a try?

He entered the first bar, the Edgington Arms. The name didn't ring any bells, but the interior seemed familiar. A fairly long, narrow-shaped room with a bar at the top end. The décor seemed more muted than he remembered. New owner, new name. He ordered a glass of fruit juice and showed the staff member a photo of Holly, asking if he recognised her as a visitor. No luck, so he finished his drink and crossed the road to the Witches Café. George remembered this place. It had opened when he was still at uni and had tried hard to capture a share of the student market. He could even remember when it had been a delicatessen before its conversion into a café and bar, where 'Every Day is Halloween!' George had always thought it was a bit naff. He looked around at the tatty interior. No reason to change his opinion.

A young woman was serving behind the bar, dressed in a punk-inspired torn top, short tartan skirt, ragged fishnet tights and clunky boots. She seemed bored, but did take the time to look closely at the photo on George's phone.

'Yeah. She was in here a few times. Isn't she the one who was attacked down in one of the posh bars?'

George nodded. 'Her name's Holly.'

'Yeah, s'right. She came in with an older bloke. Black. Much older. Like, really ancient. On crutches. He seemed kind of nervous, looking around all the time. It looked as though she was asking him questions. Maybe he was her sugar daddy. I mean, she was, like, scrubbed up really clean and fresh-looking. Not like me.' She laughed and scratched her dark mass of tangled curls.

'You seem to remember them clearly. When was this?'

She shrugged. 'Maybe a month or two ago? It was always on a Thursday lunchtime, like today. I only work here Thursday, Friday and Saturday daytimes. Fridays and Saturdays are a lot busier. I wouldn't have remembered them if it had been then. Run off my bloody feet.'

'How many times were they here?'

'About three? Maybe four? And they didn't stay long. One drink then they left. And I'll tell you summat else odd. They didn't arrive together, and they left separately. So it weren't no hook-up. That's all I can tell you.'

George took a note of her name, Lola Fulbright, and said he'd be back. Had there been something odd going on here? His phone pinged to indicate the arrival of a message from Jimmy. *The boss and I are off to the hospital again. Something's cropped up.*

He made himself a coffee once he arrived back in the incident room and started to write his report.

CHAPTER 16: HE WAS A WORM

'You wanted to see us?' Lydia said as the two detectives entered a modest meeting room at the hospital.

Holly's parents were looking even more stressed than during their previous chat. Carole's eyes were red and swollen and she was wringing her hands. Mark's face looked drawn with anxiety. Had either of them managed to get much sleep in recent days? It didn't look like it.

'Has something happened?' Lydia asked as they settled themselves on chairs.

'Well, yes and no,' came the quiet reply from Mark. 'Carole will explain.'

Lydia realised that Mark was refusing to look her in the eye. Something was clearly wrong.

Carole poured some water into a plastic mug and took a sip, her hand shaking. Like her husband, she didn't meet Lydia's eye.

'I have some explaining to do,' she whispered, still gripping the cup. 'I hoped this would never have to come out. But with what's happened to Holly, maybe it has to. We spent hours talking it through last night, then again when we got up this morning. Mark finally convinced me it was the right thing to do.'

Lydia was watching and listening carefully. The woman's hands were still shaking, so she put her cup back onto the nearby table. Then she drew herself into a more upright posture.

'You see, I'm Holly's mother, but Mark isn't her real father. Holly was a toddler when we married. We didn't bring her up to believe that Mark was her real father. We told her when she was about eight. But an old friend told us recently that Holly's been asking questions about back before she was born. She might have been looking for her biological father, that's what we're worried about.'

She sobbed and picked up her cup again. Mark slid an arm around her waist.

'Do you think this has something to do with her being attacked?' Lydia said.

'We don't know,' Carole answered. 'We just don't know. But maybe it has. How will we ever know?'

'Do you feel able to talk about it? I don't want to push you, but what you've just said might change the focus for us.'

Carole nodded miserably. 'I'll try. It's stuff that I — we — thought we could forget a long time ago.' She turned a tear-streaked face towards Lydia. She was whispering now, with every word uttered as a near sob. 'Is it true what they say? That everything in your past will come back to bite you at some point?'

'I don't think that can be a universal truth, can it?' Lydia glanced at Jimmy to check he was ready with his notebook and pen, then nodded to Carole to continue.

'I was in a mess around then. I was sixteen and in with a really bad crowd. My parents had just split up and I guess I blamed myself. I was drinking and taking stuff I shouldn't have. I failed most of my GCSEs and walked out of school. I left home too. I couldn't stand the endless arguments. I got a small, grubby room in a house in Lincoln Street, in Bournemouth. It was a squat, really, full of life's down-and-outs. I suppose I thought it would be an adventure; it was anything but.' She paused, sighing. 'I did stuff I'm not proud of. I had access to an upstairs room in a rundown pub, along with another girl, Casey. You can guess the rest. Things went downhill, badly. Casey overdosed and was rushed to hospital. There were police swarming all over the place for a few weeks. The squat was forced to close, and I had nowhere to go. One of the cops found me a room for a short while, but that was naff too. Then I found I was pregnant. That's when I first met Mark here.'

Carole gripped his hand.

'He volunteered for a homeless charity. Meeting him was the best thing that could have happened to me. He got me a place in a hostel. I had Holly. We had no proper home. We never went on holidays or trips. No money, you see. I slowly got more settled. Mark still came to see me. And my life began to turn around.'

She started crying again.

Mark spoke, still gripping Carole's hand. 'I could see what a kind and thoughtful person Carole was, even back then, at a time that must have been awful for her. She was always volunteering to help other women in the hostel. I felt drawn to her.'

Carole looked at him through her tears. 'I felt the same for him. What a lovely guy. So different to all the others I'd met. Even some of the cops.'

'We started seeing each other,' Mark continued. 'Then I got a job in town and we settled down together. We got married and Holly was our flower girl. As Carole said, Holly's known for a long time that I'm not her biological dad.'

Carole spoke again through her tears. 'I thought I was okay. My life had turned around. Now this. Is it some kind of bad karma? Paying me back for what I did all that time ago?'

Lydia didn't respond immediately. She needed a few seconds to process Carole's revelation of her time spent in a squat close to Crawley Terrace and her mention of a pub. There was a lot to handle here, and she needed to tread delicately.

And coupled with all this was an eerie feeling, akin to dread, that the investigation might be about to expand into difficult territory.

'Don't blame yourself, Carole. You were young and in severe difficulties. Take it from me. There is no causal link between any poor judgements you made back then and what's happened now. Jimmy and I have seen enough stuff over the years to know that karma doesn't exist. People who say that what goes around comes around are talking rubbish. I would like to ask you a few questions about that time, though. Things that are relevant to our investigation into the attack on Holly. What was the name of the pub? Do you remember?'

'The Lincoln Arms. It was on the corner of Lincoln Street. I think it closed down soon afterwards.'

'Okay, I know where you're talking about. This room that you were in for a short time, the one the cop found for you, where was it?'

Carole ran her hand across her brow. 'Round the corner. Not very far away.'

'In Crawley Terrace?'

'That's it. It was grubby and really tacky. No better than the squat.'

Carole's eyes dropped, as if she was reliving bad memories. Was that a shudder that ran through her? Lydia couldn't be sure.

'Can you remember the number?'

Carole's voice dropped to a whisper. 'Sixty-eight. I'm sure of it.'

Lydia breathed steadily, trying to remain calm and focussed. 'Carole, I guess this is going to be a hard one for you to answer. Do you know who Holly's father is?'

'It isn't hard. I've spent a long time thinking about it. I think Holly always wanted to know, but I really didn't want her finding out too much about those awful times, so I just said it was probably an old boyfriend of mine who joined the army but then got killed.'

'But that wasn't true?'

Carole shook her head. 'No. I made that up just to keep her quiet. I'm not sure she believed me, though. She kind of saw through me. Mark's the same. I can't keep any secrets from him.' There was a brief pause. 'It always puzzled me, though. I was so careful for the months I was upstairs in the pub. I always made sure the guys used protection. AIDS was still a big thing then. So none of it makes sense really. It must have been when I was in that room, a bit later on. I was drunk a lot while I was there. Everything is hazy and blurred, so I've got no way of being sure.' Her eyes dropped again. 'It might have been the cop.'

'Do you remember his name, Carole?'

'Phil, I think. Yes, Phil.'

Lydia momentarily closed her eyes. Surely not.

Carole was still talking. 'He came across as all helpful at first. But he wasn't. He really wasn't. He was a worm.'

Lydia gently nodded her head then glanced at Jimmy. He was studying his notebook as if his life depended on it. He knew too.

CHAPTER 17: JOINING SOME DOTS

Thursday

The early morning unit briefing was larger than usual, with both WeSCU and Lydia's team from Bournemouth CID in attendance. Sophie was in the chair.

'We've uncovered something that's bigger than we thought,' she explained. 'A set of crimes that are quite shocking when considered together. That's why I thought we needed a joint session. I called Lydia last night and told her that we'd stumbled on a name from the past, Phil McCluskie. He was a detective in Dorset CID until five years ago, latterly operating out of Blandford and Dorchester, though he did spend some time in Poole and Bournemouth earlier in his career. What we've discovered is that he was operating around the Crawley Terrace area at the time we think the child went missing. It looks like it could have been an undercover job. But that house, number sixty-eight, has cropped up too. Might McCluskie have had some kind of a connection with it? It worries me. He was — how do I put this — an unreliable cop. He had a lot of contacts in the seedier parts of the underworld. And when I mentioned his name to Lydia, she threw another spanner into the works. Can you explain, Lydia?'

Lydia looked around at the attentive faces watching her. Some of them would have crossed paths with the detective who'd so often displayed dubious morals. More recent recruits would be puzzled.

'There's a possibility that our erstwhile colleague Phil McCluskie was the biological father of the young woman who was spiked at the weekend. Holly Evans' mother opened up to Jimmy and me yesterday. She's in a bit of a state — understandably so, with Holly still in a coma and her prognosis poor. She and her husband, Mark, thought it was time to come clean with us. Carole told us she'd had a torrid time when she was in her mid-teens. She was a bit of a wild child, by her own admission. Apparently, there was all kinds of stuff going on in Lincoln Street and Crawley Terrace, and in the pub there. Its upstairs rooms functioned as a brothel, from what she told us. And Phil McCluskie was around a lot of the time, apparently upholding the law but, in reality, helping himself to anyone and anything that took his fancy.'

Sophie took up the thread. 'His personal speciality was spotting vulnerable women during the course of an investigation, offering support and help but then getting them drunk. At which point, he'd make his move.'

'Yes. According to Carole, that's exactly how he behaved with her. She was sixteen, just short of her seventeenth birthday. Nowadays McCluskie would be classified as a predator. Back then people looked the other way. The powers-that-be didn't exactly approve of what he did, but there was a shocking degree of tolerance from some senior officers that would be an absolute no-no nowadays. He was a good detective, by all accounts.'

Sophie gave a thin smile. 'Intelligent and shrewd, that was our Phil. I've had reason to look over his record several times since I arrived in Dorset. We even had him on the team once, but only so I could keep an eye on him. I knew exactly what he was like. Barry and Rae will remember him. He had a chip on his shoulder a mile wide, though I don't know enough about his background to know how it got there. It certainly didn't help our relationship when I had him demoted to DC for gross misconduct soon after I arrived. His sense of grievance got even worse at that point, but at least he reined in his inclinations. I guess he's come back to haunt me.' She gave a bitter laugh.

'This is all unconfirmed,' Lydia continued. 'We're telling you so that you know what we're dealing with. George suspects that Holly might have been trying to find out about her background. She'd grown up seemingly quite happy with the knowledge that Mark Evans wasn't her natural father. We wonder if that all changed a month or so ago, when we think she may have started digging into her mother's past. So the question is this. What did she find out and was it the cause of the spiking incident that's landed her in hospital? Jimmy's been talking to pathology experts in other areas where spiking's a problem. The amount of Rohypnol in Holly's bloodstream was high compared to most other cases. It's possible someone had the intention of killing her. Why? We're worried that it all ties in with what went on in that house in Crawley Terrace a long time ago.'

Rae chipped in. 'Surely the problem with dosage depends on the method used as well as the amount. If it's a direct injection, which it was in Holly's case, it all ends up in the bloodstream, and quickly. Whereas if it's ingested in a drink, there's a slower uptake and some might not get absorbed. Isn't stomach absorption less efficient? I thought that was the reason she collapsed so quickly after the spiking, because she got injected? If it's in a drink, doesn't it take about ten minutes or so to take effect?'

'Good point,' Lydia said. 'I can see your scientific background showing up. So it might not have been a deliberate attempt on her life after all?'

'Well, I didn't say that,' Rae added. 'It could have been. I would have thought it was worth pursuing further.'

'We're also investigating a new development — that Holly might have been trying to trace her biological father.

But it's a puzzle. If it was Phil McCluskie, then he's been dead for a few years. So why would someone want to shut her up, if that's what the spiking was about?'

Barry had been listening carefully. He'd had the same idea. 'Look, McCluskie was a very dubious cop, we know that. But he wasn't totally bent, not in my book. He was on the periphery of shady, looking for opportunities. Like here, in the goings-on in that house and around about it. He was fishing, looking for weaknesses in people he could exploit. My guess is that there were far worse people running the actual nasty stuff. If someone was targeting Holly, then it was because she'd come to their attention, all these years later. Her questions about her father must have overlapped with other, darker stuff that had a lid on it for almost two decades. Someone was worried that she was about to lift that lid.'

'My thoughts too, Barry,' Sophie said. 'And that darker stuff is linked to the death of the girl. Maybe it's not a coincidence that the spiking happened around the same time as the body was discovered. And just after Pippa Chandler had been charged with murder. Could whatever links them all be something that went on in that house?'

A moment of silence followed as the detectives considered the thought. It was broken by Jimmy. 'So, we have the body in the suitcase, that young girl, from around twenty years ago. Plus, the spiking incident against Holly Evans at the weekend. The arrest and questioning of Pippa Chandler for the murder of Joshua Quick. And the link is that house, sixty-eight Crawley Terrace? Isn't it all a bit tenuous?'

'How old is this Pippa Chandler?' Tommy asked.

'Thirty-six,' Jimmy replied.

'So she would have been eighteen at the time we think the girl ended up dead? What if she was around when all this was going on?'

It was at this point that Jackie Spring made her first contribution to the discussion. She'd sat silently until now, digesting all the comments her colleagues had been making.

'You know you asked me to do some checks on the background of that pub on the corner of Crawley Terrace, the Lincoln Arms? Well, I found something just a few minutes before we started this meeting. One of the licensees from back then was a Joshua Quick. I just spotted it a few minutes ago.'

There was another silence, finally broken by Sophie. 'Well, that's a real turn-up.' She glanced at Lydia. 'Maybe there was more to the late Mr Quick than you've been led to believe, Lydia.'

'Leave it with us,' came Lydia's somewhat angry reply. 'We'll turn his history inside out.'

'Anything else useful, anyone?'

Rae spoke up. 'Romy Mathieson is a good source of local information. She's lived in Crawley Terrace for the past twenty-five years or so, in number sixty-four, two doors away from our horror house. She's alert and perceptive. Good memory too. I expect she'll be chewing things over. Maybe she'll remember other stuff from back then. I'm just mentioning her name so, if she contacts us, you'll know she's not a time-waster.'

'Well, it's time I filled you in on what I've been up to,' Sophie continued. 'I've been tapping into the brain of Charlie Barrett, a retired cop from this area. He was a custody officer for a long while, but was also a great unofficial archivist. Knew everything that was going on. I asked him if he'd do a bit of historical research for me, and he jumped at the chance. He's managed to dig out stuff dating back to the time we're interested in, relating to Crawley Terrace and Lincoln Street. And some of it helps to open things up for us. Phil McCluskie was involved in several investigations in the area. Drugs. Protection rackets. Prostitution. It looks as though he became the go-to expert on such goings-on in that immediate area. And from what we've discovered, I think we can see why he was such an expert. The problem for us is that these events happened around eighteen years ago, give or take a year or two. Which makes it all the harder for us to get to the bottom of it. I'll be looking a bit closer into his past to see what opens up. His relationships too. But we will get there, I have no doubt, judging by the progress we've made in the last few days. Things certainly move forward when we get together like this, don't they? Well done, everyone. This discussion has given us a lot to think about. Looks like you've got your wish, Jimmy. Here we are, on the same investigation, after all. Just like old times but with the addition of a few more people. You can buy the first round when we have an occasion to celebrate. Okay?'

She winked at Barry, reached for her elbow crutches and moved towards the door.

CHAPTER 18: CAFÉ CHAT

Wayne Silverman was more than a little irritated as he opened the door of his study room. He'd been trying to get an important assignment finished and the knock on the door had disturbed his train of thought. Dan Morrow was standing in the corridor outside. Wayne was tempted to make a barbed comment, but a closer look at his friend's face stopped him. Dan looked seriously worried.

'Can I come in? I need someone to talk to.'

Wayne opened the door wide and ushered his visitor inside.

'You look stressed, Dan,' he said.

Dan ran a hand across his head. 'Yeah. I am.'

'Okay. You'd better sit down. I'll just save what I've been doing. This won't take too long, will it? I've left things a bit late on this assignment because of everything that's been going on. I've really got to finish it tonight.'

Dan didn't seem to be listening, so Wayne finished off the sentence he'd been working on and moved his laptop to one side.

'Okay,' he said. 'I'm all yours.'

Dan was frowning, his eyes dark and anxious.

'The cops asked about that guy I was talking to the night the girl was jabbed. Curtis. I told them everything I knew, and they didn't push me too hard, not that first time they saw me. But they're sure to be back, and I reckon they'll be a lot tougher. The thing is, I've been doing a bit of detective work myself. I tried to find out who he is and what course he's doing. But he's not a student here, not as far as I can tell. And his name's probably not Curtis — not according to someone I was talking to this morning. This guy told me his real name's Jerry. They were at the same school. He's local, not a student at all.'

'What? That doesn't make sense. Why would someone give you a false name?'

Dan shrugged. 'That's what I was thinking. If he's really Jerry someone or other and lives locally, why would he have told me his name was Curtis and he was a student? And before you ask, I know that's what he said to me. Honest, Wayne, I'm not joking. I just wonder if he had something to do with spiking that girl. I mean, why would he have lied to me like that?'

'Didn't the cops think it was probably someone on the dancefloor? That's what I thought.'

'No. The cops are looking for some other guy, probably this Curtis.'

Wayne felt perplexed. 'How do you know all this, Dan?'

'It wasn't from the cops, I can tell you that. They don't tell us anything. I was in a café in town having a coffee and got chatting to a group of the girl's friends.'

'So what do you want from me?'

'I just need advice on what to do. Should I tell all this to the cops? I don't want to get Curtis into any trouble.'

Wayne was still puzzled. Why was there any doubt in Dan's mind? 'But you've just told me his name probably isn't Curtis. If that's true, he's been tricking everyone. Including you. You've got to ask yourself why. If he can't be trusted, don't the cops need to know? That girl's still in a coma. She might die. If it was me, I'd tell them.'

'Yeah, you're right. I'll do it now.'

'Are you okay, Dan? It's just that you don't seem your normal self. Something else bothering you?'

Dan slumped back against the chair and momentarily closed his eyes. 'It's the business with Tanya. I can't seem to pull myself out of it. I keep thinking of her. I guess I was taking her for granted and didn't let her know how I really felt about her. To be honest, I didn't know myself until she ended it. I don't really know what to do.'

Wayne put a hand to his friend's shoulder. 'Mate, we're here for you. I can understand how you feel. But there's no point moping about it. Why don't you just message her and let her know that you want to stay friends? Keep it light but just remind her that you still care.'

Dan rubbed his head. 'Okay. Sounds good. I wonder if I came across as too controlling. I didn't mean to be.'

'Listen, I heard that someone on my course might be shifting out from a shared house to move in with his girlfriend. I'll check it out and see if it's true. If a room becomes free, I'll put in a word if you want me to. Okay?'

'Yeah, great. You're a real mate, Wayne.'

'If there's anything else I can do, just ask. Okay? Same for the others. We all wanna help you through this.'

* * *

George Warrander volunteered to visit the university to see Dan. They met in a café on campus.

'I was a bit confused by what you said on the phone, Dan. Something about that guy Curtis not being who he said he was.'

'Someone told me that his name isn't Curtis. It's Jerry. And he's not a student, he's a local.'

'Right, who told you this?'

'Some guy I met in a café yesterday morning. I don't know his name.' Dan seemed reticent to add any further detail.

'Why are you asking these questions, Dan? You should be leaving it to us.'

'Yeah, but you don't tell us anything. You treat us as suspects.'

George grimaced. 'That's because you are. Think about it. A young woman's at death's door. Someone deliberately shoved a needle into her thigh. That's attempted murder. You and your friends were all close by. We're taking it very seriously and considering all possibilities. It's not a game, Dan. This is as serious as it gets. If you know something, or suspect something, you need to tell us, not go haring off yourself. So I'll ask you again. Who was this person you were speaking to?'

Dan shrugged miserably. 'I don't know his name. He works somewhere close to the café, the one I was in.'

'What was the name of the café?'

'Café Cuba. It's down from the Triangle.'

'Okay. Let's head over there.'

Dan was taken aback. 'What, right now?'

'Yes, right now. What did you think? That I'd be happy to leave it for a day or two? Absolutely not. Get your coat.'

They drove into the town centre, where George found a convenient parking slot on a side street near the café. Dan had remained largely silent during the drive. He looked tired and vulnerable, probably not surprising after spending several nights sleeping on the floors of assorted friends. He opened up a little during the short walk to the café, once George told him that he'd been a student here, and not too many years earlier.

'I did a degree in Business Economics,' he told the younger man. 'I even worked locally for a short while after I graduated. But my job now suits me far better. It's much harder work but in a different way. I feel I'm doing something more useful. Here we are.'

They'd reached Café Cuba. George stood back and let Dan lead the way inside, where they were greeted by the enticing smell of high-quality coffee, its tantalising aroma hanging in the air. George ordered their drinks and asked the manager if they could have a few words with her. She joined them at their table a few minutes later, when George explained the reason for their visit and Dan described the man he'd spoken to.

'All I can tell you is that it might have a link to the recent drink-spiking incident — not that the man we're looking for was involved. But he might know someone who was there at the time and could be a useful witness.' George was picking his words carefully, giving enough information to get the manager onside, but not enough to cause her to hold back because of a sense of moral loyalty to her customers.

She pondered for a few moments. 'If it's who I think it is, he's a regular. He's in here for coffee most days. Occasionally lunch. His name's Greg. I don't know his last name. I think he works in an office up the hill a bit, close to the church. Groveton Insurance? I think that's its name.' She looked again at Dan. 'Yes. It was you talking to him yesterday morning. I thought you looked familiar just now, when you came in.' She turned to George again. 'There's something familiar about you too.'

George smiled. 'I used to be in here a lot, back in the day, when I was a student. Six or seven years ago. Were you here?'

She laughed. 'I was working behind the counter then. I got the manager's job a couple of years back. Good luck with your investigation. Pop back in anytime and keep me updated. Maybe have some food next time.'

George had the uneasy feeling that she was flirting with him. He put the thought out of his mind and stood up. 'Let's go,' he said to Dan.

The manager of the café had been right. The insurance office was just a few minutes' walk away, and the man they were seeking was an employee. Dan recognised him through the plate-glass window, sitting at a desk, working at a computer screen.

'Okay, Dan. Leave it with me now. We've identified him and I need to follow this up alone. I'll call you if we need to speak again.'

George waited until the student was out of sight, then entered the office. He showed his warrant card to the receptionist and soon found himself sitting opposite the wary-looking Greg Lester, as identified by the name-plate prominently in view on the front of his desk. George explained the reason for his visit. As usual, once the some-what reticent young man heard the words *drink-spiking case*, his cagey and suspicious attitude changed. George and his fellow detectives had frequently noticed the sense of abhorrence that most people felt towards the perpetrators of these drug-based attacks. Young people who might not be so willing to help the police solve other types of crimes displayed a different attitude towards spiking. He supposed the random nature of the attacks was the cause. Anyone could become a victim.

'Yeah, okay, I do know a bit about the guy you're looking for,' Greg said. 'He was at the same school as me, but we weren't friends. He was a bit odd, a bit of a loner back then. His name's Jerry. I think his last name's Murchison or something like that.'

'What school was this?'

'Northview Community. He was in the year below me.' Greg dropped his eyes. 'I heard rumours that he was involved in stuff like this. You know, getting girls drunk or drugged. It's a bit sick, isn't it?'

George nodded. 'What else can you remember about him?'

Greg shrugged. 'That's it, really. Who told you about what I'd said?'

'I can't tell you that, Mr Lester.'

'It doesn't matter, not really. I told a few people about what I thought. I suppose I should have come directly to you, but it's hard to do that, you know.'

'Well, we've got the information now. If you think of anything else, give me a call. And thanks for your help.' George pushed a contact card across the desk towards the young man, then left.

CHAPTER 19: NOT THAT KIND OF GUY

Barry's brow was furrowed as he summarised the main points of the autopsy report from the child's body found stuffed inside the grubby suitcase.

'Confirmation,' he said. 'Definitely a girl. Probably aged about ten, but lightweight for her age. Slender. Shorter than average.'

'Does that mean she was malnourished?' Rae asked.

'Possibly, but not for sure. Some kids are naturally short and thin. The report specifically mentions that, although it goes on to say that her bone density was poor. Her teeth too.'

'So she wasn't being well looked after?'

'Doesn't look like it.' Barry turned to the next page. 'Here's the key stuff. DNA results.' He paused again, still frowning. 'There's a familial match with someone already on the database.'

'Not bloody Phil McCluskie again,' Rae blurted out.

'No. A Bruce Greenfield, apparently. He's on the database because he was charged with drink-driving some six years ago.' He looked around at the WeSCU team members. 'Heard of him, anyone?'

There was no response.

'Well, he's next on our list of people to contact. But do a bit of checking first. Remember we're talking about a death that happened some eighteen years ago. And the girl, Jan, was nine or ten or thereabouts. So we're looking at a birth almost thirty years ago. There's something strange about all of this, particularly after what Carole Evans told us about what went on in that house and the nearby pub.' He flicked through the remaining pages. 'A couple of other things. She had a cleft palate. Some treatment for it, but incomplete. That could be useful. That's for you to follow up, Tommy. Nearby hospitals, clinics and the like. You're fairly local. Olivia is a hospital nurse, isn't she? Maybe she knows a bit about it and can give you some tips. Jackie, you work with Rae on trying to trace the child.'

'Could the cleft palate be the cause of her poor physical build?' Jackie asked. 'Maybe she had trouble eating, particularly if it wasn't treated properly.'

'That's a good point. Check it out, Tommy. Okay, folks. I'm off to Blandford with the chief. She's traced someone who can give us more background on Phil McCluskie from way back when. She thinks it might be useful. Let's get busy.'

Tommy had heard about cleft palates but knew few details. His first action was to send a text message to his fiancée, Olivia, asking her for background information. Her reply was quick to arrive.

Sure. I've helped with a few cases over the years. I'll get some stuff together for tonight. Remember we've got a meal out. Don't be late. 8 p.m. at the Italian but try to get home well before that.

Well, that would be a start, he thought. But he was feeling impatient.

Can't you get anything to me sooner?

It took several minutes for her response to arrive. She didn't seem pleased.

I do have to work, you know. I've got ill patients to look after. I'll see what I can do in my lunchbreak. That's if I manage to get one. So busy.

Maybe his message had come across as a bit too demanding.

Sorry. Only if you have time, thanks.

The phone in the incident room rang. Tommy looked around, hoping that someone else would answer the call, but he seemed to be the only one not studying a screen in deep concentration. He took the call. It was Romy Mathieson, the longtime resident of Crawley Terrace.

'How can I help?' Tommy asked.

'I've remembered something. That summer, the last one anyone can remember seeing the girl around, well, I was away the August holiday weekend. When I came back, the young couple in number sixty-six, right next to that house, said they remembered a tremendous row one night. Shouting and screaming. It was women's voices. And a girl. That's all I can remember.'

'The names of this couple? Do you remember them?'

'No. I've tried hard, but it just doesn't come. They were only there a short time, you see. They were Welsh.'

'Right. That's very useful, Mrs Mathieson. If you do remember anything else, get in touch right away.'

He logged the information and went in search of Rae.

* * *

Sophie Allen looked around at the small, neat flat. She and Barry were sitting in the lounge, compact but comfortably so. Several photos were displayed on a bookcase set against a sidewall. One showed two women in swimsuits posing for the camera beside an outdoor pool, the sky intensely blue and the sunlight strong. A more faded photo was hanging on the wall in a small recess, showing what looked to be a Victorian-era town pub. Doreen Butcher, the current resident, came out of the kitchen carrying a tray, which she deposited on the low table in front of them. She was a short, curvaceous woman with attractively tinted hair and a ready smile, although there was a wariness in her eyes.

'Thanks for agreeing to see us, Ms Butcher,' Sophie said. 'And for the offer of mid-morning refreshments. Always welcome.'

'There's always time for tea,' Doreen said cheerfully. 'Or in your case, coffee. Hope you don't mind. It's instant. I'm not a great coffee drinker. I only keep it for guests.'

'I'm sure it will be fine,' Barry said. 'We're used to police station tea and coffee. Everything's an improvement after that.'

Sophie looked suspiciously at the contents of the mug in front of her, a somewhat murky liquid, and frowned. Maybe what Barry had just said wasn't strictly true.

'You want to know about my time with Phil, isn't that right?'

'Yes. But don't think you're under suspicion in any way. That isn't the case.' Barry was trying to be reassuring. 'Something's cropped up from nearly twenty years ago, and Phil might have known something about what was going on. We're not aware that he kept diaries or anything like that, but it's always worth a try just in case he did and left them around when he passed away.'

Doreen smiled. 'Not Phil, no. After he died, I gave this place a good clear-out. There was nothing like that. No diaries, no notebooks. He must have got rid of that kind of stuff when he retired. That's if he ever kept it anyway. I don't think he was that kind of person.'

'How long did you know him for?' Sophie asked, taking a polite sip of coffee. It tasted as if it had been made with powdered milk, something Sophie hadn't encountered for years. Who on earth used that stuff in coffee? Surely most people kept it just for emergencies?

'I came up here to look after him in the last couple of years before he died,' Doreen replied. 'It was a good deal for us both. My life was a mess, and Phil wasn't really in a fit state to live by himself. We both gained from it.'

'How did you meet?'

'Ah, that was a year or so before, when his health was a bit better. One of my friends used to rent the flat next door. She had a birthday party and thought it was probably a good idea to invite the neighbours to avoid complaints. Bit of a party girl, was Mandy. Phil was there and I recognised him from way back, from his days in Bournemouth. We got chatting and we seemed to hit it off. We went out a few times for a meal or just a drink. No rumpy-pumpy, though. I guess that was beyond him, with his poor health and all.' Doreen sounded a little wistful.

Sophie looked at her rather more carefully on hearing this. Had she been Phil McCluskie's type anyway? She'd always imagined his preference to be slim, husky-voiced, brassy blondes looking for a good time, not more subtle women like Doreen. Maybe he'd become more discerning in his final years.

'And then you became his live-in carer?'

'Yeah, though that was a bit later. My landlord wanted me out. He had plans to develop the place I lived in. It was a tip anyway. I had no dosh and nowhere to live. Phil asked me if I wanted to move in up here. I s'pose he knew what was going to happen to him. I had the small bedroom back then.'

'I heard he started drinking again and that's what finished him off.'

Doreen frowned. 'Not entirely. He didn't booze a lot, not like his earlier days. I always told him that was part of the bargain. I'd stay and look after him as long as he did his bit to help himself. And he did stick to it most of the time. What did for him was a bad chest infection. It turned into pneumonia and that was him done for. What with his bad lungs and his liver, his immune system couldn't cope.'

'Sorry to hear that.' Sophie was impressed with the level of medical understanding that Doreen showed.

Doreen sighed. 'He wasn't a bad guy, not really. And I did well out of it. I'd be homeless if it wasn't for him.'

'So do you own this place now?' Barry asked. He sounded intrigued. 'Nice location.'

'Yeah. He left it to me in his will. He looked after me really well, did Phil. I've never had a place of my own. Now I got this. My life's turned around a bit in recent years. I got my independence now.'

Sophie took over. 'You said you recognised him from many years ago, when he was stationed in Bournemouth. How was that?'

Doreen's eyes narrowed and she looked at Sophie suspiciously. 'That was when we were a lot younger. They were rougher times. I don't want to talk about it, to be honest.' She took a sip of tea, then another, staring at her cup all of the time. Clearly Doreen didn't want to pursue it any further.

'Did Phil have any children, to your knowledge?' Barry was trying to get the conversation back on track.

Their host shook her head. 'No. Absolutely not. He wasn't that kind of guy. You know, settling down and having a family.'

'I didn't mean just in that way. Did he ever talk of having fathered a child by accident?'

Doreen looked at him quizzically. 'What are you saying?'

'Had anyone contacted him in his later years claiming he was their father?'

Doreen sat up straight in her chair. 'Absolutely not.' She stared at Barry. 'Could that put my ownership of this flat at risk?'

He shook his head. 'I wouldn't have thought so. Not if it was left to you in his will.'

'You know something, don't you? Something you're not telling me. I wondered what all this was about. Cops like you don't have a chat like this for no reason. I should have known. Did he have a kid, then?'

'We can't be sure but it's possible.'

'Who? Who is it?'

'We're not at liberty to say, Doreen. He may well not have known about it.'

'Well, that's a turn-up. But I'm not really surprised, the way he put himself about all those years ago. He could have fathered a whole tribe, to be honest. Your lot didn't know what he was like. Either that or his bosses turned a blind eye for too long.' Her gaze turned to Sophie. 'Who did you say you were?'

'Sophie Allen.'

Doreen looked her up and down for a few moments, then smiled wryly. 'It was you, wasn't it? Got him demoted? I'm not surprised, though. It took a woman to see what he was like and do something about it. He'd screw anything he could lay his hands on, back then. S'funny, he said he was really angry when he first got booted downhill. But he'd got over it by the time I met him again. He had a kind of grudging respect for you, from what he said. Maybe he finally realised what a snake he'd been.' Doreen's eyes suddenly grew wide, and she put a hand to her mouth. 'Oh God.'

'What is it?' Sophie asked.

'He gave me something to send to you. At least, that's what I think he meant. It was just a few days before he died. But he never addressed the envelope. I dropped it into a drawer and forgot about it. I think it's still there.'

Doreen hurried out of the room and came back a minute or two later looking triumphant, a slightly crumpled brown envelope in her hand. It looked to be the same type as Dorset Police used. Maybe this place also had pens, pencils and other stationery lifted from whatever police station McCluskie had been based in. Sophie couldn't really blame him. As long as it was for personal use and not being sold in bulk to market-stall holders, was it really a serious crime? She had a few pens and envelopes at home that had found their way there from the office. Not much recompense for all the thousands of hours of unpaid overtime she'd put in during her years of service.

Doreen was watching her. 'Sorry it's a bit late. You just can't get reliable posties nowadays, can you?' She gave a somewhat throaty laugh.

Sophie pocketed the envelope and the two detectives left.

'That was more informative than I expected,' Sophie said as they headed downstairs from Doreen's flat. 'What did you make of her, Barry?'

'Fairly helpful in what she told us. But her manner was inconsistent, the way she talked.'

'Exactly. At times quite astute. Then back to the everyday woman-in-the-street mode of talking. Do you think she might be hiding something?'

Barry shrugged. 'Hard to tell.'

'Maybe follow up on the flat ownership information. Probably true, but might be worth a check. It was a bit devoid of personality, to be honest, and that surprises me. She's a woman with a lot of character. I'd have thought she'd have done something with the place to reflect that. As it is, it looks to me as if it might not have changed much in the four years since McCluskie died. It's functional, which is what I would have expected of him.'

'Are you getting at something?'

'Not sure. I'll need to think about it.'

CHAPTER 20: LETTER FROM A FATHER

The envelope only carried two words, written surprisingly neatly. *Sophie Allen*. She'd always imagined that his handwriting would be poor, an untidy scrawl. She was forgetting that this was Phil McCluskie, not his long-term sidekick, the scruffy Stu Blackman. Phil had always been tidily dressed, almost always in black. Informal but smart. His writing matched that neat appearance. Sophie slit open the A5-sized envelope and peered inside. Two further smaller envelopes, one labelled once again with her name, the other carrying the words, *To my Possible Daughter*.

She opened the one bearing her name. A single sheet of paper with the same neat handwriting. She started reading.

To Sophie Allen,

I haven't started with the usual polite greeting. You wouldn't expect it from me and I'm not going to pretend that we somehow liked each other. I'll be dead by the time you read this. The thing is though, you were always straight with me. It's odd in a way but I need someone I can trust to see this through for me and it was you who sprung to mind. Weird, eh? I suppose that shows up the crappy sense of judgement I had about people and who I could trust, for most of my life.

I've heard some pretty strong rumours just in the past few months that I might have a daughter. It's too late for me to start trying to find out who and where. It'll be somewhere local, in Dorset. Probably in the Bournemouth area. That's if it's true and she's stayed put. I guess she might be in her teens.

Look, I know I've made a mess of my life. I did all the wrong things and for all the wrong reasons. But the thought of having a daughter — it worries and disturbs me. I want you to try to find her and give her the letter I've written.

The odd thing is, I know you'll do it if you can. Other people are unreliable. They're just as likely to throw it in a bin. I know you won't. Please do your best. Find out if she exists. If she does, pass the note on. I can't say I'll be forever grateful. I'll be dead.

Phil McCluskie

Sophie frowned and went in search of Barry, who studied the note carefully.

'Clever,' was all he said.

'What do you mean?' she replied, sounding irritated.

'It's vintage Phil, isn't it? Definitely not sucking up to you, yet sucking up to you, both at the same time. Manipulative.'

'Hmm. I see what you mean. I really don't know what to think. I don't know what I'd have done under normal circumstances, but we know who she is, where she is and that she's under our protection. I don't have much choice, do I, assuming she comes round? Do we leave it sealed, or do we have a peek inside?'

Barry looked horrified. 'No. Leave it. Even if Holly doesn't pull through, it'll become the property of her next of kin. That means her mother.'

Sophie scowled. 'You're right, of course. But is he just trying to be manipulative, from beyond the grave? What if he spills the beans, as it were, about her mum? Maybe there's stuff in the letter that's best left unread from Carole's point of view. He was a vindictive toad at times, was our Phil. I wouldn't put it past him to try and muck up the mother's life. After all, she kept Phil in the dark about his daughter all this time. It would be just his style to get his own back, even now.'

Barry was watching her carefully, concern in his eyes. 'Aren't you exaggerating a bit?'

'No! Absolutely not. I knew him better than you. Nothing would surprise me about that man. Look at the clever way he's trying to manipulate me in the covering letter.'

Barry nodded slowly. 'I see what you mean. You hand over the letter. It's got some hidden nasties in it. But he's dead, so you take the blame for whatever follows. Okay, you've convinced me. Let's take a look.'

He switched the kettle on, and Sophie held the envelope in the hissing jet of steam, then used a letter opener to prise it open. The two detectives stood by the window to read it.

Dear Daughter,

If you're reading this then someone has found you. If it's a detective superintendent called Sophie Allen then she's done what I asked her to do. We were colleagues for a short while but don't think that she and I were friends. We weren't. We were kind of opponents. She was senior to me. She got me demoted for unprofessional conduct but I guess I deserved it, from her point of view anyway. That's how you were created. I had too many girlfriends and nothing ever lasted. I was always a wanderer when it came to relationships.

I'm sorry you grew up not knowing anything about me. I didn't know you existed until some rumours reached me a couple of months ago. By then I was too ill and weak to do anything about it.

You'll have guessed that I was a cop, a detective. I was good but I didn't stick at it properly so stayed at a pretty basic level. I worked the more rundown parts of Bournemouth for a long time but then got transferred to Blandford a bit later.

The McCluskie family comes from Glasgow, the east end. That's where I was born. But I moved south as a kid.

My Dad was a bus driver. We moved down to Dorset when he got offered a job as a driver trainer here. He spent his whole working life on the buses. People liked him. My mum worked in a supermarket. She had a temper. They're both long gone.

I hope you had a good home growing up. I'm not thick so you should have some brains too. Use them. Don't ruin your life like I did with too much booze, too many fags, too much partying and all the other rubbish that goes with that kind of life. If I could go back and change things I would. It all seems such a godforsaken waste from where I am now, at death's door, with only a short time to live. It probably seems weird to you but you're my one hope. Have a happy life.

Your unknown dad,
Phil McCluskie

'Well, I misjudged him big time, didn't I? Maybe he wasn't all bad, after all.' Sophie reinserted the letter into its envelope and handed it to Barry. 'I feel bad about opening it now.'

'Don't. It could just as easily have been a load of spite. It's sealed back together alright, so no harm done.'

Sophie was pensive. 'Did you notice the photos she had on display, Doreen Butcher?'

'I saw one on that shelf unit. Couple of women. Maybe mid-thirties? Taken somewhere abroad, I'd guess.'

'There was another photo, hanging in the recess. It was a bit dark, but it looked to be of a pub. One on the corner of two streets, with old, terraced houses. You couldn't see it from where you were sitting.'

Barry waited. Something was coming.

'I wonder if it was the pub that's cropped up in the investigation. What was its name again?'

'Didn't someone say it used to be called the Lincoln Arms, years ago? It's on the street corner with Crawley Terrace.'

'That's right. Let's talk to Rae about it. She's visited, hasn't she?'

'It's been done up, as far as I know. Changed its name to something else.'

'Even so. And wasn't it linked somehow to Lydia's current murder case?'

'Joshua Quick was the licensee at one time,' Barry said, thumbing his lip. 'He was the victim. Stabbed in a frenzy. Lydia has Pippa Chandler in custody for it. She's admitted killing him.' Barry was pensive as he spoke. 'It's all looking a bit tangled up, isn't it?'

'You said it. It's worrying. We thought we had three separate cases on our hands. But the more we probe, the more it looks like they're connected somehow. I just wonder if the link to Pippa Chandler is deeper than we think.'

CHAPTER 21: DNA TRAIL

Mrs Magda Corcoran
Deputy Headteacher

George looked over the receptionist's shoulder at the name-plate as she tapped on the door. Magda. That was an interesting name. Eastern European, possibly?

A murmured 'Come in' sounded from inside the room, so the receptionist eased the door open and gingerly stepped inside.

The establishment he was visiting, Northview Community School, had probably been built in the sixties. Now it was showing significant signs of ageing, reflecting the underinvestment of recent years. A general look of wear-and-tear, faded paintwork, old and heavily worn flooring. Even so, the school obviously did its best, with colourful displays of pupils' work fixed to walls and on display boards. George had been at a similar school to this in his secondary years. Midway through his time there, budget cuts had forced the governors to reduce the caretaking staff from two people to one, and, within two or three years, the difference had showed. George could remember the decreasing levels of cleanliness and the increased stress on the single member of staff charged with the upkeep of the site. This place had probably gone through a similar cost-cutting process. Now, of course, it wasn't just cleaners and caretakers that were losing their jobs. Levels of teaching staff had also been cut to the bone. He sighed, probably too loudly.

'A police officer to see you, Mrs Corcoran.' The receptionist sounded more than a little nervous. Was the deputy head a bit of a dragon?

She stepped back and waved George in, then closed the door firmly behind him.

A middle-aged, dark-haired woman stood to greet him, holding her hand out for a shake. She was dressed conservatively, other than the bright green spectacles that adorned her face.

'Magda,' she said, smiling. 'Deputy head. And you are?' She had a pronounced Dorset accent, not a rather more exotic-sounding voice with a lilt from the Balkans or Eastern Europe. George felt mildly disappointed.

'George Warrander. Detective constable, Bournemouth CID.' He flipped his warrant card open, then took the seat that Magda was pointing to.

'What can I do for you, Detective?'

'I'm trying to gather information on someone, and we think he might have been a pupil here until about five years ago, give or take a year or two.'

She looked at George, as if assessing him. Grey eyes, he thought. And a good dress sense. She looked a no-nonsense sort of person. Maybe that's why the receptionist had been so deferential.

'Is it important? This would be personal information if I released anything. And we are bound by the guidelines of GDPR.'

'I'm aware of that, and yes, it is important. I wouldn't ask otherwise.'

'Hmm. I see. Is that all I get?' There was a twinkle in her eye.

'Afraid so. It's an ongoing case, a very serious one.'

'What's the name?'

'Jerry. Possibly Murchison, but we're not so sure of the surname.'

Her eyes flickered slightly.

'So you do recognise the name?' George said.

'Did I say anything?' Magda replied. 'I wasn't aware I'd spoken.'

George smiled. 'Your eyes spoke for you. For what it's worth, the case might be attempted murder.'

She frowned on hearing this. 'Yes, I see. That really is serious. And yes, Jerry Murchison was a pupil here. I always wondered if I might hear his name in that context. If it was going to be anybody, it had to be him. There are pupils we're sorry to see go when they finish their schooling. Then there are people like Jerry.'

'This hasn't come as a complete shock, then?'

She shook her head. 'No. Not one bit. Always in trouble for lying and deception. A mischief-maker of the first order. But I don't really understand why you've had to come here to find out about him. Surely you have all kinds of other records and systems you can access?'

George explained. 'Not for him, no. He's not on the voters' roll, nor does he seem to appear anywhere else.'

Magda nodded knowingly, a small smile on her lips. 'He'll have reverted to his father's surname, Busby. He sometimes used that trick here, to confuse supply teachers or new staff. Rascal. Actually, that's the wrong descriptor for him. I always think that the term rascal is better used for people with at least some endearing traits. He seemed to have none. Unscrupulous pest is probably more accurate.'

* * *

Rae and Jackie stood back and looked at the house once again. It was older than the nearby estate homes and set in larger grounds. A window was open upstairs in what was probably the bathroom, judging by its frosted glass, with another small fanlight ajar on the ground floor at the side of the house. A downstairs toilet, maybe? The presence of two open windows tended to imply that someone was in, but in that case, why had their ring on the doorbell not elicited any response?

'Try again,' was Rae's somewhat irritated instruction to Jackie. She glanced up at the increasingly dark clouds looming above them and zipped up her jacket as a particularly stiff gust of wind caught her. 'Maybe our Mr Greenfield is just being antisocial. I mean, it's not as though we can be instantly read as cops, can we? Or am I being naive?'

Jackie laughed and rang the bell again, this time giving it two hard presses for good measure. She waited, ear close to the door, and finally heard some movement from inside. It sounded like footsteps descending stairs. There was a stumble, then a curse. It was a woman's voice.

The door opened and a flustered-looking blonde-haired woman peeped out. She was fastening an animal-print negligee around her torso and looked flushed.

'No cold callers. Can't you read?' she said angrily.

'We're police,' Jackie replied. 'We're looking for Bruce Greenfield. Does he live here? We have some personal information that might be important to him.'

The woman nodded at them and then pushed her somewhat dishevelled curls away from her face, glancing around the immediate neighbourhood as if checking for peeping toms.

'May we come in?'

The woman fought to rewrap the ties on her gown, which had billowed partly open, caught by a sudden gust of wind, and was now in danger of exposing her left breast to view from the deserted street.

'Fuck's sake,' the woman muttered. 'Can't it wait? He'll go fucking ballistic. He told me not to open the door. I thought it was the grocery delivery.'

'I've got a packet of mint sweets if you want it. Does that count as groceries?' Jackie said, trying to keep a straight face.

She still had one foot inside the door, with the rest of her body outside on the top step. 'Please. Can we come in and explain? It's starting to rain out here.'

The woman stepped to one side, a resigned look on her face. Clearly, she'd been unable to decide as to the preferable course of action. Keep the two detectives out and end up looking suspicious, or let them in and possibly subject herself to the ire of Bruce Greenfield, whoever he was.

'Thank you,' Jackie said, stepping across the threshold as a flurry of rain blew into the sheltered porch area.

'Pesky weather,' Rae remarked as she too hurried inside. 'I wish it would make its mind up what to do. It was bright and sunny ten minutes ago.' She looked at the woman, now completely enclosed inside her tightly wrapped negligee. 'You are?'

'Kim,' the woman muttered. 'He's gonna go mental.'

Rae frowned melodramatically. 'Why would he, Kim? He hasn't done anything wrong, not as far as we know. As my colleague said, we've got some significant personal information for him. It's important that he gets it. Look, we'll wait if you think he needs a few minutes.'

Kim led them into a neat living room, with views across a lawn and flower beds towards the River Stour some three hundred yards away. Rae couldn't actually see the river, but she could make a guess as to its orientation by the line of willow trees that wound across the landscape. They settled onto chairs and waited. Muffled voices could be heard from upstairs. If an argument was going on, it was being kept at a fairly civilised level.

'Wife? Girlfriend? Home-help with a difference?' Jackie said.

Rae pursed her lips. 'My guess would be girlfriend. Maybe a couple of years. Sex in the late morning? Got to be something like that, hasn't it?' She looked around her at the relative tidiness of the room. 'Probably live-in.'

Jackie nodded. 'My thoughts too. Nice negligee. Suits her. Good job we're both women. I hate to think what Tommy would have made of that unplanned display.'

'I'm jealous, to be honest. Well, I would be, wouldn't I?' Rae replied, grinning.

'You do pretty well. Don't underestimate yourself, boss.'

'You're so loyal, Jackie Spring. And you know just how to get round me.'

Their conversation was interrupted by the sound of footsteps descending the stairs. Two figures entered the room, with the man leading. He looked irritated, tugging at a loose shirt. Kim hung back, somewhat sheepishly, moving towards a window seat.

'What's all this about?' he said, as he settled into a chair. 'Kim said you had important information for me.' He was trying to look calm and in control, but his face showed signs of exertion, a slight pinkness in his cheeks, and his clothing had clearly been thrown on in a hurry.

'It's complicated, sir,' Jackie answered. 'But you are Bruce Greenfield? We need to check.'

'Yeah, that's me.'

'How long have you lived here?'

'More than fifteen years now, I guess. Look, I don't have all day. Can you get on with it?'

'Of course. It's about an ongoing investigation. We had a DNA sample to analyse. It turned out to have a close link to you.'

The man looked taken aback. 'How did you have my DNA?'

'Your drink-driving charge some six years ago. You were found guilty, so your DNA was retained.'

Bruce's eyes narrowed. 'Whose DNA was the match?'

Rae broke in. 'It's historic, sir. We haven't completed our investigation yet.'

'Who?'

Rae took a breath. This needed to be explained carefully. 'A child's body that we found recently. She lay undiscovered for many years. DNA indicates you're close family.'

His face became pale, losing its previous ruddiness, and he slumped back in his chair, his eyes wide. 'Jesus.'

CHAPTER 22: SO YOU SAY

Bruce was still slouched in his chair, brooding, despite the two detectives having left some ten minutes earlier. Kim was pretending to read a magazine, wondering how she could best end this awkward silence.

'Do you wanna talk about it?' she finally asked. Why did she feel so nervous?

'What?' he barked.

'I said, do you want to talk about it? It's obviously eating at you.'

He stared at her, scowling. 'I should have got out while the going was good,' he muttered. 'Fuck.'

'Waddya mean, you should have got out? What you talking about?'

'Ah, nothin'. It's all a fucking mess.'

'Who was she, this kid they found? I mean, she was obviously closely related, but how close, Bruce? You can trust me. I'll stick by you, whatever. I wouldn't spill the beans on you, no matter what. You've been too good to me for me to land you in the shit now.'

He seemed to flop back in his chair as if he'd somehow accepted the inevitable. But the inevitable what? Kim was genuinely puzzled.

'It's what I told them. I dunno about the kid. I got no idea she existed. What was she? Niece? Cousin? Granddaughter? That's what they said. I never knew she was related.'

This last comment set Kim's brain working. What did he mean, he had no idea she was related? Did that mean he'd known about her, despite telling the cops that he didn't? Was it just the fact that the girl had been related that was new to him? The trouble was, Bruce was such a closed book. He'd never really opened up to her, not in the two years they'd been together. He never talked about his past, and the few times she'd asked about it had sent him into a moody silence, curtailing any further questions. She had no idea of where he'd lived in his earlier life or what he'd done to earn his money. She just knew that he seemed to have plenty. Better to remain silent and enjoy the fruits of his impressive bank balance. She cooked and cleaned for him, shared his bed and pandered to his comparatively unimaginative sexual desires. He liked vanilla sex, and plenty of it.

Was the stability of the past two years now under threat? If so, she needed to be extra vigilant. After all, she had nowhere else to go and no real skills she could use to move into ortho-dox employment. Sticking with Bruce was her best hope for a tolerable future.

'You never told me much about your family, babes. You got brothers and sisters, then?'

He shrugged. 'One of each. My brother's dead. In the army, killed in Afghan. Never had a kid.'

'And your sister?'

He shook his head. 'She's long dead. You don't wanna know the details, believe me.'

Kim frowned. 'But the cops will want to know. That's what they said. They said they'd be back.'

'I know, for Christ's sake. I don't need reminding. I just need some time to get my thoughts together. Chalky used to be good at sorting out stuff like this, years ago. But lately? Well.'

Kim glanced across at Bruce. He was staring out of the window at the back lawn, his mind apparently miles away.

'Do you fancy summat tasty for lunch, babes?' she asked.

'What?' came the curt reply.

'I said, do you want something tasty for lunch? I could do you a sausage sandwich, if you like. Or something really special. I got some nice steak in the fridge. How about a steak and onion sandwich? Your favourite.' She paused. 'Or we could go to the pub. They do a curry deal at lunchtimes midweek. What d'you say, babes?'

'Yeah, whatever,' was his response.

Clearly something was worrying him, and badly. He enjoyed his food, and Kim's cooking in particular. Yet here he was, being vague and distant about it.

'Steak and onion sandwich it is, then.'

That would be the best option. If they went to the pub, they'd probably be there for much of the afternoon, and he'd fall asleep once they returned home. This way she might be able to manoeuvre him back to bed for the afternoon and continue their interrupted session from earlier. He might open up a bit more to her after a good screw. She'd need to be cautious, mind. He seemed super touchy at the moment, ready to snap and snarl at the slightest provocation. That was so unlike him. He'd always been such an easy-going individual. Well, in comparison to some of the other men she'd known in her life. And she'd known a fair few.

* * *

Dan Morrow was feeling angry and betrayed. He was sitting in a quiet corner of the bar in the student union, talking to Ollie Morgan.

'I feel tricked,' he was saying. 'That guy was using me. The cops don't even think Curtis is his real name. They won't tell me who he really is, but I've been doing a bit of finding-out by myself. It might be Jerry. He's probably a local.'

'How'd you find that out?' Ollie asked, taking a sip of beer.

'Some guy I was talking to in a café a few days ago. It makes me sick to think he was just using me to get into that club and come across as one of us. Then he did that to that girl.'

'Have you heard any more about how she is?'

Dan shook his head. 'Not officially. The cops just told me she was still in a coma. But that's been days now. If she was gonna come out of it, wouldn't it have happened by now?'

'I dunno, mate. Don't they sometimes keep people in a coma deliberately until the brain swelling goes down? Maybe that's what they're doing with her. I heard she hit her head badly as she fell. Maybe it isn't just the stuff she was spiked with. Maybe she got really bad concussion too.'

Dan didn't feel reassured.

'Whatever. It doesn't change the fact. That guy spun me a pack of lies and used me. I want to get my own back, but I need someone to help me. Are you in, Ollie?'

Dan's friend pondered for a few moments. 'I hate it when people get away with things. Cops have their hands tied by all the stupid rules and regulations. I told them that. I could see they agreed. They didn't say anything, though.'

'So, are you in?' Dan sounded insistent.

'Yeah, okay.'

'We don't tell the others. Not yet, anyway. Wayne thinks we should just leave the cops to do their job. And you know how much the others listen to him.'

'So what's your plan?'

'Well, I wanna know where he lives, this Jerry bloke. I thought we could find him, find out where he hangs out and pay a visit. Pretend we think his name's still Curtis and we don't know any different. We'll decide what to do then, once he thinks we're just pals. He won't know what we know.'

'Okay, Dan. But nothing too bad when we do start to pin him down. I don't want to end up in court myself.'

'Course not.'

* * *

139

Pippa Chandler had become an avid reader of newspapers since she'd been in prison, awaiting her trial. She devoured them, scanning for updates about the investigation into that kid's body, disappointed at the lack of detail in the news accounts. So much of it was regurgitated from earlier stories. It was obvious that the cops weren't going to release any new information until it suited them. And when would that be?

She had to time her move just right. Tell them that Bruce might be someone interesting to talk to. That he'd had his fingers in lots of pies back then. That he'd known everything and everyone.

She sidled up to one of the warders.

'You know that cop who came to see me a few days ago? The ginger-haired one?'

The warder just looked at her, giving nothing away.

'He asked me to search my memory, think back to when I was younger. He's looking for a name.'

The warder kept her eyes on Pippa's face but still didn't react.

'See, I've remembered summat. It could be important. He'll wanna know.'

'So?' Finally, the warder spoke, although her distrustful look didn't alter.

'He needs to come back in, don't he? So's I can tell him.'

'And what do you want me to do?'

'Oh, for God's sake. Do the business. That's what you're here for, innit? Get him back in. He'll want to know what I've remembered.'

'Tell you what, Pippa. I'll think about it, shall I? Maybe I'll mull it over for a few days, just like you claim to have done. God's sake, why didn't you tell him at the time? Don't try to kid me on with this *I've only just remembered* garbage. I know, and you know, that this is just a part of some scheme of yours, half-baked probably.'

Pippa clenched her fists, her face turning red with fury.

'Don't you dare,' the warder said. 'Don't even think about raising a hand to me, or you'll be in solitary quicker than shit sliding down a sewer.' She paused. 'Give me a name. If you're a good girl, I'll pass it on. If I feel like it. Depends on my mood.'

'Bruce Greenfield,' Pippa hissed. 'He's a snake, though the cops won't have heard of him. He's the one they need to do a bit of digging on.'

'So you say, Pippa. So you say.'

CHAPTER 23: PIPPA OPENS UP

The information on cleft palates that Tommy's partner, Olivia, had managed to email to him was useful in enabling him to understand the medical issues relating to the problem. She'd also sent across some notes that gave an insight into the possible psychological effects on a child of not being treated fully and early enough in their life. Even if the child did go through the tried and tested sequence of operations, it would still prove to be traumatic to some degree. As far as he could see, all children in the UK and other developed countries received treatment, and this had been the case since the post-war years. But it could leave speech problems. And he was well aware of how those kinds of issues attracted the attention of bullies once children started school, having had a slight lisp himself in his infant years.

He messaged back to Olivia. *Thanks that's all great.* Then he researched the hospitals in the region that would have offered surgery and subsequent support for cleft palate work several decades earlier, and tried to identify where he might find old hospital records, though a search job like that wouldn't be easy. Data protection legislation would probably mean that the treatment records of young Jan would have been destroyed long ago. It might still be worth a try, though. What might prove more useful would be the support groups, often run by local charities, with people dedicating decades of their lives to helping out. He might be lucky and find someone who recalled the child they were interested in.

He put together a plan and presented it to Rae, just returned with Jackie from their visit to the man who was some kind of close relative of their child victim. Maybe 'close' was the wrong term to use. In Tommy's mind it meant something rather more than a mere genetic link. Surely a close relative should play a more caring part in the child's upbringing and show some responsibility towards the youngster, if the child had been orphaned? He voiced these thoughts to his boss.

'Well, that idea certainly doesn't apply in this case, Tommy,' came her reply. 'He claimed he didn't even know the young girl existed. And he certainly couldn't confirm who the parents were. He was almost catatonic.'

Jackie was even more condemnatory. 'Irresponsible idiot,' she said, before turning towards her own desk.

'Now, now, Detective Constable Spring,' Rae said, with a mischievous look in her eye. 'Remember, a responsible police officer is never judgemental about people.'

Jackie stopped and turned. 'I was thinking of describing him as a shallow-minded, self-centred wanker, but I thought better of it.'

'I didn't hear that. And neither did you, Tommy. Your plan looks fine, by the way. Maybe start with the support groups, since there's one backed by the town council. I'll make a quick call to Lydia since she's local, keep her up to date. Back to work, everyone.'

Tommy found progress slow, as he'd expected. The problem was the historic timeframe he was interested in. A delay of a couple of years would have been okay. An eighteen-year wait was an utterly different matter. Some of Tommy's subsequent calls lasted a mere minute or two, often with a snorted comment along the lines of, 'Eighteen years ago? You must be joking!'

By late afternoon he was experiencing that despondent feeling that was all too common in this type of investigation, a reaction to the repetitive negative results and the continuous crossing out of entries on his carefully constructed list of contacts. Then, out of the gloom, a pinprick of light. He'd somehow been put through to someone at a support group in Bournemouth.

'Wait a tick,' the woman said. 'We've got someone with us who's been here for yonks. She's not in at the moment, but she'll be here tomorrow. Do you want me to make an appointment?'

'Please. I can be with you first thing. And thanks.'

* * *

Barry glanced at his watch. Did he have time to visit Pippa Chandler in prison or should he hand the issue over to Lydia to deal with? She was in charge of the case being brought against the woman, after all. But the message that had arrived for him from the deputy governor at the prison that was housing Pippa while she was on remand sounded intriguing and had specifically asked for him. Lydia had told him previously that Pippa's moods were extremely unpredictable. She might be in a co-operative mood today, but that gave no indication of how she'd be feeling tomorrow. He sighed to himself. Better strike while the iron was hot.

Who could he take with him? Tommy was on the phone, engaged in a conversation that looked as though it might yield something fruitful. Rae and Jackie were writing up the details of their visit to Bruce Greenfield and making plans for some follow-up enquiries. He considered Jimmy Melsom, but he'd prefer a woman officer. Really, it ought to be Jackie, the detective who'd accompanied him on his previous visit. She and Rae also had the advantage of having just visited the Greenfield man, whose name had cropped up, according to the short message detailing what Pippa wanted to talk about.

Barry told Jackie not to mention the DNA connection they'd discovered, the puzzling link between Bruce and the young child victim. He hadn't had time to discuss the implications fully with either Sophie Allen or an expert. The complexities of DNA profiling were too often overlooked, he knew that. Better to hold fire and see if Pippa mentioned something that helped to make sense of it.

An hour later the two detectives were inside the prison, entering an interview room, to be followed shortly by Pippa, who was led in by a warder. The stockily built woman sat down and looked at them. Was that a look of wariness or something more calculating?

'You have something for us,' Barry said.

'Got a name for you. Bruce Greenfield.' She looked almost triumphant, rather like a young child who, after a prolonged period of mediocrity, had just won a gold star for a piece of schoolwork.

'We've already visited him, Pippa. My colleague here was talking to him just a couple of hours ago. We already had his name from a different source. Isn't that right, DC Spring?'

'Yes. I saw him with my boss, the DS. We learned quite a lot.'

Jackie was watching Pippa's face closely. Pippa's eyes narrowed, as if she was wondering whether to believe them or not.

Jackie went on. 'He didn't mention you very much, though. He talked a little about events in the Crawley Terrace area in the distant past. Eighteen years ago, in fact. Your name cropped up in the conversation once or twice.'

Pippa scratched nervously at her left wrist. 'You might be talking bullshit. Spinning me a yarn.'

Jackie shrugged. 'We don't really care what you think, Pippa. If you want to impress us, we'll need more than just a name we've already got. Someone we've already visited as a person of interest. You need to do better.'

Barry was watching this interplay with interest. Clearly Jackie was getting her own back for the insult she'd received from Pippa at the end of their previous visit. He decided to sit back and let Jackie get on with the exchange. She seemed to be doing well in her new role, her confident and buoyant personality helping her to interact positively with people. How would she handle this prickly and tense interchange with the devious Pippa Chandler?

Jackie continued as Pippa just glowered sulkily. 'So, we either need more names, ones that we don't yet know, or stuff about Bruce Greenfield that we haven't already found out. Or both, of course. That might make us feel particularly benevolent towards you.'

Pippa dropped her head and swapped her scratching position, using the fingers on her left hand to scratch her right wrist. The skin looked sore and inflamed.

'Why is everyone getting on at me?' she moaned in a low voice. 'It's so fucking unfair. It's always me that's gotta deal with stuff. Someone like Bruce just swans through life.'

'We're waiting,' Jackie said quietly.

'Chalky,' she finally muttered with an exasperated sigh.

'Who's he?'

'Guy you need to talk to,' Pippa replied. 'Prob'ly knows more than me.'

'About what?' Jackie clearly wasn't going to allow the woman to get away with vague assertions.

'That house, the one I just got ownership of. Who was in it. Why they was there. What went on there. That kinda stuff.'

'Okay. If you tell us his last name, we'll check up on him.'

A long silence followed before Pippa shrugged hopelessly. 'I dunno. He was always just Chalky.'

'That's not much use, is it, Pippa? I'll tell you who we do want to know about. A young girl. Jan, maybe Janice. Who was she? Was she there? Did you ever meet her?'

Pippa gave her wrist a final rub then wrapped her arms around her torso as if she was cold.

'What do I get out of it?' she said in a dejected half-whisper.

Barry broke in. 'I already told you. All I can do is mention it to the judge, that you've been co-operative in a separate case and that you helped us voluntarily.'

He got a grunt as a reply. This was followed by another silence. Then she spoke again, still in a near-whisper, as if they might be overheard by other prison inmates.

'Yeah, I met the girl. Jan. She was a weird one. Deformed, like. On her face.'

'We think she had a cleft palate,' Jackie said. 'That would have probably shown in the shape of her top lip. Maybe up to her nose.'

'Yeah, that was it. She was a scrawny little thing. Fucking nuisance at times.'

'What do you mean?'

'Listening at doorways, moping around where she weren't wanted. That kind o' thing. She got under people's feet.'

'Why was she there at all?'

'I dunno, do I? She used to run errands for them.'

'For who, Pippa?'

'The guys I already told you about.'

'What kind of errands?'

'Just stuff. Taking stuff to addresses. Collecting stuff.'

'Do you mean drugs?'

'Yeah, well, I guess so. What else would it be?'

'Who was telling her to do all this? Who was the organiser?'

Pippa shrugged. 'I dunno. I wasn't there much.'

She was lying, of course. Her body language gave her away. Someone on full alert might well be able to control all the little signs that facial features beam out into the world, but Jackie knew that someone with a serious drug habit who was having to endure the stresses of enforced abstinence would find it almost impossible. And Pippa was most definitely a member of that group. And not by choice, not here in prison, awaiting trial. Previously, the drugs would have given her a false sense of her own abilities and importance. But without them as a confidence-booster she was having to rely on her own wits, currently almost non-existent.

Jackie raised her eyebrows. 'Really? Not there much? Even though your uncle owned the place and told people that you were the apple of his eye?'

Pippa glared at her. 'Who told you that? They was lying, whoever it was. They're setting me up.'

'And why would they do that, Pippa?'

Pippa almost snarled out her response, her eyes black with anger. ''Cos I'm already goin' down for murder, en't I? So what difference does it make if I get done for another one? Shunt all the bad stuff onto me and they all get away with it. Someone'll be telling you I killed the girl next.'

'I never said she was dead.'

'I ain't stupid. I can read. I knows about that girl's body being found.'

'As far as I can see, your way out is to tell us everything you know. It needs to check out, of course. We can't just take your word for it. But be honest with us. You can see it's in your best interest.'

Another sullen silence ensued while Pippa looked to be thinking through her options, her face clouded with frustration. Finally she spoke, her voice hoarse, as if it was resisting her efforts to get the words out.

'Bruce, he lives somewhere posh, up near the river. But I ain't seen him for years. I ain't seen the others much, neither. I knows a bit more about Chalky. He's stayed local and I caught sight of him last year, down in the town centre, sunning hisself in the gardens, pot belly and all. He used to have a strip club in a street somewhere at the back of the station.'

'Used to? That's not very useful now, Pippa. How long ago? Anything else we'd find useful about these men?'

Pippa shrugged. 'They must both be about fifty. Devious. They've left me here to rot, ain't they? They ain't got in touch.'

Jackie smiled thinly. 'No honour among thieves, Pippa.'

'Too fucking right.'

'Describe them to us. What they looked like.'

'Chalky thought he was God's gift to women. Dark hair, always combing his quiff. Wore tight black trousers and a poncy leather jacket. Right poser. A bit taller than the others. Always had a big wad of cash with him. He used to flash it around, showing off. The opposite of Bruce. He was always careful, used to watch everything and everyone. Chalky was a real Flash Harry.' She took a sip of water. Jackie watched her carefully. She seemed to be warming to her task. 'He looked so innocent. As if butter wouldn't melt. People trusted him. Fucking idiots. He could wangle money out of any poor sod. He had a partner and a family. Last I heard he was living somewhere near Boscombe.'

'Do you know his real name?'

'I already said I don't know his last name.' Pippa looked at her blankly for a few moments before realisation dawned. 'Oh, you mean not Chalky? Dunno. That's what everyone called him. Dunno why.'

'That's all very useful, Pippa. But how were they connected to the young girl, Jan?'

'She hung around the house, and the pub too. The girl, I mean. Maybe she lived there. I never asked. Look, they was all into all kinds of drug shit. So was I. So was the girl. We was out of our heads a lot of the time.'

'Where did the pub come in?'

'What, the Lincoln?'

'That's the one. The Lincoln Arms.'

'Bruce owned it back then, but he kept quiet about it. He rented it out to the people who ran it. But they had to do what he said. He ran the upstairs rooms as a knocking shop.'

Jackie was surprised by the amount of information that was now pouring out of the lips of the woman sitting across from her. It was as if, once she'd made the decision to open up to them, she couldn't stop.

'One thing we do know, Pippa. Joshua Quick was the licensee at one time. Is that how you met him?'

Pippa's eyes narrowed again, and she stared suspiciously at the detective. 'Yeah.'

'When was that? Was it at the same time as the girl was there?'

Pippa shook her head. 'Nah. A lot later. He had the idea of changing the name of the pub and doing Jamaican food.

Bruce wanted to sell up. Some local group bought it and kept Joshua on. That's when they changed the name to the Watermelon. I worked there. Then Josh had a beer keg fall on his legs. He had to give up.'

'Is that when he moved to his flat?'

'Yeah.' Pippa's eyes dropped to the table.

'And you moved in as his lodger and carer?'

'Yeah. Listen. You got enough from me. I ain't talking no more.'

Barry cleared his throat. 'You've given us some useful information, Pippa, assuming it all checks out. I'll find a way to inform the judge when your case comes to trial. It won't affect the trial's outcome, but it might help in the sentencing. But there is one name I want to check with you. Did you ever come across a police officer around that time? Name of Phil McCluskie?'

Pippa stared hard at him. 'Is this you trying to trick me?'

'No. Just answer the question.'

She paused, her eyes flickering between the two detectives once again, as if she was trying to decide their motives in asking this question. Finally, she responded.

'Yeah. But I ain't gonna tell you more. It might still be fucking dangerous to talk about a cop, even if it was from back then.'

Barry raised his eyebrows. 'He's been dead for four years, Pippa. Liver failure.'

The woman uttered a sound midway between a chuckle and an exclamation.

'No surprise there,' she finally said, as she rose from her seat. 'But I still ain't talking about him. He had friends. That's what I always thought. They're still around somewhere, ain't they?'

CHAPTER 24: VULNERABLE CHILD

Friday

Sophie Allen's leg injuries were healing steadily but at a slower rate than she'd like, and this left her feeling frustrated. She still needed her elbow crutches to get around, and the agreement that she'd made with her consultant had included the proviso that she'd work from home every third day, resting the injured femur. She knew better than to put her recovery at risk by trying to cheat the process. She might have got away with bending the rules a decade or so earlier in her life, but she was now into her sixth decade and had been made well aware that the healing process took longer. Besides, her younger daughter, Jade, now in the middle of her medical degree, was the one person who could bully her mother into submission in a situation like this. Sophie might be able to manipulate most other people, but Jade was an entirely different kettle of fish. She would just eye her mother suspiciously and say, 'I know what you're up to, Mum. Just do what you're told.'

Sophie had several folders of administrative items to work on, with one of high priority that she started on first. It was from the chief constable, after all. Even so, she kept

glancing at the folder of material collected by Charlie Barrett, and it was the first thing she reached for after her initial task was completed. She'd had a quick glance after Charlie had handed it over, but she now started a more detailed study of its contents. Charlie had offered to help her with the task, but she'd politely turned him down. On this type of research, she worked better alone and in silence. She began to read through the material, separating it out into several piles by considering each item's relevance to the ongoing investigation.

She soon realised that Charlie had done a thorough job in amassing material on police investigations into various goings-on in the Crawley Terrace area. Not all of them involved the late Phil McCluskie but a high proportion did. Drug abuse, prostitution, betting shop fraud, intimidation, underage drinking. The small piles of notes and papers grew slowly. And as the material accumulated, she could see a pattern emerging — one of incidents not being followed up thoroughly or being shifted down side avenues, only to be forgotten as time went on. She was having to rethink her previous assessment of the erstwhile detective as someone who was rebellious and lazy, but ultimately not seriously corrupt. This stuff showed he was rather worse than she'd suspected. Clever Phil, to have kept all this hidden by the shrewd manipulation of personnel, ensuring that he was kept informed of any reported crimes in that particular area of the town, then quietly moving in to see if he could benefit in some way.

Why hadn't it been spotted? She already knew the answer to that one, of course. Charlie had pointed out that all this had occurred while McCluskie and his great buddy Stu Blackman had been under the protection of Blackman's uncle, the area superintendent. All three of them were long gone now. And good riddance, as far as she was concerned. Three cops, using inside knowledge to line their own pockets. And what else besides? From the records in front of her, it would appear that McCluskie probably had early access to any new girl working the area, looking for clients. Charlie Barrett had said that he'd

sometimes suspected it, but these records provided clues as to how the detective had operated. McCluskie was often first on the scene when police intervention was called for. The same was true for betting shop disagreements and disputes in the pub. Who had been the senior officer in attendance? DS McCluskie, more often than not.

After just over an hour, Sophie sat back and looked at the records spread out on the table in front of her. Where to go from here? And was there any point? There had been no mention of any young girl, no clue as to their victim. Other names had appeared. Busby. Greenfield. But no Janet or Janice. Something Charlie had said about McCluskie was niggling away at her. The long-dead cop's wife, Moira. She'd probably still be around somewhere. If so, would she be willing to speak after all these years? Sophie had never met the woman. She'd obviously separated from her errant husband well before Sophie had appeared in Dorset. Maybe it was worth trying to track her down. Would someone like Charlie Barrett recall anything about her? She'd suggest to Barry that Tommy or Jackie might be put onto the search for a short time. It was always worthwhile trying to tap into people's memories.

* * *

Tommy Carter looked again at the nondescript building in front of him. He guessed that the place had once been a shop, part of a small row of similar premises that fronted onto the busy street. Busy in terms of traffic, that is. Not at all busy in terms of pedestrians and potential shoppers, partly because most of the other buildings were either empty or had become charity shops. A café was still operating two doors away, and a betting shop at the end of the row. Even they looked as though they might be struggling financially.

He checked the number once again and re-read the small nameplate on the door. Dorset Smile Charity. He pushed the door open, stepped inside and looked around. Bright primary colours. Children's artwork pinned on the walls. A toybox in the corner.

A middle-aged woman with curly grey hair looked up from her desk and smiled.

'Police?' she said.

'DC Tommy Carter. I have an appointment.'

She stood up and walked around the desk, holding out her hand in greeting.

'Yes. It was me you spoke to when you phoned. Helen Murray. I'm the admin person. I'll let Morgan know you're here. She runs the place and is one of the trustees. We were intrigued by your request.'

She pushed open a door into a backroom and leaned around the frame. 'The detective's here, Morgan. Shall I make some coffee?'

Tommy heard an indistinct reply that must have been an agreement, because Helen moved to a corner unit and switched on a rather battered kettle that had seen better days.

'I'll take you through,' she said. 'Coffee okay? I could do you tea if you prefer.'

'No, coffee's fine.'

He followed Helen through to a small office where an older woman with even curlier hair and somewhat mischievous blue eyes stood waiting just inside the door, as if ready to ambush him.

'Sorry for the lack of space,' she said. 'I thought it would be better to talk in here rather than out front. We're less likely to be disturbed. I'm Morgan Shandwick. I set the charity up almost twenty-five years ago and I've been involved ever since.'

'Shall I run through the nature of our enquiry?' Tommy asked as he sat down on the chair Morgan had pulled out for him.

'No real need, Officer. Helen is a good listener and gave me the details of your request. I guess it might be that child's body? The one that's been in the news?'

Tommy looked at her a little nervously. 'I can't really comment. It's a very sensitive investigation.' He wondered if he'd chosen his words carefully enough. Had he uttered an inadvertent confirmation?

'It's a historic case, the one you're interested in? Almost twenty years ago, you told Helen on the phone.'

He nodded.

'We've been supporting children with cleft palates for longer than that. And their parents too. It's often the mums and dads who are the more distraught. Everyone expects a perfect baby, you see. It can be a stressful time for everyone involved.'

'And you set the charity up?' Tommy asked.

She nodded, just as Helen appeared with a tray of steaming mugs. 'There were three of us back then. We all had children with cleft lips or palates. The medical support has always been really good. In this area, the surgical stuff is carried out in Salisbury. But we felt more opportunities were needed for Bournemouth-based parents and children to get together, so we set this place up for drop-in support. You know, chatting over tea and biscuits. Letting the kiddies play with each other. It all helps to normalise things, let the parents know there are others in the same boat.'

Tommy nodded gently. 'I know the value of that. My partner's a nurse. She talks a lot about the importance of that kind of support. Making people feel less vulnerable.' He paused and cleared his throat, a nervous habit he'd had since he was in his teens when it was time to get serious in a conversation. 'The girl we're interested in — we think her name was Jan, maybe short for Janet or Janice. She was about nine or ten. Probably thin. This was about eighteen years ago or thereabouts. We can't be too sure. The hospital records don't seem to stretch back that far. Or if they do, she's not on them.'

'No, I can see your problem. Our records don't cover that period either. That's why you've come to see me, isn't it? To use my memory, such as it is. You want to know if there's a child that sticks out a bit from back then.'

She paused and looked Tommy in the eye, as if she was trying to read his mind. He found it somewhat disconcerting.

'Yes, that's right.'

'I'll assume it is that girl's body, found in the old suitcase.'

He said nothing.

'It makes a difference to me, you see. I'm a great believer in keeping personal and medical information away from prying eyes. We're all entitled to our private lives, I feel, unless there's a strong reason for sharing such information.' Another pause. 'Yes. She was here a few times, about twenty years ago, when she was quite young and had undergone a couple of rounds of surgery. Her name was Janice. But for the life of me I can't remember her surname. I used to worry about her because she always looked thin and a bit malnourished. She'd eat as many biscuits as she could when she was with us, but that wasn't as often as I'd have liked. Her mother only brought her here occasionally, not as regularly as everyone else. I sometimes wondered if the woman who came along might not have been her mother. Their facial features were very different, and they didn't appear to be close on an emotional level. I have a vague notion that they came from the old part of town. You know, that warren of streets near the railway station. Can't be sure, though.'

Tommy was carefully noting all this down. Once he finished, he looked up. 'Anything else that you remember?'

Morgan frowned. 'Yes. I don't think she completed her course of surgery. I talked to her mother about it, if that's who the woman was, but I didn't get anywhere. She didn't seem particularly interested. I couldn't afford to be too harsh with her. I got the distinct impression that she'd leave and never come back if I upset her, and I wanted to maintain some degree of contact. I was right in that assessment. When one of the other mums gave her short shrift for her perceived negligence, we never saw either of them again.'

'What did you do?'

'We tried to contact her, of course. What did you think? That we'd have just left it? No, we tried everything. Social services, schools, hospitals that might be involved in her treatment, even churches in the area. Nothing ever came of it, though. We were all running around trying to find her but none of us ever did. The address we had for her was an empty house. We had no idea what had happened. You have to ask yourself, how could such a thing happen in this day and age, a vulnerable child just vanishing like that? Of course, we now know why. It's so tragic. You can't tell me more?'

Tommy shook his head. 'Sorry. Look, you've helped a lot. Here are my contact details. If you think of anything else, no matter if it seems unimportant, please get in touch.'

He thought she looked desperately sad as he left.

CHAPTER 25: SPIN A FEW YARNS?

Kim Brogan flounced out of the bar in a huff, heading towards the toilets. Bloody men. Why did they have to be so buttoned up and secretive? Why hadn't Bruce warned her that their evening out in a quiet pub on the fringes of the town centre would be rather more than a social occasion? All he'd told her was that they'd be meeting an old friend of his from years ago. Quite naturally, she'd thought that it would be the ideal occasion to wear her new dress, particularly since it perfectly matched a pair of leopard-print heels she owned. She thought he'd be pleased. But when she'd come downstairs, feeling glamorous, he was already waiting at the door, car keys in hand, looking irritably at his watch. His eyes had swept across her and he'd frowned. God. There was no pleasing some people.

Now this. This guy, Bruce's old friend; his other half proved to be the most boring woman Kim had ever met. She showed no interest in anything. She just gazed around vacuously. When Kim tried to start a conversation with her, she just smiled weakly and said next to nothing. After half an hour of trying to get some sort of chat flowing, Kim had finally given up and walked away for a short while to escape the atmosphere at their table. Talk about toxic! A woman who was a moron, a man who spoke in monosyllables and kept looking around nervously, and Bruce in a bad mood. Kim wished she'd stayed at home watching the telly. She'd been wondering when to wear her new dress, considering what kind of event might be suitable, sure that it would please Bruce. She'd thought tonight might provide that occasion. How wrong could you be? To cap it all, she'd forgotten that these shoes pinched her toes. What a miserable night.

Kim returned to the lounge via the bar, collecting another bottle of prosecco on the way, feeling eyes on her, and not just the lonely men who were propping up the bar.

'Bottoms up!' she said loudly as she refilled her glass and offered the bottle around.

The other woman, Ivana, or something like that, covered her glass with her hand. Bruce accepted a small top-up, while the other man merely glowered at her. What was his name? Chalky? What kind of name was that, for goodness' sake? If someone felt they had to use a nickname, surely they could come up with something a bit more original? Tiger. Waspy. Jag. Gio. How hard was it, for God's sake? No fucking imagination, that was the problem. Well, not the only problem. No fucking personality, either. And what were the men talking about in their whispery voices that she couldn't quite make out? Stuff from years ago, by the sound of it. People's names. Places. Pub names. Money. More names. And was that the word 'prison'? It sounded like someone they knew was expected to start a long sentence soon. Why did it sound as if they were talking about a woman? Had she, Kim, misheard something?

Bloody hell. This was so boring. They all just needed to lighten up a bit. As far as she was concerned, all three of her companions were badly in need of personality transplants. She shifted her chair and leaned in more closely to try to hear some of the details of the conversation. Phil. That was the only name she managed to make out. Was it the same Phil she'd known from way back when? Kim listened for a bit longer. Pippa. Was that the woman they'd been talking about earlier? It rang a bell, somehow. Something worrying. She extracted her mobile phone from her bag and googled the name, sticking in the word Bournemouth after it, then gaped at what came up on the screen. Arrested for murder. A knife attack on someone called Joshua Quick. Now in custody, awaiting trial. Possibly pleading guilty. There was some kind of link to another story of a house in the town centre, near the railway station. Ah. She remembered reading about this in the local paper the previous week. A child's body had been found in a house in Crawley Terrace. Kim gaped. Was this what the two men had been discussing? No wonder they'd been keeping their voices low. But why?

'What you looking at, Kim?'

Kim switched her phone off and put it away, then glanced sideways at Bruce.

'Just my horoscope,' she replied. 'It's a good night for love. That's what it said. You and me, both. How about it, big boy?'

He looked at her with distaste, as if she'd just farted. 'Not right now.'

She was indignant. 'I didn't mean right this minute, obvs. What did you think I meant? On the table, in front of all these people?' She paused. 'Mind you, it might wake the place up a bit. It needs a bit of a kick up the arse.' She turned to the other woman. 'How about you, Ivana? Up for a threesome? Or even a foursome? Anytime you fancy it, just let me know.'

Kim had deliberately raised her voice for those final few comments. She glanced around to see the effect and caught the eyes of several people around the room. She gave a throaty laugh and winked at them, mischievously.

* * *

Bruce was livid. 'What the fuck was all that about?' he growled as he grabbed her arm and dragged her towards the car. 'I wanted a quiet chat with an old mate, with no one taking any notice of us. I told you that. So what do you do? Talk all kinds of fucking rubbish, and do it so loud, everyone looks at us. For fuck's sake, what kind of moron are you?'

'A bloody bored one,' she hissed in reply. 'That was the pits. Who were those people? I mean, what an airhead. She hardly said anything.'

'She's from some place in Eastern Europe. She can hardly speak English. That's why she didn't say much.'

'How was I to know?'

'From her name, maybe?'

Kim was forced to hold onto Bruce's arm as she wobbled the last few yards to the car. These shoes were hell. She'd bin them once she got home and look for a new pair before the weekend. The thought cheered her up.

'So, you wanna have sex tonight? Hmm? You know getting angry makes you horny. Let's do it, yeah? I got a really sexy bodysuit on under this dress. Have a feel.'

She pulled his hand down to her waist and around her buttocks.

'God, that feels good,' she said, momentarily closing her eyes.

They separated and climbed into the shiny Jaguar. Bruce started the engine and steered it out of the car park. Kim watched him out of the corner of her eye. Yes. He was definitely interested. Temper successfully defused. Result!

CHAPTER 26: WHIRRING COGS

Rae tapped on the door of Barry's small office and poked her head through the gap.

'You wanted to see me, boss?'

He looked up from the documents he was reading. 'I've asked Lydia if George and Jimmy can follow up on this Busby character. It's another name that's cropped up a couple of times in different contexts. I was double-checking through stuff with Lydia a few minutes ago and we realised that Chandler mentioned a Busby when we saw her. But George reported the same name for the young man who's on the list of suspects in the spiking case, the one we thought was Curtis. Again, there's probably a difference in ages. But we're wondering if it's the same family. It'll need a light touch, though. There's stuff being uncovered here that's worrying. So tangled up. And just to complicate things more, the chief has been on the blower. Phil McCluskie might have been involved a lot more than we thought. One of her old pals has lifted the lid on a lot of murky stuff he was probably involved with, under the pretence of investigations.'

Rae snorted. 'No surprise there. Don't you think it fits in with the other business he was tangled up with?'

'She also wants someone to pay another visit to that woman who was McCluskie's carer, Doreen Butcher. There was a photo hanging in an alcove in her living room. A pub. She wonders if it was the one we're interested in, the Lincoln Arms, now called the Watermelon. Can you do that first? It would be useful to get another opinion on the woman, as well as finding out more about the pub and if she has any links to it. That's if the photo is what the super thinks.'

* * *

Rae was irritated when there was no response at McCluskie's flat, the one now occupied by Doreen Butcher. She moved towards the top of the stairs and glanced out of the window, spotting the arrival of a sleek Mercedes. The woman driver swung out of the car and walked towards the building. Doreen Butcher, possibly? She matched Barry's description. Expensively dressed and with a nice car, Rae thought. She moved back towards the door to the apartment and waited. Finally, Doreen Butcher arrived at the top of the stairs. Rae felt the woman's eyes on her.

'DS Rae Gregson,' Rae said as an introduction.

Doreen said nothing as she unlocked and opened the door, indicating that Rae should follow her inside. She was led into the sitting room.

'I'm sure this won't take long,' Rae said, glancing around.

She couldn't see any photos on display, although the recess showed a slight shadowy mark. Maybe dust, or an area less faded by light than its surroundings. So Doreen had removed the photos.

'How can I help you?' Doreen asked, politely and formally.

Rae was intrigued. The woman wasn't acting at all like Barry had described from his visit, when she'd been light-hearted and cheery. She now seemed tense and watchful, making Rae wonder if she'd been warned off by someone. The interesting thing was, of course, that by taking down the pub photo, she'd pretty much confirmed that it was of importance. She seemed guarded and, if so, might well be prepared for possible questions that followed on from Barry and Sophie's visit. Something different was required, something that would shake her up a bit.

'Do you know Pippa Chandler, Doreen?'

Doreen's mouth opened as if in shock and her eyes narrowed. *Well, that worked*, Rae thought. *And much better than I'd ever have imagined.*

'What do you mean?' Doreen said. Then, finally, when it was already too late, 'Who?'

'Pippa Chandler, Doreen. She had close links to the area around Lincoln Street. Didn't you used to live around there once? Or am I getting you confused with someone else?'

'I never said I lived around there, not to anyone.'

Rae felt that she was onto something. 'Oh, well, maybe I've got my wires crossed.' She paused and fixed the woman with a stare. 'But do you know Pippa?'

Rae could almost see the cogs whirring. Doreen might well know that Pippa was in custody, awaiting trial for murder. If so, she would have no idea what Pippa had told the police. How would she answer? Doreen appeared to draw herself together.

'The name rings a bell. I might have come across her. Years ago, though. Memory's a bit hazy. If I did, I've forgotten.'

'She's awaiting trial for murder, Doreen. Didn't you know?'

Doreen shrugged. 'Don't keep up with the news, not really.'

'She's charged with killing Joshua Quick. Did you know him?'

'Did he run a pub in the area?'

'That's right.'

'Maybe it's the name, Joshua. It kind of sticks in the mind. I never met him, but an ex of mine mentioned him, just in conversation. It's biblical, isn't it? That's why I remember.'

'Can you remember the name of your ex?'

Doreen shrugged again. 'Nah, not definitely. It was probably Phil. Anyway, what you here for? Surely the other two got what they came for?'

'It was to ask those questions about the pub. My colleagues thought they saw an old photo of it on your wall.'

'Must be mistaken. Look around you. No photos like that.'

She seemed to clam up after that, giving minimal information in response to further questions about the pub. Just the one slip-up, then. Even so, Rae was pleased with the visit.

* * *

Barry and Sophie were intrigued when Rae returned to the incident room and summarised her visit. Sophie had dropped in to catch up on news and tell Barry of her findings about McCluskie.

'What did you do?' she asked Rae.

'I had a good look around for that photo, the one you mentioned. There was a photo lying face down on a nearby shelf, but I didn't have an opportunity to take a close look at it.'

'What did you make of her?'

'Difficult to read after the initial slip-up. I got the impression she was playing a role.'

'Interesting,' Sophie said. 'So she might be in on it too. Whatever it is, it just gets worse and worse.' She glanced at her watch. 'I nearly forgot to mention the other reason I've called in on you all. Holly Evans came out of her coma this morning. I'm going across to the hospital with Lydia. It'll be bedlam over there, I expect, with press people coming out of the woodwork once news gets out. I expect some kind of statement will be called for. Not that Lydia can't deal with that. She has just the right kind of pugnacious attitude when it comes to putting journalists in their place.'

Sophie made her way down to reception where she met Lydia, and the two women drove north to the hospital, arriving at the same time as Holly's family. Her parents looked relieved but exhausted, no surprise to either of the detectives considering the nightmare they'd been through. The duo waited until Carole and Mark Evans came out from Holly's room after a fifteen-minute session at the young woman's bedside, then moved across for a chat.

'How is she?' Lydia asked.

'Tired. But she was aware of us and said a few words. Well, murmured them, really.'

Carole was struggling to stay upright and looked around for the nearest chair. She was holding tight to her husband's arm. Lydia pulled a chair a little nearer to allow the exhausted-looking woman to sink down onto its plastic surface.

'Thank God. Maybe this nightmare will soon be over,' Carole sobbed, dabbing at her eyes with a paper tissue.

'I'd better introduce my boss, Detective Chief Superintendent Sophie Allen,' Lydia said. 'Although I'm the SIO on the case, DCS Allen is involved, keeping an eye on things.'

'I can't tell you how relieved we all are that Holly seems to be recovering,' Sophie said. 'And I want to reassure you that we'll do everything we can to find who did it and why.'

Mark looked at Sophie carefully. 'When you say keeping an eye, do you mean there have been other cases?'

'Good question,' Sophie replied. 'There may be other connections that we need to consider. With your agreement, and that of the doctors, we'd like to talk to Holly as soon as she's well enough. I need to be honest with you both. You deserve openness after the trauma you've been through, and the frankness Carole showed a couple of days ago. It couldn't have been easy. I'm talking about when you mentioned to Lydia last week that Holly's biological father might well have been an ex-police officer, Phil McCluskie. I'm involved because of that possibility. He died four years ago but some connections and concerns relating to him have recently resurfaced. Holly is just one of them. I got to know him slightly in his last few years before he was forced to retire through ill health, but he was rarely under my direct command. I can't say any more because it's an active investigation. But trust me when I say that I will tread delicately, for Holly's sake.'

'Is there any way of being sure?' Carole asked in a half-whisper.

'Only with Holly's agreement. We can look at her DNA profile and compare it with McCluskie's. It's something that you could broach with her once she's a lot better. Rather you than us, I think. Would you consider it, please?'

CHAPTER 27: RECOVERY

Ollie nudged Dan with his elbow. 'There he is, just come in.'

The two friends were standing at the bar of a pub located in a side street near Bournemouth town centre, each sipping at a glass of lager.

'Stay cool,' Ollie added.

Dan did his best to remain relaxed. He turned around slowly, as if he was letting his gaze wander over the end of the bar nearest the entrance, then lifted his hand in a vague wave.

'Hi, Curtis,' he called. 'You okay?'

'Yeah,' came the reply. 'Ain't seen you in here before.' He looked at the two students somewhat suspiciously.

'First time visit,' Dan answered. 'We thought we'd check the place out as a possible stop on a pub crawl we're planning. Seems okay. Can I get you a pint?'

'Sure. Same as you've got, I guess.'

'Haven't seen you for a while,' Dan said as the extra drink was handed across by the barman.

'No. Been quiet. Short of cash.'

Ollie laughed. 'Aren't we all.'

'You remember Ollie,' Dan said to Curtis. 'One of my best mates.'

'Yeah,' came the reply from a still-cautious Curtis.

'What course are you on?' Ollie asked.

'I'm not at the uni,' Curtis replied. 'I'm a local.'

'I didn't know that,' Dan commented. 'I thought you said you were a student. Must have mixed you up with someone else. Anyway, it isn't a problem. Me and Ollie, we're friendly with everyone. Isn't that right, Ollie?'

'Yeah. Totally. So what do you do, Curtis?'

'This and that. While I get myself sorted, I've been doin' a bit of car mechanics at a local garage.'

'Any particular make of car?'

'Nah. Anything that comes in, really.' Curtis swallowed a large mouthful of lager.

'Whereabouts is the garage? Near here?' Ollie slid these questions into the chat as smoothly as possible, just before taking a sip from his glass and looking around the pub's interior, as if he was only half interested in the conversation. He and Dan had discussed the role he'd play on their way to the bar. He would ask the more probing questions but try to keep them low-key.

'Over in Boscombe.'

'I don't know that area very well. What's it like?'

Curtis shrugged. 'S'okay. Too many old people, clogging everything up.'

Ollie laughed. 'What, even the bars and clubs on Saturday nights?'

Curtis seemed to relax a little. 'Nah. But they're pretty crap, the bars around there. Anyone with any sense comes across here to the town centre. There's loads more going on.'

Dan broke in. 'I know a few students who share houses over there. Good bus service, isn't there?'

'S'okay. They run through the night.'

'Is that from down in the square? Most of the buses run from there, don't they?'

'Guess so.'

'I'm not a great bus user,' Ollie said. 'I get a bus if it's raining but otherwise I walk. Saves me money.'

'Takes longer, though,' Dan added. 'And late at night you need to be careful if you're not in a group. I know a couple of guys who ended up getting on the wrong side of thugs. It worries me too much. That's why I use the bus. What's it like getting late-night buses out to Boscombe, Curtis? Are they okay?'

Curtis shrugged again. 'Yeah. Never had a problem.'

'Do you have far to walk at the other end? From the bus stop to your place?'

Curtis finished his glass of lager. 'Nah. Just a couple of minutes.'

'Maybe the biggest danger is getting spiked,' Ollie said, after taking another sip of his own drink.

Curtis suddenly looked wary. 'What do you mean?'

Dan explained. 'Blokes get spiked as well as girls. People who do it think it's a laugh, seeing someone falling about, maybe being sick. Creepy.'

Ollie added a further explanation. 'It's been in the news a lot since that girl collapsed down at Suki's. A lot of people at uni have been talking about it.'

Curtis remained silent, so Dan decided to stir the pot a little. 'I bumped into one of her friends this morning, coming out of a lecture. She was talking to someone else, but I couldn't help overhearing. She was saying that the girl might be coming out of her coma. The hospital was swarming with cops, she said.'

The two friends each took another sip from their drinks, hoping to disguise the fact that they were watching Curtis closely. They both noted his rigid jawline, pale face and stiff stature. That news had shaken him.

'Whoever did it deserves everything the cops will throw at him,' Ollie said. 'I mean, doing that to someone with a heart weakness. Must be sick in the head.'

'Yeah, but he wouldn't have known that, would he?' Dan suggested.

'Makes no difference. Loads of people have disabilities that aren't obvious,' Ollie went on. 'He won't be able to use that as an excuse once the cops catch him. God, if it was my sister who got spiked, I'd go after whoever did it myself. He'd be sorry.'

'Gotta go,' Curtis said. And with that, he turned and left.

The two students quickly finished their drinks and followed their quarry out into the street. He was about twenty yards ahead of them. Ollie crossed the road to the opposite pavement and the duo started trailing the young man they knew as Curtis. In their minds, his behaviour had confirmed their suspicions.

What they didn't realise was that they were being watched themselves. A man in grey trousers and a nondescript darker grey jacket, clothes that helped him to blend into the background, was observing them with interest. He, too, sauntered along the street, keeping a steady distance behind Dan.

* * *

Holly Evans still couldn't make sense of where she was and why she was there, despite trying hard to listen to what her parents were saying to her. She could see their lips move, she could hear the sounds they uttered, but her brain still refused to do its job properly and make sense of it. Her last memory was of a university tutorial in the Business Studies building when an assignment had been returned, one where she'd received the top mark in the group for the first time. She could remember feeling thrilled. That warm glow had lasted beyond the tutorial itself. She could remember suggesting to Josie that a night out clubbing was called for, that coming weekend. Now here she was, in a hospital bed, wires and tubes snaking away from her body to various screens and machines. A cluster of people were standing by her bed, looking at her but also keeping an eye on the display panels. It was all so confusing.

Her mum, dad and brother were sitting at her bedside, her mother clutching her hand, stroking her fingers. The other three people in the small room looked like medics. One was probably the nurse who'd been with her when she came to. She was wearing pale-blue scrubs and looked as though she was a caring sort of person.

She felt her eyelids fluttering, so closed them and sighed. Had she had an accident? Had she suddenly been taken ill? Her head felt weird, as if all her thought processes had got jumbled up. She opened her eyes again and tried to concentrate once more on what her mum was saying. She raised a hand.

'Sorry, Mum. Say again. Can't think. Feel so tired.' Her voice was little more than a hoarse whisper.

She felt the squeeze of her mum's hand on her fingers and saw her glance at one of the doctors.

'She needs to rest,' the doctor said. 'I think she's had enough for now. You can stay, along with Nurse Gibson. She'll feel more alert after another sleep, I think. Is that okay, Holly?'

Holly nodded. It was so tiring trying to sift through her thoughts and put them into some sort of order.

'Yes,' she whispered, then closed her eyes again. What was wrong with her?

* * *

Sophie and Lydia were waiting in a visitor's room, and rose as the small group came towards them.

'Holly may not realise it, but she's doing really well,' the doctor said. 'I don't think we've been introduced. I'm Riya Banerjee, Holly's consultant. She's not ready for a formal interview yet, and won't be for another day or two. The brain swelling is subsiding, but we need to be very cautious and take things step by step.'

'Of course,' Sophie said. 'Her recovery must come first, we both recognise that. I'm Chief Superintendent Sophie Allen, by the way.' She held out her hand, grasped firmly by the doctor's. 'You've already met DI Pillay several times, I understand.'

Dr Banerjee nodded and glanced at the two detectives. Sophie thought she looked tired. 'Well, here we are. Three women in charge of things. I'm parched. Would you like to join me for a cup of tea? I've been on the go for almost four hours without a break.'

'Why not?' Sophie said, looking the doctor in the eye. 'I bet it's a good one, isn't it?'

'Assam,' came the reply. 'My father gets it sent across from family in India.'

'Sounds ideal.'

'Colin here can give you a rundown of what we know from a medical point of view, and anything Holly's said. I expect it will all help?' She glanced across at the junior doctor standing to one side. Sophie guessed he'd been directly responsible for much of Holly's treatment, and had been present, along with the nurse, at her bedside for much of the time since she'd begun to come out of her coma.

'That would be useful,' Sophie replied.

CHAPTER 28: PILLAR-BOX RED

Bruce Greenfield slid his phone back into his pocket after receiving a call from one of his informants, someone who kept an eye on goings-on in the local underworld. Bruce had known that Chalky's son, Jerry, would be a weak link. He was a careless and arrogant moron of the first order, always drawing attention to himself. Stupid prick. Chalky should never have trusted him. He was unreliable and cocky, a combination of traits that could prove problematic when things got tough. Now Jerry seemed to have come to someone's notice at the worst possible time. It was worrying, but the real puzzle was why those two lads were so interested in him. What had he been up to? Word was, the two were students, part of a larger group who had been interviewed by the cops about something. What could it have been? Drugs? Intimidation? But Bruce's source had told him that the students didn't seem to be in any trouble with the cops. They were more likely to be witnesses. But witnesses to what? And did the Busby lad need a bit of help, even though he wasn't aware of it? Nip it in the bud. That had always been the way that Bruce had dealt with things years before, when he'd been in his prime and still active. His methods had worked. He'd been able to retire with a lot of dosh in the bank, living the quiet life for more than a decade. Of course, he'd had the help of old Phil McCluskie to keep him out of the cops' spotlight back then.

Kim came into the room, pulling a vacuum cleaner behind her. Bruce suppressed a smile. He knew of no other woman who would even consider cleaning a house while wearing a tight, low-cut dress in pillar-box red. She was unique in so many ways. Did she realise how much she'd come to mean to him, despite her occasional outrageous outbursts? She must have realised he was watching her.

'Okay, babe?' she said, giving him that sexy smile of hers.

'Yeah. Listen, I need to ask your advice on summat.'

'Me? Babes, I got no real brains. You're a lot savvier than me.' She switched the machine off. 'Okay. Give it a go.'

'You know a lot more about local gossip than me. You heard anything about local students? Young guys? Summat we might need to worry about?'

Kim perched on the arm of the couch. 'Could be that drink-spiking stuff. Actually, it wasn't drinks. I think someone jabbed a needle in her arse or summat. Down in one of the clubs by the new cinema.'

'When was this?'

Kim shrugged. 'Last weekend? But I heard the girl's just come round. She's been in a coma all this time. Old Mrs Whatsit next door was just telling me when I was hanging the washing out. Her daughter works at the hospital. The place is crawling with cops and newspaper reporters.'

Bruce nodded. That would fit. Jerry Busby was just the kind of arrogant knobhead who'd do that kind of thing. He tuned back in to Kim, who was still talking.

'Her name's been in the local paper. Let me check.' She picked the folded pages out of the nearby magazine rack and flicked through them. 'Holly Evans. That's her. Her parents live in Basingstoke. Carole and Mark. Carole with an E. It says here she used to live in Bournemouth years ago. The mum, I mean.' Kim looked at the clock. 'There's a local news bulletin on the BBC in a few minutes. I bet there'll be a mention. Shall I switch it on?'

'Okay. Just interested.'

In fact, Bruce was more than interested. He had a foreboding that yet more messy stuff from the distant past was about to resurface and create problems. Carole with an E. It couldn't be, could it?

He and Kim settled on the couch and watched as the local news broadcast unfolded. A land slippage on the Isle of Wight. A delay to the introduction of new trains running on the route into London. And then, finally, a reporter standing outside the hospital. Holly Evans was coming out of her coma after being spiked a week earlier. There were her parents standing by a police spokesperson as a statement was read out. Fuck. It really was Carole.

Kim gasped. 'It's her! I remember that face. Wasn't she around way back? You know . . .' Her voice trailed off for a few seconds. 'Listen, babe. Do we want to hang around here if things are gonna unravel? Wouldn't it be better if we got away somewhere a bit safer?'

'You might be right, Kim. It's that stupid fucker Jerry Busby, Chalky's son. I reckon it could've been him who jabbed that girl. The cops could be onto him at any time. Then they'll start asking questions about his family. It won't take them long to get into Chalky's backstory. Then my name'll crop up, and they've already been to see me about that kid's body. Before we know it, it'll all be spilling out like muck from a broken sewer.'

Kim put her hand on his, resting on the arm of the sofa. 'How long we got, d'ya think, babe?'

He shrugged. 'I need a couple of days to get stuff sorted and the money together. I need to shift it all into an account the cops won't be able to find. One thing's for sure, I ain't gonna tell Chalky. He blabs too much to that Jerry. I think he's tryin' to train him up to take over his operation, but it's pointless. The lad's a useless pillock of the first order.' He turned and faced Kim, looking her in the eye. 'Where d'you fancy headin'? Spain?'

Kim looked at him, uncertainty on her face. 'Babes, the cops asked us to stay put. You sure you wanna do this?'

He smiled slyly at her. 'Sure. I been thinking about it on and off for a while. Get out while the going's good. Just you and me, Kim.'

She leaned across and kissed him full on the lips. 'Babes, that's the best idea ever. Maybe we shoulda done it yonks ago. Let's get things started.'

* * *

Doreen Butcher set her mobile phone down on the table-top, picked up her cup of tea, took a sip and sat thinking. Things were beginning to happen. People were a little like chess pieces, remaining in place until set in motion by a master manipulator, and these recent events in and around Bournemouth had a similar set of tendencies. It was too easy to view a chessboard from the perspective of an observer, but how would it appear from the viewpoint of one of the pieces? That was how it should be considered. Maybe a pawn, like Jerry Busby, or a bishop, like his dad, Chalky. That was a laugh, comparing the notoriously devious Chalky Busby to an important religious figure. Though some real bishops might have secretly dubious morals, hidden away from public view. Maybe someone even more powerful, a rook-type personality, like Bruce Greenfield. Possibly someone who has unexpected, even unpredictable powers, like a knight. Someone like Kim Brogan. And what role would she, Doreen Butcher herself, fulfil? Maybe the queen? But a queen without a king — not in recent years, since Phil had died. Not that it mattered, though. This was real life, not a game of chess.

She glanced again at her phone. Interesting, what Kim hadn't said, the gaps between the words and phrases. She was hiding something. Some important decision had been made, but Kim had been trying her hardest not to give anything away. Doreen could sense the effort her friend was having to make. Kim was a natural gossip. A bit of an innocent, really, someone who wore her heart on her sleeve.

It was pretty obvious what it would be. Bruce had learned something that he didn't like. He must have realised that things were finally starting to unravel, so what might he have learned that had sparked that line of thought? After all, the discovery of the kiddie's body might have provided a spur, yet he hadn't acted then. Nor had he following the arrest of Pippa Chandler.

Doreen tapped her fingers on the arm of her chair, thinking hard. Maybe it was just an accumulation of problems. But she couldn't help thinking that something had happened, something unexpected. Whatever it was, it had spooked Bruce. Of course, she could guess what he'd decided. He was planning to cut his losses and do a runner. Heading for sunnier climes, probably. And he was going to take Kim with him. Now, that was a turn-up, very unexpected. Doreen had suspected for some time that there'd come a day when Bruce would quietly slip out of the country. But taking Kim along? She hadn't realised that Bruce and Kim had become so close on an emotional level. She'd always thought their relationship was just down to sex, pure and simple. Maybe it was an age thing. Or maybe, finally, he'd realised life was so much more comfortable with someone around. Just like her and Phil, right up until he'd buggered up their plans by snuffing it.

She finished her tea and set the bone-china cup back on its saucer, looking around at her beautifully decorated lounge, this one in her luxury house in Poole. Very few people knew about this place. She'd kept quiet about it for years. Most people only knew of her flat, the one Phil left her.

Her thoughts returned to her friend. Kim would be an obvious weak link if they were pulled in by the cops and questioned hard. There was no way she'd get through an intense police interview without giving something away, and, in all likelihood, they'd all end up in prison as a consequence. It would be to everyone's advantage if Kim could be separated from Bruce and helped to make a smooth escape from Britain. Maybe she, Doreen, could instigate it. Do some planning. Maybe what was needed was a really serious talk with her close friend, if only to impart some sensible advice. After all, they'd once had that one important link, in the dim and distant past. Shame that they'd both been out of their heads at the time.

CHAPTER 29: A SHADOW OF A PRESENCE

Moira Gamble had chosen not to retain her married name, McCluskie. She explained why as she dropped into her seat at her home in Poole, having deposited two mugs of steaming tea onto the low coffee table in front of Sophie. Moira was a slim, well-dressed woman of medium height, her hair showing a few grey streaks. Sophie guessed Moira was of a similar age to herself, in her early fifties. She'd explained her reason for wanting to pay a visit during a phone conversation earlier in the day.

'Why would I want to keep his name?' Moira said. 'That man destroyed all my young dreams and nearly ruined my life into the bargain. Our marriage lasted five years. Five years of duplicity and treachery. Bastard. I still think that, twenty-five years after finishing with him. He was a slug. I didn't want anything more to do with him once we separated. I went back to using my maiden name as soon as I possibly could, even before we divorced.' She blew onto the surface of the hot liquid and took a careful sip. 'You see how it gets to me, even now, years after the divorce came through?'

'You never had children with him?' Sophie asked.

Moira snorted loudly. 'You must be joking. I suppose it shows that I always had my doubts. The thing is, people told me what he was like before we were married, but I refused to believe them. I was living in pink petal land, not in the real world. But I found out pretty quick, and thought, do I want someone like him to be the father of my children? In the end I got fed up giving him yet more chances. It was ruining my life.'

'You said this was twenty-five years ago?'

Moira nodded. 'That's when I kicked him out. I changed the locks and just refused to answer any of his calls. I knew one of his bosses in Dorset Police, a really nice guy, and told him what I was doing and why I was doing it, just to be on the safe side. He kept an eye open for any signs that Phil was looking to get even with me, but it all went quiet very quickly. In that respect, he still had a s of decency.'

'Did your relationship stay acrimonious after you divorced?'

Moira sighed. 'I suppose we mellowed. We exchanged Christmas cards. But that was the extent of it. I did keep in touch with his father, Donald. He moved back to Scotland and settled in Dumfries. I always had a soft spot for him. He was a lovely guy, thoughtful and kind. He claimed he had no idea why Phil turned out the way he did, but I wonder if he took after his mother. I always thought she had a bit of a wild streak, particularly when she was boozed up. The two of them separated too.' She looked Sophie in the eye. 'I don't know why I'm telling you this. I haven't thought of Phil for a few years, not since his funeral. I went to it, but only as company for Donald. He was doddery himself by then. He died shortly afterwards.'

'I was there,' Sophie said. 'Just out of respect as a fellow officer, not out of any personal feeling. Like you, I distrusted him. But I was one of his bosses in his final years with us. We never got on, though.'

'Yes, I vaguely remember you. Weren't you with a ginger-haired man?'

'Well remembered. Barry Marsh, now a DCI in my unit.'

'And you're even higher? Well done, you. I bet that annoyed Phil. He didn't think women were made for serious work. He got demoted, didn't he, in his later years? Isn't that right?'

Sophie nodded but offered no explanation of the part she'd played in the ex-detective's downfall. He'd deserved what he got, and it was obvious that Moira felt the same way.

'Did you ever get to meet the woman who acted as his live-in carer during his last few years?' Sophie asked.

Moira frowned. 'Her name's Doreen. She organised his funeral. Didn't you realise? I only exchanged a few words with her. A complicated sort of woman. I always thought she must have done well out of it. Why else would she look after him like that?'

Sophie felt like kicking herself. She'd been to the funeral. So why hadn't she recognised Doreen when she and Barry had called on her a few days previously? And why hadn't Barry? It was so unlike both of them. Had the woman changed her appearance?

'He left her his flat in his will,' Sophie finally said, still trying to think back to the funeral, some four years earlier.

Moira sighed. 'Ah, that explains it. I can't complain, not really. The divorce settlement was good to me and saw me through the next few years. Phil wasn't a vindictive man. It's just that I very soon decided that I didn't want any children by him. I can remember my thoughts. What if it was a boy and took after him? I couldn't stand the thought of a son of mine behaving like that towards women. Maybe Phil viewed me differently compared to other women. He was never violent or manipulative towards me. Anyway, once I got settled into my career and met Doug, I had everything I ever wanted. I'm a hospital pharmacist. I have a stable life, a reliable partner and a couple of lovely children. I could forget about Phil McCluskie and pretend it never happened. I didn't really want anything more to do with him.'

'I don't recall Doreen at the funeral. Yet I saw her just a couple of days ago. It's a puzzle.'

Moira laughed. 'She's had a complete makeover and cosmetic surgery. Lost weight, expensive hair-dos, facial skin treatment. You wouldn't know it was the same woman. I only know because she's been in the pharmacy a couple of times, collecting medicine. I wouldn't have recognised her otherwise.' She paused. 'Maybe I shouldn't be telling you this, but that Bournemouth flat she got from Phil, I don't think it's her only house. The address on her prescription was a place here in Poole. She drives a Merc. She's not poor, not by any means.'

Sophie filed this new information away in her already brimming brain. There was obviously more to Doreen Butcher than she'd thought. The woman warranted further investigation.

'I attended Phil's funeral, but only popped into the reception for a few minutes. Did you go to that?'

Moira grimaced. 'Yes, for a short while. If you remember, the funeral was late morning, up at the crem. I only went to the reception because I would have had to find some lunch somewhere else. It wasn't a particularly great experience, though. Some of his ex-police colleagues knocking back the booze and being a bit loud. Are they all like that? One of them even tried to pick me up.' Moira curled her lip in distaste.

'No, it's a minority. But they make their presence felt at an event like that. Dinosaurs from a previous age. Thankfully, many of them have been pensioned off by now.'

Sophie realised that Moira was frowning. Had she remembered something else? She waited.

'That was another odd thing. Most of the women there steered clear, staying with their husbands or whoever they were with. Not Doreen. She was in the middle of that group, larger than life, along with another woman. Swigging back the booze and giving as good as they got. I found the whole thing distasteful and left as soon as I could.'

'Did you ever find out anything else about Phil's relationship with Doreen? Was it just in recent years, or did you ever wonder if they knew each other from years back?'

'You mean, was she one of his many flings when we were first married? She certainly could have been. In some ways she's just the sort of woman he went for. An obvious party animal who likes a drink and a good time. Your other question is a bit more difficult to answer. Was she around way back when? I don't know. Phil was secretive. I know there was a pub he used to hang out in, somewhere in the back-streets in the area around the railway station. I went with him once. That was enough. Not my kind of place. For all I know, she might have been there. There were a number of women around, even though it was largely men. The atmosphere kind of gave me the shudders, but Phil seemed to fit right in. He was in his element. I think that's when the doubts started to creep into my head.'

'When would this have been, Moira?'

Moira pursed her lips. 'Maybe about a year after we were married? It all seemed a bit odd to me.'

She was still frowning. Sophie waited.

'Look, I don't know whether I should be telling you this. It was at Phil's funeral. One of the retired cops was sort of on the periphery of the rowdy group but hanging back a bit. I recognised him from the early days and decided to say good-bye to him just before I left. He was looking at Doreen as we spoke. He said something quietly, almost under his breath. It was something like, *She dragged him down.* I wondered if I'd heard him right, but I didn't stop to check. I'd had enough and just wanted to get away as quickly as I could.'

Sophie didn't respond immediately. She was thinking hard. Doreen Butcher had originally just been a person she and Barry had decided to visit because of her role as McCluskie's carer in his last few years of life. Now she'd become a person of interest in her own right.

'Did you ever hear talk of a young child back in those earlier days in or around the pub? Possibly about nine or ten.'

Moira shook her head. 'No, not that I recall. What are you saying? Is this the girl whose body was found in the suit-case in that old house? My God. What was going on back then?'

'Maybe only a minor connection. We wonder if she was somehow linked to the pub. The house where her body was found was only a couple of doors away.'

'No, honestly.' She looked distraught.

'This has all been very useful, Moira, but keep it to yourself, please. It's been a pleasure talking to you. There were things going on in Phil's life that are only becoming clear just now. Once the investigation is complete, I can fill you in on it if you wish.'

Moira shook her head. 'I don't think so. He's been out of my life for over two decades. I don't want even a shadow of his presence back.' She looked keenly at Sophie. 'That kiddie. She wasn't Phil's, was she?'

Sophie shook her head. 'No, we know that.'

She decided not to tell Moira of their discovery about McCluskie's possible living daughter, Holly, still in hospital. There might be time for that later, if Holly should ever want to find out more about her biological father. Would that be likely? Sophie didn't think so, but these things could be so unpredictable.

CHAPTER 30: BREAKTHROUGH MOMENT

Saturday

Sophie and Lydia paid another visit to the Bournemouth Royal hospital the next morning, having received a message from Holly's mother that her daughter was starting to show more awareness of where she was. The two detectives shared information on the progress they'd made in their investigations during the drive to the large hospital on the northern edge of the conurbation, its bright blue roof visible from afar.

'I still wonder if all these incidents can really be connected.' This was Sophie, as she steered her car into a parking space. 'I know it's beginning to look that way. And there might be something murky at the bottom of it all. The trouble is, I can't see what it is, not yet, and that makes me doubt it.'

Lydia pushed her umbrella open as a few raindrops started to fall from a dark cloud that had mysteriously appeared above them in an otherwise sunny sky. 'You mean, is it just coincidence that the different strands have all opened up at about the same time? Or is there a reason for it? It puzzles me too, to be honest.'

'I've always been suspicious of coincidences,' Sophie replied, as she squeezed under her fellow detective's umbrella.

'You know that. I know they happen. I'm not an ignoramus when it comes to statistics and probability. But let's think. Joshua Quick's murder and Pippa Chandler. On the one hand we have to ask ourselves, why then, at that time? It was just when Holly was starting to ask questions about her biological father. Did her probing set off warning bells in someone's mind because of the link to Quick's pub, twenty years ago? We know that link was the long-dead Phil McCluskie, but she didn't. But if that was one of the causes of Quick being knifed, why wasn't his murder planned better? You arrested Pippa Chandler the next day, didn't you?'

'Fingerprints on the knife and all over his kitchen. Her DNA everywhere. No evidence of anyone else being involved. And she admitted it pretty soon after we arrested her, mainly due to the evidence we had. No doubt about it.'

Sophie continued. 'And then there's Holly's subsequent spiking. Is there a link or was it just an accident that went disastrously wrong? As for the discovery of the kiddie's body, I can only see it as a lucky break for us. How could it possibly have been planned that we'd find it? It was so well hidden. It could only have been a coincidence, surely. Or am I wrong, Lydia? Could there be a master manipulator at work?'

Lydia frowned and shook her head. 'I don't see it. I'll tell you one thing, though. I'm not happy with the supposed motives for Pippa murdering Joshua. I don't really understand why she did it, and she's never let on, other than that she was out of her head on drugs, and he'd somehow upset her. I accepted it at the time. But now? With all this other stuff? I'm not so sure. Was Holly the real catalyst for it all? Did she find out something that might have lifted the lid on some dark history?'

'Well, we can't press her on it, not yet. All we can do is hope that her memory starts to return.' They reached the hospital entrance. 'Let's play it gently. We've got to keep her onside. Her and her mum.'

Sophie suddenly stopped walking, eyes gazing into the distance but seeing nothing. She put a hand on Lydia's arm.

187

'That could be it. It's not Holly that's the problem at all, not for the people behind this. It's her mum. She knows too much but probably doesn't realise it. They were worried that Holly might start asking her mum the wrong sort of questions.'

Lydia turned back, watching her boss's face carefully.

'You know what, Lydia? It's possible this whole case could revolve around what two or three women were involved in all those years ago. Pippa Chandler. Doreen Butcher. And Carole Evans. And that house, the one in Crawley Terrace. Was it Pippa's uncle who left it to her?'

Lydia frowned. 'Yes, Gus Gibson.'

'Well, maybe him too. Listen. Once we've finished here, maybe we should pay that house a visit. Just you and me. Get a feel for the place. And we need to know more about him. Maybe he was the focus around which everything else revolved. What do you think?'

'Sounds good. I'll set Jimmy and George onto it.'

By now they were well inside the hospital, approaching Holly's ward, and it was Lydia's turn to stop dead, right in the middle of the corridor.

Sophie turned. 'What is it?'

'How did Phil McCluskie die?' Lydia had a startled look in her eye, as if she'd just been given a mild electric shock.

'His liver packed up. He'd started drinking again. That's what we heard at the time.'

'But he had a live-in carer, didn't he? He couldn't leave his flat. How did he get hold of the booze?'

Sophie shrugged. 'Online orders, maybe?'

'But surely she'd have spotted bottles of booze? Doreen Butcher. That's her name?'

Sophie nodded, intrigued.

'What if it was deliberate? What if she got him hooked on the drink again? An easy way to get rid of someone in his physical state. Tidying up loose ends. People who were around back then and knew something. Him, McCluskie. Then Joshua Quick. Holly when she started to probe into

188

her background and might have been getting close to some hidden truths. What if our Mr Quick had also started asking the wrong sort of questions? Or there were worries that he might start to blab?'

Sophie grabbed her arm. 'Hold onto those thoughts. We need to talk to Barry about all this.' She paused. 'God, I love this job when we have breakthrough moments like this. Lydia, it's just great working with you again.'

* * *

Holly's parents met them outside her room, still looking tired but happier and more relaxed. A doctor was with them and explained that the two detectives should remain with Holly for a maximum of half an hour, but would need to leave if the young woman showed any signs of mental agitation or exhaustion. A nurse would be with them, monitoring Holly's state.

Holly was still in bed, but she was in a more upright position than on their previous visit that the detectives had made, with her head and shoulders resting against several pillows. There were also significant improvements in her facial appearance. Her eyes were livelier compared to the previous day, and her skin showed a little more colour. She was clearly recovering.

'You look a lot better, Holly,' Lydia said. 'Your parents must be so pleased. Well, elated I expect.'

'I know,' came the reply. 'They must have been really worried about me.' She gave a soft but tired smile.

'We don't want to put you under any strain, so if you feel things are getting too much, just let us know right away. We can always come back again.'

'Remind me who you are,' Holly said.

'I'm DI Lydia Pillay from Bournemouth CID. Please call me Lydia. This is Chief Superintendent Sophie Allen from the Wessex Serious Crimes Unit. One of my bosses, I suppose. Though she doesn't rub my nose in it.'

'Sophie to you,' Sophie added.

'You were in yesterday?' Holly said. 'I sort of remember.'

Lydia answered. 'Yes. We've been given half an hour with you just now, Holly, so we may need to come back several times over the coming days.'

'I'll try to help, but my memory is still a bit vague.'

'That's understandable. Just take it easy, as I said. We're not in a rush.'

'Fire away.'

Despite these words, Holly was looking anxious again. No wonder, Sophie thought.

Lydia started her questioning. 'Do you remember much about that evening, Holly? When you were spiked?'

The young woman frowned. 'Not much. I sort of remember getting ready, then catching a bus into town with Josie, Katie and Simon. There were probably others with us, but I remember being with those three. They're my best friends. We ended up in Suki's. We'd always planned to go there. It's great for dancing.'

'Who suggested it?'

'Me and Josie. It's our favourite place and we feel safe there. The staff are great. We go every Saturday night.'

'What do you remember after that?'

'Nothing. I remember going in with the others. But that's it. I don't know whether I'll ever remember.' She was beginning to look upset and the nurse cast a meaningful glance at Lydia.

'Let's not worry about it,' she said. 'We've got pretty clear information from the other people you were with, so we're fairly sure we've got a picture of the sequence of events that night.'

Holly gave her a pointed look. 'Do you think I was deliberately targeted?'

'What makes you ask that?' Lydia replied.

'It's what I said. Suki's is normally so safe. And Mum said something that got me thinking. I don't think I was meant to hear it. Something like, *I hope it wasn't a message for me.* I didn't understand at first, but it got me thinking.'

'You may have got the context wrong, Holly.'

'Suppose so.'

Sophie spoke for the first time, leaning forward to do so. 'Do you suspect that there might have been more to it, Holly?'

Holly frowned. 'I don't know what to think.'

'Have you been trying to find out more about your background? Just in the past couple of months?'

She nodded anxiously. 'Yeah. My real dad. I love my dad, Mark. I get on better with him than my mum, to be honest. Mum's always been kind of nervy. He's just the best dad. But coming here to Bournemouth for uni, where my mum used to live. Well, it was a bit deliberate. I never told her that, though. She always told me my biological dad was probably a bit of a waster. I just wanted to settle the doubt in my own mind.'

Holly watched closely as Sophie stood up and had a few quiet words with the nurse, who checked the digital displays, felt Holly's forehead and gave a nod.

'Holly, we have a fairly good idea who your biological father is. I told your mother just before we came in, and both her and your dad gave us the go-ahead to let you know if you seemed well enough. Your doctors agreed too. Your father was probably an ex-colleague of ours, a Dorset Police officer. But he wasn't an easy man to get on with. He died four years ago. In his last few months, he began to suspect he had a daughter. He left a letter for you, kept by his carer until a few days ago, when she passed it to me. Would you like it? I have it with me.'

Holly closed her eyes for a few seconds, then spoke. 'I think so. It can't do any harm, can it?'

Sophie frowned. 'Well, it could do, if it was a spiteful letter. But I don't think it is, not in this case.'

'Do you know what's in it?'

'I have an idea. It was inside a bigger envelope addressed to me, with a note that explained a few things. He was seriously ill and knew he had only a few weeks to live. He was clearly in a reflective mood.'

'Okay. I'll have a look.'

Sophie passed the small envelope across, and Holly slit it open and pulled out the single, small page.

She started reading, leaning forward and holding the small sheet of paper in trembling hands. Tears formed in the corners of her eyes, and she wiped them away, somewhat irritably. Finally, she folded the page and placed it back in its envelope, then reached for a paper tissue and blew her nose.

'It's kind of sad.'

'Yes. I can imagine.'

Holly looked at her keenly. 'Can you?'

Sophie nodded. 'Oh, yes. I grew up not knowing much about my father. He disappeared before I was born. A different time and a different situation, but I can empathise, Holly.'

'He says you got him demoted but that he probably deserved it.'

'True on both counts, I'm afraid. What else can I say?'

'So, if I want to know more, at some time in the future, can I ask you?'

'Of course. But keep your mum onside, Holly. And, if anything, your dad will be even more scared, probably worried sick. Don't get sidetracked into ignoring the people who brought you up and love you.' She paused. 'Holly, before we go, I need to ask you something. Did you get anywhere with your investigation into your birth father? Did you meet anyone about it?'

Holly nodded her head, somewhat tiredly. 'Just before all this happened. I met someone who said he might be able to help.'

'Who was it?'

'He was a disabled guy, originally from Jamaica. An odd name. Something biblical, I think. Told me he used to run a pub.' Holly closed her eyes momentarily.

The nurse had been watching her patient carefully and felt her brow. 'I think that's enough for today.'

Sophie squeezed Holly's hand as she stood up. 'We need to nail whoever did this to you. We'll see you again tomorrow, if you're happy with that. It's unlikely to be me, though. If you remember anything else at all, phone us.' Lydia slipped a contact card onto the tabletop.

CHAPTER 31: SHE MADE A RUN FOR IT

Barry set Jackie the task of tracing the interactions between Joshua Quick and Holly Evans, but keeping a low profile while doing so. Lydia's Bournemouth CID unit had a legitimate interest in finding out more about the murdered ex-publican. The WeSCU detective, now temporarily transferred to CID, had a different aim in mind, that of trying to pin down how the original contact had been made and then what had transpired during the couple of occasions the young student had met with the retired publican. Of course, much of her initial work would come from Holly's own recollections and, with that aim in mind, she arranged to accompany Lydia to the follow-up visits to the hospital. But the young woman's memory was still woolly, with haphazard gaps in what she could recall in the weeks leading up to the assault.

Meanwhile, Rae was set the task of finding out more about Doreen Butcher, the woman who they guessed might know rather more about the whole messy background than she'd been letting on. Not, of course, that she'd ever been asked directly, for the simple reason that they'd never considered her a person of major interest until very recently. Even now, there was some doubt about how important she was. A person of interest, yes. But major interest? Possibly; possibly not. And that was the essence of her own task. To get a definitive answer to that very question.

Where to start? Records of births, deaths and marriages. Who were her parents? Her siblings? Was Butcher her surname at birth or was it acquired later, through marriage? Where had she been born? Where had she gone to school? Did she have children of her own? Qualifications and career? The answers to these questions would help to construct a skeleton on which Rae would slowly flesh out Doreen's life with facts and opinions, gleaned from a range of online sources.

Doreen Louise Butcher had been born in Camden fifty-three years previously. Rae looked with interest at the school she'd attended: a fee-paying day college for aspirational young ladies. Rae gained this information from a press photo in a local Camden newspaper that had reported the success of the school hockey team under its captain, a compact and fit-looking Doreen Butcher. Her next press entries were in the family news section of the same periodical, in the marriage column. Doreen Butcher was now a Hopgood, but within four years she'd reverted to her previous surname. Rae could see why. Doreen Hopgood had received a suspended prison sentence for possession of Class C drugs. The story reported that her husband had decided to wash his hands of his 'errant wife'. His family were prominent members of the local community and were reported as supporting several worthwhile local charities. It seemed as though Doreen simply hadn't fitted in with them. This puzzled Rae, until she spotted another story that reported a police raid on a notorious local escort club. It looked very much as though Doreen Hopgood had been one of the scantily clad women arrested at the scene. She was found guilty of soliciting but had received a suspended sentence. No wonder she'd decided to revert her surname back to Butcher at some point before she made the move to Bournemouth.

At least this tended to indicate that there was more to Doreen's involvement than had first been assumed. So what had really caused her to become Phil McCluskie's live-in carer so many years later? Was it just a case of mutual benefit, in which the ailing retired cop gained the help he needed to live out his final years in some degree of comfort and Doreen gained a stable home in return? Or was something deeper at work, a situation in which someone was around who could keep a watchful eye on the increasingly unpredictable ex-cop?

Rae was intrigued by the report that Sophie Allen had supplied after her meeting with McCluskie's ex-wife, Moira, that Doreen owned another property somewhere in Poole. She switched the focus of her research and soon found a possible address — a detached property in Parkstone, one of the upmarket areas of Poole — and decided to pay the place a visit, just for a look. She didn't want to meet Doreen Butcher again until she was good and ready. She had a niggling feeling that there was a lot more to find out about Phil McCluskie's former live-in carer and she wanted all the facts to hand before facing the woman.

The address she'd found for Doreen was a secluded bungalow in a quiet, tree-lined avenue. Rae examined it through her car's windscreen with interest. What would it be worth? A good half-million or thereabouts? How could Doreen ever have afforded to purchase or rent such a property? Particularly given the running costs of the flat in addition. Something just didn't add up.

* * *

DC Tommy Carter was plodding on with his investigation into the historic background of the child discovered in the old, battered suitcase hidden behind the loft partition of that grim house in Crawley Terrace. It wasn't easy, but he hadn't been left completely on his own. He had regular progress meetings with his DS, Rae Gregson, and was often visited by Barry. Both of the senior detectives recognised that he'd been given a difficult task, possibly the hardest one that had been allocated to members of the team. Even so, he'd made steady progress and had a small list of people who might be worth seeing for face-to-face visits. A retired teacher. A social worker. An ex-volunteer for a local orphans' charity. A concerned parish-link volunteer from the local church. All four had got back to him after his initial contacts with them about the young girl, Jan. Of course, their memories may yet prove to be suspect, given the number of years that had passed, but the process of tracing local people who may have come into contact with Jan had generated something useful. He rose from his desk, stretched and walked across to Rae with his list.

'This is really good, Tommy. I didn't have high hopes of you finding much. But four names to add to Romy Mathieson and that charity worker. What was her name again?'

'Morgan Shandwick.'

Yes. Now comes the tricky bit. With a bit of luck, some of these people will have vague memories of the girl. But they'll all be incomplete. We need to put them together to build a bigger picture.' She looked at him.

'Boss, I'm happy to make a stab at it, but you know I'm not the best person for this kind of stuff, to do with personalities. I'm a bit useless at putting emotional stuff together.'

Rae thought for a few moments. 'Look, you do the initial work with these people. I don't expect all of them will have something useful for us, but they've all got to be seen. Talk it over with me after each one. I may come with you once I've got this Doreen Butcher stuff sorted, but make a start yourself. Visit Romy Mathieson and the Shandwick woman first. I know they've already been seen once, but it's an odd thing about people's memories. A lot of them don't remember much on a first visit. But give them a few days to mull things over and all kinds of stuff can pop back into their heads. Okay?'

Tommy didn't look particularly enthused.

'It'll be good for you, Tommy. If you say you're still a bit rubbish at this kind of work, then you need more experience. How else will you improve? Not that I believe you, by the way. You might not realise it, but you've been getting steadily better. Maybe it's Jackie's influence.'

Tommy shook his head. 'It'll be you, boss. That's if it's true. You're the biggest influence on me. Well, you and the DCI. Jackie thinks so too.'

He collected his coat and moved to the door. Rae was left feeling curiously moved. *Maybe I still doubt myself too much*, she thought. *Goes with the territory of being trans, I suppose.*

* * *

Rae proved to be right in her judgement. Tommy called into the Dorset Smile office and found Morgan Shandwick free to see him. She looked at him in surprise.

'I was about to phone you,' she said, running a hand through her grey curls and adjusting her hairband. 'I remembered something. It came to me in a kind of spark out of nowhere. The girl's surname. It was Gibson. Well, to be honest, I don't think it was her real surname. It was just the one they used for her, the people she lived with. I've also been thinking about what I told you a few days ago. I'm pretty certain the woman who came with her wasn't her real mother. Might she have been the girl's foster mother? Or just someone who lived in the same house? I don't know.'

Tommy nodded. To him, of course, the name Gibson was important. Hadn't the owner of the Crawley Terrace house been a Gus Gibson? The man who'd left the house to his niece Pippa Chandler in his will?

'That's really helpful, Mrs Shandwick.'

'That's all, I'm afraid. Nothing else has occurred to me since I saw you last.'

'My boss tells me that you never know what bit of information is going to help make the breakthrough. Please keep thinking and let me know right away if you remember anything else.'

Tommy, a natural pessimist about his abilities as a detective, felt buoyed up as he made his way back to his car. This had been the first of his six visits, and it had proved productive. Sadly, this feeling didn't last long. Romy Mathieson wasn't home, and neither was the ex-teacher, who'd indicated on the telephone that she'd vague memories of the girl. The next person on Tommy's list was the volunteer from a local parish church situated about half a mile from Crawley Terrace. Graham Parkinson was a tall, thin man with wispy grey hair and a slight limp. He met Tommy at the door to his house but suggested that they should take a short walk to the church for a coffee.

'They're open for hot drinks most mornings,' he explained. 'It gives people somewhere warm to linger for a few hours. And we'll pass the place where I met the young girl, if it's the same one.'

'How did you remember?' Tommy asked as they made their way towards the church hall.

Graham frowned. 'It was so odd. Don't think I can remember other random stuff from back then because I can't, but this one stuck in my mind because I was worried about her. I'd just started volunteering as a street pastor on Friday and Saturday nights. You know, looking out for people in difficulty who might need some help. We just wander around in twos or threes keeping our eyes open. The main problems are drink, drugs and homelessness. Back then it was early days, something fairly new here.' He pointed to the church, still a hundred yards or so away. 'See the old stone wall running away from the street? It's got an open grassy area in front of it. A few bushes and trees.'

They stopped as they reached the spot. Tommy could see how the strip of rough grass might attract people with nowhere else to congregate.

'All sorts of people used to gather here at times. Bottles of cheap wine. Drugs sometimes. It was a quiet spot, close to the main street but a bit out of view. That old stone wall would keep the worst of the wind and rain off.'

Tommy looked at the ground. 'Is it still used? Look at the fag ends and bits of litter. Some broken glass.'

Graham nodded. 'Sadly, yes. It's the proximity of the church hall, you see. They might get a hot drink or soup if they hang around here.'

'So how did the girl come to your attention?'

'It was dark, but not very late at night. Must have been autumn or winter. She was staggering around even though she could only have been about nine or ten. Someone had obviously thought it was funny to give her some wine or a puff on some cannabis. There were a few other people here as well, you see. That street lamp lit up her face and I saw the remnants of her cleft lip.'

'What did you do?'

'We had a very quick discussion and decided to get her into the church hall. We contacted the police because of the grubby, uncared-for state she was in. It was my colleague who made the call; she was the team leader. But she had to let go of the girl's hand to get to her phone. As soon as the girl heard the word *police*, she made a run for it. She dashed across the road in front of some cars and vanished up that side street.' Graham pointed. 'I still think of her occasionally. It was one of my first outings as a street pastor. I won't forget it.'

Tommy peered up the side street indicated by Graham's outstretched hand. It looked as though it could lead to the Crawley Terrace area, possibly through a warren of side streets. Perhaps the girl had headed for home.

The two men walked to the church hall, entered the welcoming interior and bought a coffee each.

'What was she wearing? Can you remember?'

'I think it was jeans and a pink anorak. Can't be sure, though.'

And that was it. The volunteer pastor couldn't remember any other details. Tommy thanked him and prepared himself for the next person on the list.

CHAPTER 32: THROUGH THE NET

'Yes, that's right. I'm Pretty Nkomo, the person you spoke to on the phone.' The speaker was standing at her front door, smiling somewhat warily at Tommy. 'I used to volunteer for the local orphans' charity. Do you want to come in?'

'Please. It's a bit chilly out here.'

'Ah well, a good hot cup of tea might be needed, then. Just take a seat in the lounge and I'll be through with it in a moment.' She pointed to a doorway on one side of the tiny hall.

Tommy found himself in a room filled with small ornaments on every shelf. They must be a nightmare to keep free of dust, he thought. But they were attractive, with an African feel, many made of carved wood.

Pretty soon joined him, bringing two mugs of tea and a plate of cookies.

'Always time for chocolate,' she said as she sat down opposite him.

She certainly didn't look as though she gorged herself on plates of chocolate goodies, Tommy thought. She had a neat, dainty build, despite being of pensionable age.

'You said on the phone that you remembered having some kind of contact with the girl I'm trying to identify,' Tommy prompted.

'That's right. It was a long time ago. What, almost twenty years?'

He nodded. 'Yes, a long time. A lot of people wouldn't remember something from that far back.'

Pretty grimaced, the corners of her lips turned down. 'I wouldn't have, not normally. But this . . .' She shook her head.

'What do you mean?' Tommy was intrigued.

Pretty was still shaking her head. 'It was all wrong, that girl.' She frowned heavily. 'I'd better explain. A local lad, Ritchy, was one of my cases. He was an eleven-year-old and was on our books at the charity, you see. We'd had a report that he was truanting from school, very unusual for him. He was one of our better kids and was doing really well. I went to his home, but his foster father said he'd set off for school as usual. He was really concerned. I thought I'd have a quick look in the local playpark. There he was, with a girl I hadn't seen before. Ritchy looked really worried when he saw me, but the girl was brazen. I wondered afterwards if she'd been drinking. I asked him why he wasn't at school, and he just looked sheepish. He knew it was wrong. The girl laughed. It was then I saw she had a cleft lip, though she'd obviously had surgery on it. But it was what she said that shocked me. I've never forgotten it.'

Tommy was intrigued. 'What was it?'

Pretty was clearly reluctant to tell him. Finally, she said, 'Bear in mind she was only about nine or ten, even younger than Ritchy.'

'Yes, I get that.'

Pretty cleared her throat and spoke quietly. 'She said, "Everyone knows Black men have big cocks. But do Black women have big fannies to cope with them? You must know. How big is your cunt?" She thought it was funny. I really didn't know what to say. I just ignored her and told Ritchy to come with me. He looked shocked too. He went back to school as meekly as anything.'

'Did you find out any more about her?'

'I asked Ritchy. He just said her name was Jan, that she lived somewhere nearby, but he didn't know where exactly.

She wasn't at his school. I reported it to social services, but I don't think they found her. Ritchy was as good as gold after that. I don't think he saw her again. Well, he never owned up to it.' She paused. 'I think she was drunk. And at that time in the morning.'

'What was she wearing?'

'I can't be sure. But I think it was a pink anorak. A bit grubby.'

'And this Ritchy. Is he still local, do you know?'

Pretty shook her head. 'No idea. I do know he stayed on at school and got some good grades.'

'What was his surname?'

'Brown. His foster parents were Fred and Georgina Hughes. No idea where they are now either. Lovely couple.'

'Do you think he knew more about the girl than he let on?'

'I expect so. He was at that age when sex-related stuff starts to become interesting, and she obviously knew a lot more than she should have. In today's world she'd be deemed as being at risk and seriously so. She might even have been sexually active. There was something in her eyes, that knowing look that kids shouldn't have.'

As soon as Tommy left the house, he made a call to his boss, Rae. She told him that she'd bring Barry up to speed and not to move to the next person on his list until he heard back. The return call came within five minutes. This line of enquiry was obviously of prime importance and needed more resources put into it, she explained. Jackie had been freed from her own task and would be joining him, particularly since she'd just completed a training course on child protection issues a few weeks before this case had opened up. Meanwhile, he'd done a great job and would remain the lead investigator. Rae finished with a simple comment that made his heart swell.

'This boy may be key in helping us get to the bottom of things, if we can find him. Fantastic work, Tommy.'

* * *

He met up with Jackie some fifteen minutes later in a café, where they discussed plans over coffee.

'Jan appearing to be drunk and speaking in a lewd way caught Rae's attention. Put together, they're signs of a child who's experienced or witnessed sexual acts that are inappropriate for their age. Grooming gangs ply children with booze and drugs to prime them for sex. I know this case was a couple of decades ago, but methods haven't changed much. I'm probably the team member who's most up to date.'

'I was planning to see the social worker next,' Tommy said. 'She's one of the managers now but back then she was newly qualified. She said on the phone that she had vague memories that might be relevant. She should be at the council offices.'

'Sounds good. Let's get moving.'

The two detectives were optimistic that things might start to open up further now they were working together and had a better understanding of the young girl's character. Sadly, it was not going to prove as straightforward as they'd hoped. Tommy's social-work contact could add nothing to their picture of Jan. All she could do was confirm a couple of the facts they were already aware of, that the girl's name was Janice and that she had undergone top-lip surgery at some point in her young life. It did give them an opportunity to discuss the procedures that had been in place twenty years earlier, and to see that those procedures had been followed. The problem had been that Jan's plight had never been brought fully to the attention of the social work team. The girl's erratic educational attendance across several different schools, coupled with her now-obvious lack of home care, had seen to that.

They walked back to Tommy's car feeling despondent.

'Where to now?' Jackie asked.

Tommy consulted his notes.

'The last of the professional people, a retired teacher. He said he remembers something but wasn't very forthcoming on the phone. The name's John Murray. Then I want to speak to

204

this Romy Mathieson. I saw her briefly last week, with Rae, but that was before we knew exactly what we were dealing with. She might have remembered something more since then.'

John Murray lived in a bungalow in the northern part of the Bournemouth suburbs, an area favoured by middle-class retired professionals by the looks of things. Neat homes, well-tended gardens, relatively clean cars parked in driveways. A far cry from the more vibrant and chaotic streets around Crawley Terrace. John was a slightly stooped man, slim and of medium height, almost completely bald but well-dressed in a sand-coloured shirt and slacks. He looked relaxed but alert as he opened the door to the two detectives and welcomed them inside. Was this another case of retired people welcoming disruptions to their otherwise mundane lives?

They sat in a neat living room, sipping at coffee brought in by a petite woman, Claire, who John introduced as his wife. She then left them to talk.

'Janice Gibson, I'm fairly certain that was her name on the register,' John said.

Tommy nodded as he noted this recollection. That would make some sense. The girl could well have been living in Gus Gibson's house; that's where her long-entombed body had been found.

John continued. 'There were several things that made her stick out in my mind. The hare lip, for one. She'd had surgery, partly successful, I suppose, but it had left that shape. That's why people called it hare lip sometimes, rather than the more medically correct cleft palate. She was a somewhat solitary child. Kept herself to herself. Then there was the fact she started school late in the term. Her attendance was erratic. I think I used to get notes explaining that her frequent absences were due to her ongoing medical treatment. But there seemed to be a lot of them. I hardly ever met a parent or guardian. They never appeared at any formal parents' evening or any school event, even when Janice was taking part in something like a performance.' He took a sip of coffee. 'She was very quiet. Didn't mix much. Educational progress was slow. I got the feeling she had little encouragement at home.' He paused. 'By little, I really mean none.'

'Did she make friends?' Jackie asked.

The retired teacher shook his head. 'Not really. It wasn't just the fact that her attendance was poor. She seemed very withdrawn and self-conscious. I tried to get a couple of the other girls to take her on, as it were. But she didn't respond in any meaningful way, and they finally lost interest. Then, six months later, we were told she was moving schools.'

'Was there a reason for that?' Tommy asked.

'I was aware that she lived on the edge of our catchment area. We got a message from her home that a neighbouring school was more conveniently situated. And that was that. I prepared a report and sent it off. I checked with the other school after a few weeks and was told they'd seen a girl with a cleft lip. I wonder if her guardians strung that school's staff along in the same way?'

'How old was Jan when you had her in your class?' Jackie asked.

'It was in Year Five. She'd have been nine or ten.' He paused again. 'You know I find all this deeply troubling. The fact that a young girl could find herself in that kind of situation. I can't understand it, not really. Why did her parents or guardians allow her to be manipulated so? Or were they the manipulators?'

Tommy frowned. 'That's what we're trying to find out. Why she ended up like she did. She appears to have slipped through so many nets.'

'Tragic.' John paused, a worried look on his face. 'There was something else, but I can't be sure about it.' He stopped.

'Please go on,' Tommy said. 'If there's something else bothering you about her, we need to know. If it's not relevant, it doesn't matter. We'll just ignore it.'

'It was something the two girls told me, the ones I'd asked to look after Janice when she first joined the class. They were really embarrassed by it, squirming almost. I had to prise it out of them gently. They said she could be really rude. I don't mean rude in an aggressive way. I think she knew a lot about sex, rather more than a girl of that age should.'

'In what context?' Jackie asked. 'Some parents are very open with their children about sex, right from an early age. I was with mine. I always thought it was better that they knew the basics to avoid any issues as they grew up.'

'I agree with you. But that's not what I picked up from the other two. It wasn't in that context. It was very hard trying to get the two of them to open up, but I got the impression that Janice had witnessed stuff. Possibly even some type of prostitution. Maybe I was reading too much into what they told me.'

'What did you do about it?'

'I reported it to the headteacher. I know she told social care. But it was about then that Janice moved school, so we lost direct contact.'

'Is there a chance that her so-called carers found out she'd told someone? Could that be the reason they moved her?'

John shrugged, looking somewhat pensive. 'I never thought of that at the time. But looking back now, it might explain things. She obviously slipped through the net, as you just said, considering what happened to her afterwards.'

Tommy switched the line of questioning. 'Did you have a lad in your class at the same time as Janice? Name of Ritchy Brown? They might have hung around together a few times at the local playpark.'

A shake of the head. 'No. That name doesn't ring any bells.'

* * *

'Mrs Mathieson, I wonder if you have a few minutes to talk to us again?'

Tommy and Jackie were back in Crawley Terrace, visiting the woman who lived two doors away from the house that had held Jan's body for all those years.

'Of course. Come in.'

Romy Mathieson led the two detectives inside and offered them tea or coffee, but they refused.

'I hope you don't mind, Romy, but we've been offered drinks at every place we've visited. My stomach couldn't cope with any more,' Tommy replied.

Romy giggled. 'I can think of worse problems. Wait 'til you get to my age.'

Tommy explained the purpose of their visit more fully. 'We wondered if you'd thought of anything else that might be of help. Particularly about the girl, Janice. I'm digging into her background, trying to uncover more about what she was like. What kind of a child was she?'

Romy's smile disappeared. 'I felt sorry for her. To be honest, I was never sure that she actually lived in that house. She used to hang around the area at odd times, looking a bit lost.'

'Do you mean when she should have been at school?' Jackie said.

'Partly. But it wasn't just daytime. Even evenings sometimes, she'd be outside without a coat on. Did they throw her out? I don't know. I never got to the bottom of it. Sometimes she'd talk to me. Other times, she'd move away when she saw me. I always thought she looked sad.'

'Was the house noisy at all?'

Romy looked uncertain. 'I don't remember it being too much of a problem. I talked about it once with the neighbours in number seventy, right next door to them. They said they didn't hear a lot of noise or anything. Although it had people coming and going at odd times, it was all fairly low-key. There were more down-and-outs hanging around the pub at about that time. There were rumours that the upstairs at the pub was a bit of a knocking shop, if you know what I mean. I was a bit worried about young Janice then, because she used to hang around that place too.'

Tommy took over. 'Do you remember a boy of about the same age, Ritchy Brown? We've heard a report that he might have been friends with Janice for a short while. He was fostered.'

Romy's frown deepened. 'There was a family who lived a couple of streets away. They fostered five or six children over the years. Mostly well behaved. I don't remember their names, though.'

'Whereabouts was that? Where they lived, I mean.'

'Taplow Street, I think. Bigger houses there. Posher area.'

Tommy finished noting this down. 'Was that area served by the same school?'

'I don't think so. It was closer to Birchwood Primary, as far as I remember.'

Tommy was intrigued. This might explain why Janice changed schools, to be with her fellow foster-child, Ritchy.

They left Romy's house, grabbed a quick lunch in a nearby café and then drove back to the incident room.

'We need to trace that lad, Ritchy Brown. How old would he be now? About thirty or thereabouts?'

Jackie agreed. 'Just what I was thinking.'

CHAPTER 33: GO WITH THE FLOW

Bruce Greenfield felt somewhat cut off from his usual information sources. The short but revealing phone conversations of earlier in the week had been educational for him. He was obviously no longer viewed as the kingpin of old. People had been reticent about talking to him, so something was up. It was particularly worrying that his old pal Chalky Busby was keeping silent. It only confirmed what he'd begun to suspect, that Chalky's son Jerry was involved with the spiking of that girl, the one who was in hospital. Bruce had been keeping an eye on the young troublemaker and had spotted quickly that the lad was being watched. Not only were a couple of students interested in him, but it looked as though he was being investigated by the cops too. Crazy idiot. Why on earth had he targeted the girl in that way? It just didn't make sense.

Nothing else made sense either. His whole world had turned turtle after that cop visit, when he'd been told that he was closely related to the kiddie found dead in that house. He'd spent a couple of days wracking his brain for memories of that time, but they were all too hazy. Too many women. Too much booze. He remembered the girl, of course. She'd always been hanging around. But he never knew she'd been closely related to him. A quarter DNA link, that's what they'd said. Grandchild? Niece? Fuck. What a turn-up.

Bruce thought back through his recent conversations with Chalky. The latest one had been the worst. That night out in the pub when Kim had got bored and drunk. In a way it was no wonder. Chalky had been acting weird. He'd been shifty, not wanting to answer any of Bruce's questions about the old days. No wonder Kim had got restless. It had been a painful evening for him too. Had something been mentioned at a previous chat? Bruce tried to think back. It had been a month or so earlier. Chalky had muttered something about Joshua Quick. What had he said? That Quick might be a weak link? That he'd been spotted talking to someone outside of their circle? Bruce hadn't taken much notice at the time. They'd talked on the phone, mainly about old times. Thinking about it now, Chalky had been a bit distant then too. Maybe Chalky was getting paranoid as he got older. Unless, of course, he was seriously worried about something.

Bruce scratched his head. What had Chalky said? That Quick needed to keep his mouth shut. That was it. Well, it was permanently shut now, after the job that Pippa Chandler had done on him.

Fuck! Was there a link? Surely not. Those two planning something together. It just couldn't be, surely. Could they have been closer than he'd thought, back when Chalky had been one of the area tough guys and Pippa had been a wild teenager? The two of them, along with that devious cop bloke who'd go for anything in a skirt. Maybe they'd all known something that he hadn't. Deliberately kept him in the dark.

God, that was it! Chalky had said that Quick had been spotted talking to a blonde girl, a student. Bruce's blood turned cold. Could it have been the girl who'd got spiked? Had she learned something? That might explain why Chalky's nutcase son had spiked her. And why Pippa had put an end to Quick.

But those two didn't have a whole set of brains between them, which is why Pippa was on remand for murder and

Chalky seemed to have lost his marbles. Was there someone else pulling their strings? But who? With Gus Gibson dead, Bruce was the sole remaining senior figure from back then. And none of it made any sense, not unless Chalky was letting his wayward son start to run things. If that was the explanation, God help them all. That boy was trouble.

Bruce looked up as Kim came into the room.

'You're looking worried, babes,' she said, standing directly in front of him and running her fingers through his thinning hair. 'It's never worth it. Worry gets you nowhere.'

She looked fantastic as usual, wearing a mottled blue dress and blue wedged sandals. He leaned forward to rest his face against the softness of her stomach and slipped his hands around her buttocks. Maybe her simple approach to life was the right one after all. *Go with the flow* was one of her favourite phrases. But he couldn't dispel the worry that occupied his brain constantly, the one that niggled away at him, even in the middle of the night. If he'd been so closely related to that dead girl, the one found stuffed inside the suitcase in Gus's old house, who were the parents? And where were they now?

For her part, Kim was more worried than she was letting on. Clearly something was bothering Bruce, it was obvious. Should she ask him if he wanted to talk about it or was it better to ignore it and continue to play the happy-go-lucky woman that he clearly liked her to be? It was a role that suited her. After all, she really was happy-go-lucky in her approach to life. She always had been. Maybe she'd just continue as she was for the time being and only ask him about his worries if he got worse.

'Cup of tea, babes?' she asked. 'I got some chocolate eclairs too, if you want one.'

'Great,' he said.

She leaned lower and kissed him on his lips. He was a good bloke, really. It was this bother over that kiddie's body that was at the root of it, the fact that he'd been genetically linked. The discovery must have set some things in motion that had been lying undisturbed for years. She'd known Bruce a long time ago, well before she came to live with him. Back when she was a bit of a wild child herself. Had that young girl been around then? Kim couldn't remember. To her, the past always had a hazy veil pulled over it.

A sudden thought struck her. The cops had told Bruce that he was closely related to the girl, but they hadn't mentioned anything about the mother. Did they know who she was, and was she still alive?

* * *

Ollie and Dan had lost track of their quarry, Jerry Busby, known to them as Curtis. They'd spent Friday evening hanging around on the street corner near to where Busby lived with his father in Boscombe. They'd discovered that a mousy-looking, fair-haired woman lived there too. She had a thick foreign accent and used the local minimarket to buy her groceries. But Curtis seemed to be staying holed up inside the house.

They were in the street outside now, trying to appear nonchalant, when they became aware of an angry-looking middle-aged man walking towards them, staring at them. They didn't have time to slide away before he was directly in front of them.

'What are you two fuckers up to?' he demanded. 'You bin watching our place on and off since yesterday. I seen you. Everyone else has seen you. What's your game?'

Ollie started to protest, but the burly man grabbed his lapels and pulled him close to his red face, his lips curled in fury and his stubby finger jabbing Ollie in the chest.

'Don't you fucking try to bullshit me, you creepy turd. If I see you round here again, you'll be dog meat. You stay away from my house and my son. Get that? Now fuck off.' He turned to Dan. 'And you. You're not wanted around here, so stay in your poncy university where you belong.'

With that, he let go of Ollie's jacket and pushed him back against the nearby lamppost, where Ollie only just managed to stay upright by curling an arm around it. If he'd fallen into the road, it would have been directly in front of a delivery van that roared by at that very moment.

'Christ!' Dan said as the man stomped off along the street. 'Are you alright, Ollie?'

Ollie brushed himself down. He was clearly shaken by the incident. 'I think so,' he said, his voice quivering. 'I think I need a strong coffee.'

'Do you think we need to tell the cops about this?' Dan asked.

'I can't think straight. He was a total thug. Who the hell was he?'

'I'm gonna guess that he was Curtis's father. He had the same kind of face shape, and when he screwed up his face at you, it was just the way Curtis looked yesterday. I think we've rattled someone badly.' He gave his friend a wry grin just as a shop assistant came out of the nearby newsagents.

'Are you okay?' she asked. 'I saw that Chalky guy having a go at you. I was all ready to call the police, but he went off.'

'Chalky?' Dan said.

'Yeah. It'll be a nickname, won't it? Sure you're okay?'

Ollie nodded. 'Tougher than I look.'

She laughed as she returned to her shop. 'I bet you're not.'

* * *

It was only half an hour later that they were sitting in a town centre café, sipping coffee and talking to George Warrander. The police detective looked annoyed.

'I told you to leave it to us,' he said. 'You could have got yourself badly hurt. With people like that, you've got to leave it to the professionals. Not to mention the fact that you might have put them on their guard. If you've mucked up our investigations, my bosses won't be at all pleased, I can tell you.'

'Yeah, but surely some of the stuff we've found out is useful?' Dan protested.

'Of course it is. It adds to the picture. But we've already found out a lot of it, and more besides.'

'What?' asked Dan, looking expectant.

George smiled somewhat grimly. 'No, I'm afraid it doesn't work like that. What I will say is that it's a wider issue than it appears, and that's why we're playing our cards close to our chests. And, in case you haven't heard, Holly came out of her coma the night before last. It looks as though she might make a full recovery.'

'That's good news,' Ollie said. 'Does it mean the pressure's off?'

'Not at all. Spiking is a serious crime, and we have to try to put a stop to it. The best way we have to do that is to catch the culprits and take them to court. That's the way justice works in this country. If we were to drop the case, what kind of message would that send out?'

'The press would have a field day,' Dan said.

'And a lot of people would feel let down by us,' George continued. He thought for a while. 'I'd like a statement from you about everything you've done in seeking out this man Curtis, along with what just happened across in Boscombe. Can you come along to the station just now to get it done while it's fresh in your minds?'

The two friends looked at each other and shrugged.

'Don't see why not,' Dan replied.

George thought that Ollie was looking uneasy, awkward even.

'Something bothering you, Ollie?' he asked.

'Well, yeah. The girl, Holly. Would we be able to visit her? I don't mean right now. I just feel so bad about what happened to her. She came close to dying, didn't she?'

George nodded.

'And we heard that she's got some kind of heart defect. That's the reason for her coma, isn't it?'

'I can't comment. We can't divulge people's personal details.'

'No, but that's the talk. She needs to know that most guys aren't like that. It's the bad few that create all the problems.'

'I can get that passed on to her.'

Ollie looked disappointed. 'No chance of seeing her? Is that what you're saying?'

'I'm not saying anything. I can get the message passed on if it's that important to you. But I haven't spoken to her, nor has my own boss, the DS. It's just been the DI and her boss. She's only been out of her coma for a day or so. We've got to be gentle and slow.'

'Even so, I feel really angry about what happened.'

George watched him carefully. 'And that's why you decided to try a spot of investigating yourself?'

'Suppose so.'

'Well, your attitude does you credit. As I said, I'll get your request passed on. No guarantees, though.'

Ollie nodded. He was happy with that.

CHAPTER 34: UNCLE, AUNT
OR SOMETHING ELSE?

Lydia was chairing a briefing with Jimmy and George in the CID room at Bournemouth police station. Jimmy was explaining the presumed sequence of events that had occurred at Suki's Bar when Holly had been spiked.

'This guy Jerry Busby, or Curtis Murchison as he sometimes calls himself, he's clearly our prime suspect. And we've worked out how he got out of the place after he'd spiked Holly.'

'I'm all ears, Jimmy,' Lydia said wryly.

'Well, it has taken a bit of figuring out, boss,' came the reply. 'He jabbed her as she went past, then he quietly headed off in the opposite direction, keeping out of the camera's vision. He didn't hang around to see the effect on her.' Jimmy pushed the floorplan of Suki's across the table. 'This area here, just a few yards from the door, is out of CCTV range. He waited until the kerfuffle started when the girl collapsed. The security staff headed into the main part of the bar to see what was going on. That's when he slipped out, just in the few seconds when no one was on the door. He kept close to the wall in the entrance lobby and avoided the camera. That's why he wasn't on any of the CCTV sequences or on any of the lists made up by the staff. He'd already gone by then.'

'Sounds good. Anything to add, George?'

The junior detective shook his head. 'It's the only thing that works, boss. We've checked the idea with the staff there and timed everything. We've gone through the videos really carefully. Anyone spiking her once she was on the dancefloor couldn't have got away after jabbing her. There just wasn't enough time and they'd have been caught on camera. But this way, yeah, it works. Add to that the fact that Holly and her friends were there every Saturday night. Predictable. He knew she'd be there.'

Lydia looked thoughtful. 'So, this guy, Curtis or Jerry or whatever his name is, he's the one? You're sure?'

'Absolutely. Add up everything else we know about him. He's lied about his identity to these other students. He's been acting suspiciously, according to two of them. He was in a lot of trouble as a teenager, according to his school, and used both names then if he felt like causing trouble. His father seems to be a bit of a thug too.'

Lydia spoke sharply. 'What's the father's name?'

'Alan Busby, though everyone calls him Chalky. No idea why. They live in Boscombe.'

'Ah.'

'Exactly,' Jimmy added. 'The place with the worst drug problem in the area.'

'Do you think he's involved, this Alan?'

Jimmy shrugged. 'It fits with what we know, though he isn't on anyone's radar, not according to vice. Should we bring them in?'

Lydia shook her head. 'No. Not yet.'

Jimmy looked puzzled. 'Why not?'

'Because the father, this Chalky bloke, has been seen out and about with Bruce Greenfield. And his number's on Pippa Chandler's phone. There's something deeper and murkier going on here. At the moment we just watch and wait. I need to see Barry about this. Find out what you can about these two Busby men, but do it quietly. I want to know about the father's backstory. Going back about twenty years or thereabouts.'

George sat forward in his seat. 'You think it links to the kiddie's body?'

'Dead right, George. We think there's been a conspiracy of silence for all that time. People who knew or guessed what happened to Jan. And it's all finally opening up, thanks to Holly Evans and the fact that she started probing into her own background. The chief super is convinced all these bits and pieces are linked. Someone didn't want the lid lifted and they acted quickly once Holly did exactly that.'

George was frowning. 'But how did they know about her heart weakness?'

'Family and friends knew. She didn't try to hide it.'

'So you're saying someone might have been quietly keeping an eye on her all this time?'

'In one way or another. Someone more subtle than that Busby bloke or Pippa Chandler. Jackie Spring, over at WeSCU, is convinced that Holly had been speaking to Joshua Quick about her biological father. That's when all this kicked off. Makes you think, doesn't it?'

* * *

Lydia had time to pay a short visit to the hospital before her strategy meeting with Barry and Sophie. She found Holly sitting on a high-backed chair beside her bed, supported by cushions. She looked well on the way to recovery and Lydia told her so. The young woman smiled.

'I'm beginning to feel better too. Have you come here to ask me more questions or to tell me how you're getting on with your investigation?'

Lydia laughed. 'Very perceptive. Both, I suppose. We are making progress, Holly. But it's proving to be a more complex case than we first realised. And that's partly why I'm here.

We'll be keeping a security presence at the ward entrance for a few days.'

Holly looked concerned by this news. Her previously relaxed demeanour was replaced with a worried frown. 'Why? What's happened?'

'It's not definite by any means, but what happened to you might be part of a wider issue. We wonder if your meeting up with Joshua Quick, the disabled guy from Jamaica you mentioned, set a chain of events in motion. We're still investigating. What you may not be aware of is that he died in suspicious circumstances within a week of meeting you last. Is it connected? We can't be sure, but it's a possibility. We can't take any risks with your well-being, not at present.'

Holly's face paled noticeably, and she gripped her chair's armrests tight. 'What are you saying? How can me trying to find out about my birth father cause problems like that?'

'Look, Holly, I can't explain, not at the moment. We've been assuming that your spiking was a random act. But in the last couple of days a few niggling facts have come to light, and we have to probe into them. I really can't tell you more, not just now.'

'It's like it said in that letter, isn't it? The one from my birth dad. He was a detective who got himself into trouble. Is that what you mean?'

'It's complicated by that fact, yes. What I've really called in for, other than to see how your recovery is going, is to see whether you've remembered much from your chats with Joshua Quick.'

'I didn't get a lot out of him. He seemed a nice guy, but he was a bit nervous, I thought. He was on crutches. He told me he used to help run a pub and my father might have been a regular there a long time ago. He clammed up after that, though. He said he needed to think things through before telling me more. I couldn't understand why. If he knew stuff, what was the problem with telling me? I got a bit angry.'

Lydia nodded. 'I can see why you'd find that frustrating. I would have felt the same.'

'It kind of makes sense now though, doesn't it? After that letter you brought me. Was there something a bit dubious going on? Way back then, I mean.'

Lydia shrugged her shoulders. She needed to be careful here, and only pass on hard facts that wouldn't put the investigation at risk. And what hard facts did they possess, in reality?

'Possibly. That's the subject of our enquiries, Holly. You must realise that I can't tell you much, not while it's all ongoing. Please trust me. We'll tell you everything when the investigation is wrapped up. But not before, I'm afraid. As I said just now, we need to keep you safe, and that's why there'll be an officer stationed outside. I've got you a security alarm button to wear around your neck. If there's an emergency, don't hesitate to use it.'

She passed the device across to Holly and talked about its use, then glanced at her watch.

'Sorry, got to go. I've got an important meeting with my bosses about your case, but I'll be in again tomorrow. Just give me a call if you think of anything, or something's worrying you. Okay?'

Holly nodded, a look of worry on her face. Lydia squeezed her hand and left.

* * *

The three senior detectives were grouped around a table in a meeting room at Bournemouth police station, studying a set of summary notes and decision points that Barry had prepared. All three of them realised they were at some kind of crossroads, a moment at which important decisions had to be made about the course they were to follow from this point on. But the way ahead was still not absolutely clear.

Sophie spoke first. 'This is fine, Barry. It helps us to get our thoughts in order. It would have been so much easier for us if that child's DNA profile had shown a fifty percent match to this Bruce Greenfield character, but sadly it's just a quarter.'

'So what are the possibilities?' Lydia asked.

Barry explained. 'Uncle or aunt. Grandparent. Half-sibling. I think that covers it.'

'What's it more likely to be?'

Barry shrugged. 'It's a guess, isn't it? With normal generational age differences, it's more likely that he's Jan's uncle. But we can't rule the others out. People have children at all ages, don't they? We tend to think that secret love children are a thing of the past and people are more open now, but it isn't always true.'

'Can't we get more from the DNA? You know, information about the exact relationship.'

Sophie shook her head. 'Not currently. The guidelines limit us to identification of an individual and we can't probe any further unless it's a fifty percent link. Parents and siblings, in other words. There are too many practical and ethical issues with going any deeper. I have to say, I agree. It could be a real can of worms. That's why those limits have been set.'

Lydia grimaced. 'Well, you're the expert, boss. These legalities are a closed book to me. But I trust what you're telling me.'

Sophie gave her a hard stare. 'I'm glad I have your trust, Lydia. Things wouldn't work between us otherwise, would they?'

'I didn't mean it quite like that, and you know it. Maybe we should just move on.' Lydia's prickly side was something that Sophie and Barry had got used to over the years. It had surfaced before and would again, no doubt.

They were interrupted by a knock on the door. Rae's head poked through the crack.

'Sorry. Something important has cropped up. You need to know.'

Sophie beckoned her inside the small room.

'It's the house. Sixty-eight Crawley Terrace. Solicitors have just got in touch with me about the will Gus Gibson left. Apparently, he amended it just before he died. He didn't just leave it to Pippa Chandler. It was left jointly to her and to Joshua Quick.'

CHAPTER 35: GUS GIBSON

'We need to think this through. What it means and how it changes things.' Sophie indicated for Rae to join them, taking up the fourth position at the table. 'How come it's taken so long for us to find this out?'

'A slip-up at the solicitors, as far as I can tell. This man Gus Gibson had a long-standing will and the beneficiaries knew what was in it.'

Lydia interrupted. 'Pippa Chandler had a copy. Jimmy and I have seen it. We checked with the solicitor and weren't told of any update.'

Rae looked at her somewhat apologetically. 'No, the guy who called me said that. Apparently, Gibson called in to lodge a new will just a few days before he died. It was witnessed by neighbours and left with a staff member in the office who set off on holiday the next day. He guessed it was late on a Friday afternoon. It got covered over with other stuff. He admitted it should never have happened.'

'How come this came to you?' Lydia asked, still sounding irritated. 'It was my unit that was in charge of the Pippa Chandler investigation. Why didn't he contact me or Jimmy or George?'

'I was on the phone to him about Phil McCluskie's will. I've been following up stuff related to the flat he left to Doreen Butcher. Same solicitor, you see. I asked if he knew whether McCluskie had ever owned property in Crawley Terrace or the area around there. That's when he told me he'd just uncovered this change to number sixty-eight.'

Lydia looked as if she was only just managing to control her temper, muttering under her breath.

'The important thing is what it means for us,' Sophie said. 'It casts a new light on things, doesn't it? What's the place worth? Come on, someone must know. About two hundred thousand? Maybe a bit more? With Joshua Quick alive, Pippa would have seen half of its value lost to her. Was she the type of person to sit back and meekly accept that?'

Lydia gave a grim laugh. 'Absolutely not. But she's also totally incapable of organising anything. Bad-tempered. Huge mood swings. Pops any drug she can lay her hands on. Her brain's all over the place. I don't see her as someone who can mastermind any kind of plan.'

'But the loss of that much money would be a pretty strong motive for getting rid of Quick.'

Barry nodded. 'I would say so.'

'So, was the relationship between Gibson and Quick closer than we thought? Was this some kind of reward, leaving half of the house to him?'

'Maybe Quick helped to keep Gibson out of jail some-how. Him and Phil McCluskie.' This was Rae speaking for the first time. 'He must have done a great job of keeping the lid on all their activities. I hated him when he was still working as a cop. He made me shudder. But hat's off to him, in a warped kind of way. He must have smoke-screened all the stuff they were up to.'

Barry was feeling frustrated. 'Look, this is all very interest-ing. But it's not getting us anywhere. We need facts. Evidence we can use. My view is similar to yours, boss. That we need to dig into this shady bloke, Gus Gibson. I know he died a couple of months ago, but so much of what we're investigating seems to revolve around him and his house. We've been checking into everyone else's backstories and still haven't made the key breakthrough. What does that tell us? Maybe we've been concentrating on the second tier without realising it. Missing out the kingpin. It could well be Gibson.'

Sophie summed up. 'Well, let's get both units onto it as soon as they're in on Monday morning. We need to know more about Gus Gibson and his background. And I think we need to look at Greenfield in a bit more depth. And there's this Busby character. Isn't he a person of interest? And what about the Chalky person that Chandler mentioned? How important might he be? Can the two of you split the work up?'

'What about Doreen Butcher?' Lydia asked.

'Leave her to me. I need to keep my hand in, just to stop me drowning in a sea of spreadsheet cost–benefit analysis and budget planning.' She grimaced. 'Can I suggest that you both give your people some time off this afternoon and tomorrow? They're all looking a bit tired, and we need them on the ball next week.'

Rae interrupted. 'I've been a bit worried about Jackie, to be honest. I think she could do with a day or two back in Watchet to make sure her love life with Tony doesn't go down the pan.'

Sophie laughed. 'You're showing your soft side, Rae. Good for you.'

'But leave me out of your R & R plans, please. Craig is away on a course this weekend. I'd prefer to be busy on something, so leave me with the Gus Gibson research. It'll stop me getting bored.'

Barry nodded. 'That would be ideal, Rae. Depending on what you find, we might be able to hit the ground running on Monday morning.'

Sophie was fidgeting awkwardly in her chair. She looked at Lydia. 'Um, and maybe try your best to get George to take the rest of the weekend off, even though he might resist the idea. He could visit Oxford.'

Lydia laughed. 'Has Jade been getting onto you?'

Sophie rolled her eyes. 'You have no idea.'

* * *

Sophie Allen went home with the hope of spending at least a few hours relaxing, though not physically. She joined Martin, her husband, on a visit to the RSPB's famous Arne nature reserve. They might have considered walking there from their Wareham home prior to the serious assault that had led to her leg injury, but currently such a distance, about four miles in each direction, was out of the question. The visit fulfilled its purpose though, and helped to soothe her somewhat ragged mood. She'd been told by her therapist that although her physical injuries might be healing well, the mental scars of her near-drowning could take a good bit longer. Well, occasional trips out to beautiful scenery like Arne helped. Even so, she sent a quick text message to Rae telling the DS that she was available should she be needed.

Barry shared a quick lunch with Rae, spent some time clearing a backlog of administrative work, then headed home to work on the garden with his wife, Gwen. Were fruit bushes a good idea? Only one way to find out. He messaged Rae to remind her that he was available on the phone if she needed advice.

Lydia was still in the process of softening the fittings in her office. She'd admired her previous boss, Kevin McGreedie, but he'd had a very minimalist approach to decorating the DI's lair. Now it was hers, she wanted to adapt its appearance to match her own personality. She spent an hour there before setting off for the shops. Even so, she found time to pop her head around the door of the incident room to speak to Rae and offer her support if it was required.

Jimmy Melsom was off to a football match. Now that they were back in the top tier of English football, some of Europe's finest teams came to play against Bournemouth. For a football addict like him, that was heaven. Today's home match was against Chelsea. Bliss. He messaged Rae telling her where he was, and that he was contactable once the match was over, if she needed him.

Tommy was visiting IKEA with Olivia. They'd moved in together and had decided that they needed some new furniture for the living room. He was wondering when might be the right time to pop the all-important question, but his shyness was holding him back. Maybe once this case was over? Before setting off to the shops he shot off a short text message to Rae, wishing her luck in her task.

Jackie climbed into her car and headed directly for the North Somerset coast and her home in Watchet. She needed to feel Tony's arms around her. What was that saying? Absence makes the heart grow fonder? It was certainly true in her case. He'd promised to cook her a fish-based pasta meal this evening. To be honest, it wasn't the food that she was most looking forward to, but she hadn't yet told him that. She intended to play coy at first and wait until they'd finished eating before pouncing on him. Would her willpower hold out, though? She had her doubts. She was home inside two hours and stopped off at her own house for a shower and a change of clothes. Plus a short message to Rae, offering her help should it be required.

George was in Oxford by early afternoon. He peered ahead as he approached Keble College from the south. There she was, standing outside the entrance, waving like a mad thing. He lengthened his stride for a few seconds, then broke into a trot. He whirled her into his arms and nuzzled his mouth into her ear.

'I love you, Jade,' he said.

The sound she made was halfway between a laugh and a sob. It made him wonder how Rae was getting on, back in the incident room on her own. He'd message her once he had a spare moment. She'd probably welcome a bit of support.

* * *

Rae settled down to work after sharing a snack lunch with Barry, in which he'd outlined some ideas. When she'd first joined Sophie's unit some six years previously, this kind of task had proved to be her strong point. Digging into people's backgrounds, looking for motivations and connections. Since she'd got her promotion to DS she'd done less of it, handing the task over to Tommy Carter, but she still had the skillset required and relished dusting off the techniques she'd honed back then and getting stuck in.

Gus Gibson. Angus, probably. Latterly a Bournemouth resident but where before that? Rae had the Crawley Street address. Start with that and then move outwards, and backwards in time. Criminal records. Electoral roll. Registers of births, deaths and marriages. Death certificates. Health records. Possibly social media, but that might be less likely considering his age when he died. News media.

Stage one, construct a timeline of his life. Stage two, fill in the details of where and who else was involved. Stage three, look for connections and possible motivations.

Rae was in her element. The only thing that distracted her during the next few hours was the seemingly constant pinging of her phone to signal incoming text messages from her colleagues, offering help if she needed it. Nuisance.

CHAPTER 36: STORMY MONDAY

Monday

Although Monday morning dawned wet and windy, the detective teams arrived early and were gathered in the incident room waiting for the summary Rae had put together, to be followed by the allocation of tasks for the week ahead. All apart from George Warrander. His drive south from Oxford had been delayed by a fallen tree, but he'd messaged to say he should be with them by nine.

Rae had a photo showing on the large display screen. She was keeping an eye on Sophie and Barry with interest. Both seemed tense and were talking to each other in near-whispers, pointing to dim figures in the background of the shot, as she'd expected. Something important was happening. She could feel the air almost crackling with tension.

When everyone had settled, Rae started talking.

'These photos are key. They link so much together. Can I introduce you to the three men in the foreground, all important to our investigation? On the left, Bruce Greenfield. Next in, Gus Gibson, then owner of the house in Crawley Terrace. Third, Alan Busby.' She pressed a button on her remote and the display changed. The new image showed two well-dressed women. The group of three men in their dark suits could still be seen in the background.

'Doreen Butcher and Kim Brogan.'

Jackie leaned forward for a closer look, trying to discern two figures on the edge of the photo. Surely not?

Rae continued. 'And you might just be able to make out the chief superintendent and the DCI on the edge of this shot. You might want to explain, ma'am.'

Sophie nodded. 'Phil McCluskie's funeral four years ago. Barry and I were there, representing Dorset Police.'

Rae pressed the button again. There, leaning against the bar of the function room, was a seemingly inebriated Pippa Chandler.

'I remember a drunk woman being there,' Sophie continued. She sounded embarrassed. 'She was pretty obvious. We popped into the post-funeral reception for the minimum amount of time possible, just to show our faces. We spoke to his ex and a couple of other people, then left.'

'You don't have to justify it, boss. I don't think any of us think you're bent.' Lydia was trying hard not to laugh.

George arrived at that moment, looking flustered and apologising for the road disruption that was beyond his control. Lydia put a hand on his arm as he sat down next to her.

'Don't worry, George. I'll fill you in on what you've missed.'

He looked up at the screen as Rae cycled back through the photos.

'Hold it,' he said, pointing at the display. 'That's Alan Busby, on the right.'

Rae checked the photo. 'So he's this shady Chalky character we've heard mentioned?'

George nodded. 'He's the father of the lad we think spiked Holly Evans. He's an intimidating thug of the first order, according to two of the students. He came out and threatened them. They sent me a photo of him late on Saturday.'

'That's interesting to know. Okay to move on, boss?'

Sophie nodded. 'Where did these photos come from? They've got that press look about them.'

Rae nodded. 'They're from an old bank of photos held by the local paper. They were never used. I got access through a reliable contact of mine who's a freelance press photographer.' She moved away from the screen but left the group photo on display. 'My guess is that those are the people we're interested in. I spent yesterday looking through the information we have on each of them, then finding out a bit more, particularly on Gus Gibson.' She took a sip of water from the bottle that stood on the tabletop in front of her. 'From our point of view, Gibson is the big unknown. He's been dead for a few months. Lung cancer. He seemed to have come across as an ordinary, law-abiding individual, almost a pillar of the local community, although we suspect differently after hearing Pippa Chandler's account of his behaviour. He owned and ran an off-licence for most of his working life, at the eastern end of Crawley Terrace, a few hundred yards from his house. Would that have given him access to some suspect people? I don't know.'

Sophie looked unsure. 'This is all good. It helps us pick apart more of the background. But remember we need to concentrate on Jan. I know you've been working hard, and it's not easy trying to probe into a murder that dates back twenty years or so, but we still don't know much about her, and it's been more than a week now. Has there been nothing from the public appeals?'

There was an all-round shaking of heads.

'Do we need to make it a bit more high-profile?'

Tommy cleared his throat nervously. 'I think we're finally getting somewhere, ma'am. It's slow, but Jackie and I have a couple of leads to follow up. The girl was friendly with a local lad, according to a couple of people we spoke to. That's our next plan. To trace him and speak to him if we can. His name was Ritchy. He was in foster care at the time.'

'So do you want me to hold back on a public appeal, Tommy?'

'I'm not sure. Could it make people even less likely to help us? The people we need to find might have shadowy backgrounds.'

'I see what you mean. Well, let's review it again in a couple of days. You and Jackie keep at it.' Sophie looked at Rae. 'Anything else?'

'I did a bit of thinking about this Bruce Greenfield character. He looked genuinely shocked when we told him about his DNA link to the girl, Janice. A quarter link. That means he could be her uncle. Maybe a half-sibling, but that's less likely because of the age gap. Maybe another visit is called for. Has he thought a bit more about it now and got some idea of who Jan's mother was? The other thing is that his current partner is Kim Brogan, there on that second photo from McCluskie's funeral. When we visited Greenfield, we kind of thought that's all she was, his partner. But she was at the funeral. Why? Did she have some kind of link to what was going on? And she's very close to Doreen Butcher in the photo.'

Rae switched the display back on. 'See the way they're arm in arm, with drinks in hand? It looks as if they're really close friends. There are a lot of connections here, boss. Connections that we need to dig into. Look again. They've got different jackets on, but their dresses look identical. And I recognise the style. Phase Eight. Very upmarket. Not cheap. I remember trying the same dress on myself about then. Couldn't afford it, sadly.'

Barry smiled. 'Okay, I'm convinced that it needs following up — how close the friendship was between them and whether it's still ongoing. Can you do that, Rae, in addition to following up on this Gus Gibson?' He looked at Sophie. 'Anything else?'

'Another visit to Chandler. She must know more than she's letting on, though maybe her brain is too ruined for her to access memories from twenty years ago. And Busby, our man Chalky. He's in the mix.'

'Leave my team to deal with him,' Lydia said. 'George has got those couple of students to keep him occupied. They're a kind of upmarket Baker Street Irregulars. I bet you they're still meddling in some way, despite him warning them off.'

The meeting started to break up and Rae found herself standing next to Lydia.

'Who would be top of your list? For murdering the girl, I mean?' Rae asked.

Lydia rubbed her top lip with a finger. 'Pippa Chandler,' she replied after a few moments. 'I think she's worse than any of us think. But the big problem for us is that it could have been this guy, Gus Gibson. For all we know, he was another psychopath. And we're not going to be able to confirm it one way or the other, not now, not with him being dead for months.'

CHAPTER 37: RITCHY

Ritchy. Or Ritchie. From Richard, maybe? With a probable surname of Brown. His foster parents at the time of the boy's friendship with Janice had been Fred and Georgina Hughes. That's all the information Tommy and Jackie had, apart from the fact that he had been fostered as a child, like young Janice, and had lived somewhere nearby. Granted, they also knew a little about his character and personality, but it wasn't much to go on.

'Foster records? Schools? Criminal records? Is that where we start?' Jackie asked her more experienced but younger colleague.

'Foster parents, I think. School next. We're fairly certain which school he went to, at primary level anyway. And we know what street he lived on, from the information Pretty Nkomo sent in. She's a good place to start and she was keen to help. You or me?'

'You, Tommy. You obviously got on well with her, judging from what you told me. Or how about seeing her together? I worked on that case back in Watchet with my then boss, Sarah, and we got things done brilliantly. It increases the dynamic — that's what the DCI, Polly, said.'

Tommy shrugged. 'Fine by me. Let's get going.'

Pretty greeted them in a low-key way when she answered her front door. 'I've been doing some reading of press reports since you came last,' she explained to Tommy. She shook her head sadly. 'Awful about that child's body. Just terrible. It's been worrying me. I can't seem to shift it out of my brain, what happened to her.'

'Have you remembered anything else?' Tommy asked.

Pretty frowned even more. 'Not about her, no. I only met her that once. But I have been thinking of young Ritchy Brown since you phoned about coming back. I keep asking myself, how well did he get to know her? He was a shy boy, and didn't talk much. He probably didn't tell anyone all he knew about the girl.'

'That's why we're here, Ms Nkomo,' Jackie said. 'We're hoping he can still remember things about her, but we've got to find him first. Can you help us in any way?'

'Are you his boss?' Pretty asked, indicating Tommy.

Jackie laughed as she shook her head. 'No. It's the other way round. I'm a probationary DC, still learning the ropes. Tommy has got infinite patience. He needs it with me. I'm much more impulsive.'

'Well, it's nice to know that police detectives are human too.'

'Can you remember Ritchy's school?' Jackie asked.

'Birchwood Primary,' came the reply.

'Did he ever say which subjects were his favourites?'

'Ah. I see what you mean. Science. Well, animal science and nature, anyway. He used to chat to me about helping to look after the animals at lunchtime and after school. They kept rabbits and a few lizards. Fish in tanks. That kind of thing. They also had a garden and grew fruits and a few vegetables. Flowers too. He got involved in the heavy work, digging and stuff. He was a bit of an outdoor type. Makes sense, considering where he works now.'

Pretty sat back and watched the effect of her bombshell.

235

'What?' Jackie said, a look of astonishment on her face. 'You know where he works?'

Pretty nodded and smiled. 'I get a bit bored, you know, since I retired from full-time work. I didn't have a lot to do over the weekend, so I did a bit of investigating. I feel quite pleased with myself.'

'What does he do?' Tommy asked.

'He works for the Environment Agency, looking after Dorset's rivers. His name's on the website. His rivers are the Stour and its tributaries.'

'That's great. You've saved us a lot of effort, Pretty. How did you do it?'

'Found details of his old foster parents, the Hughes couple. I phoned them, then popped round. They still live in the same house. And they keep in contact with him. They said he's one of their better foster children. Well, for keeping in touch, anyway. They went to his wedding, apparently. He lives in Ringwood. Nice area, so they say.'

Pretty handed across a slip of paper with an address and phone number on it.

* * *

An hour later, the two detectives entered the reception area of the Environment Agency premises on an industrial estate just north of Blandford Forum, where they met the manager Tommy had spoken to on the phone. He showed them to a small meeting room, having arranged for Ritchy Brown to drive in from his current location upriver.

'He shouldn't be long,' the manager said. 'One of our best employees. Very reliable. Dedicated.'

Jackie watched through the window of the room as a compact four-by-four displaying the EA logo drew up outside in the car park. A tall, gangly man clambered out, looked around and made his way towards the building. He was frowning and running his fingers through his untidy, sandy-coloured hair.

Surely this was the man they were here to see? Jackie's instincts about people were good, she knew that. He looked slightly anxious and uneasy. Was it just down to the fact that he was due to be interviewed by police? Maybe he'd always been that way, since his days of being fostered as a child. She imagined the lack of close family contact would do that to a youngster, particularly if they had the type of personality that preferred some emotional reassurance. It all depended on the way in which the foster parents interpreted their role. And some people never lost that childhood-learned sense of deep insecurity.

A couple of minutes after the man disappeared from view, there was a knock at the door of the small office they'd been allocated. It opened a few inches and his head peered through the gap.

'Police?' he asked. 'DC Carter?'

So he'd obviously bothered to ask the receptionist for the name of the officer waiting to interview him. Jackie was already impressed.

'Come in,' Tommy replied. 'Take a seat. We shouldn't keep you long. I'm Tommy Carter. This is my colleague, DC Jackie Spring. And you must be Ritchy Brown.'

The man settled his lean frame into a chair, then looked at them warily. 'That's right. How can I help you?'

'We're involved in an investigation into a death that occurred some twenty years ago, maybe a year or two less. You may have read in the press about a child's body being found in a house in Crawley Terrace?' Tommy waited.

'Yes. It sounded awful.'

'It was a young girl's body. We know her to have been Janice Gibson. Jan. We believe you knew her?'

The man put a hand to his mouth. 'Oh no. I had no idea it was her. Oh my God. That's just awful.' He looked genuinely shocked.

'Did you know her?'

'Yes, for a short while.' He slumped back in his chair, shaking his head from side to side. 'This is terrible. It's hard to believe. Wasn't she killed deliberately? Or at least hidden away, out of sight? That's what was in the papers.'

Tommy nodded. 'That's right. We're treating it as murder. Because you knew her, we have a few questions. You can understand how hard it is trying to find out what kind of person she was. And the details of her life.'

'I can see that.' He frowned.

Jackie spoke for the first time. 'How did you meet?'

Ritchy sighed. 'It was just before I moved in with the Hughes. They were just the best and I stayed with them from then on. But the previous people, well . . .' He almost shuddered. 'They were the opposite. I hated them. I ran away one day but didn't know where to go. I slept rough that night, then ended up at a church hall, one that had some soup for people who'd run out of luck. She was hanging around outside, so we got chatting.'

'You were, what? Ten? Eleven?'

'I think I was just eleven. Jan was ten. She still had a few months to go until her birthday. It was meeting her that made me realise there were kids worse off than me. She wouldn't come inside the hall. I got a soup for her and took it out.'

Jackie was puzzled. 'Why wouldn't she go inside?'

'She said something like, she'd be for the high jump if she let on to anyone. She'd been warned never to come to the attention of the police. Though Jan didn't use the word police. It was cops and pigs. She seemed really scared when she told me that. I never found out why.'

'How long were you friendly for?'

'A couple of months. Maybe three. At first, we just chatted when we bumped into each other. Then she started at my school, in my class. It wasn't a new year or term or anything like that. She just turned up one day. She told me the teachers at her old school were getting too nosy.'

'How did she fit in?'

Ritchy sighed. 'She didn't. She was thin and ill-looking. And she had this awful scar on her top lip. No one knew how she'd got it, so a lot of the kids thought she'd been slashed

238

there, with a knife or something. They kept their distance. They must have thought she knew some scary people. She never explained what it really was to them, a cleft lip. I found out because my new foster mother told me when I asked. The thing is, Jan wasn't at school very much. She must have been playing truant a lot. Then it was the end of the school year, and we were all due to move up to secondary. I lost touch with her. She wasn't around at all. And I went to a different school to everyone else. I got a scholarship to a private school. It was through a foundation of some type. My new parents must have arranged it somehow. That's when my life changed completely. Did Jan make it to secondary? Do you know?'

Jackie shook her head. 'We don't think so, Ritchy. We think that's when she died.'

'That's awful.'

He looked upset. No wonder, Jackie thought. He'd probably been a nice kid way back then, judging by what he was like now. Someone just waiting for the right opportunity to present itself, even though they didn't know it themselves. He'd obviously struck it lucky, able to make a huge leap forward in his life. Whereas Jan — well, it was as if she'd fallen down a pit of evil.

Jackie watched Ritchy. He looked as if he was having the same thoughts.

Tommy cleared his throat. 'Mr Brown, we need to press you a bit harder about what Jan may have told you about her life. As far as we can see, it was a mess. We don't think anyone was really taking care of her. We even wonder if she was living in an environment that might have been totally inappropriate for a child. Was that ever your feeling?'

He nodded slowly. 'There were some things I couldn't share with my own parents. Jan swore me to secrecy. Nothing was to get out. Otherwise, she might be killed. I didn't take that very seriously but, even so, I was wary of saying anything that might get her into trouble. I didn't know whether to believe what she told me. It all seemed so strange.'

'What kinds of things?'

'It's hard to remember any clear details. At first she told me she'd seen people having sex. Men and women. She told me the kind of things they did. That's what seemed so strange to me. Then she said she'd had sex herself.'

Tommy tried hard to control his sense of shock at this revelation. Even Jackie, the older detective, looked stunned.

'She was only ten,' Tommy said. 'Do you think she was telling you the truth?'

Ritchy looked troubled. 'I had no reason to doubt it back then. I believed her. Now? I still think she was telling me the truth. Why would she have lied about something like that?'

'Did you tell anyone about your concerns?'

Ritchy shook his head. He looked pale and drawn, as if speaking about his memories of his childhood friend had drained him emotionally. 'No.' His voice was little more than a whisper. 'She made me swear not to. She said they'd kill her if word got out. And they did, didn't they? Whoever it was? They did end up killing her.'

'That's if it was the same people,' Tommy interjected. 'We can't assume that unless we have evidence.'

'But it's likely, isn't it?' Ritchy persisted, tugging at his earlobe. His anxiety was obvious.

'We'll grant you that.'

'Maybe she told someone else, and they didn't keep quiet about it. Is that possible?'

'We don't speculate, Mr Brown. We might have ideas, but we never discuss them outside the team until we find some hard facts and need to follow them up. I want to ask you now about any people she may have mentioned to you. Names. Descriptions, possibly. I know it was a long time ago and we're asking a lot of you. But can you help us?'

Ritchy put a hand to his head, stroking his forehead. 'She lived with her uncle. His name might have been Guy or Gus. Gus, I think.'

'That's helpful.'

'She had another uncle. Bruce, maybe? I think he was only around for some of the time. She liked him. He gave her sweets and sometimes a bit of pocket money.'

'Did she ever mention her parents?'

'It's hard to remember. I think I asked her once, but she clammed up. I don't think they were around.'

'Okay. Any women in her home life, can you remember?'

'I know she said she didn't like them. They seemed to come and go from where she lived. I think she said there were two who were really nasty to her. I just can't remember their names, though. Sorry.'

Jackie spoke. 'Don't worry, Mr Brown. Maybe now you've had some initial thoughts, names might pop into your head when you're not expecting it. My memory's certainly like that.'

'Just get in contact with us as soon as you can if anything else occurs to you,' Tommy added. 'Any names. Here's my card. Phone at any time, even if it doesn't seem important. We'll probably want to speak to you again in a couple of days to go over what you've told us, so you'll hear from one of us soon. Thanks for your time.'

They stood up and started towards the door.

'Pippa,' Ritchy said. 'It just appeared in my head. Something about a Pippa. I have a feeling she was another teenager, but an older one.'

Jackie glanced at Tommy before turning. 'That's very useful, Mr Brown. As DC Carter said, phone one of us if you remember anything else.'

CHAPTER 38: SPIDER, UNKNOWN

Lydia was discussing the case with Jimmy and George. 'I'm uneasy about those two students. Ollie and Dan? Have I got their names right? They might be putting themselves in danger if they keep poking their noses into the Busby duo. The father might be a thug of the first order, up to his neck in what's been happening for twenty years. We're dealing with two murders in addition to the attempt on Holly's life. Those students don't know about the other stuff and probably still think it was just a spiking gone wrong. Can you warn them off? But don't tell them any more than you have to.'

Jimmy was his usual confident self. 'Sure, boss. Leave it with me.'

'And we need to think through this convoluted house-ownership business. If Quick was part owner, along with Pippa Chandler, how does that feed into things? Did Chandler find out somehow? How well does she know Busby? Could she have arranged the whole thing? Might it even explain the murder of Joshua Quick?'

Jimmy broke in. 'I always thought the motive was a bit thin for that. This makes more sense if she saw Quick as some kind of obstacle. But I can't see how that would be the case, not exactly.'

'Maybe he knew,' George suggested. 'Do you think he could have stayed friends with Gus Gibson? After all, Quick was the landlord of the local pub, years ago. Even when he moved out, his flat was in the same area, just a couple of streets away from Gibson's house. That house. Number sixty-eight.' He almost shuddered.

Lydia was trying to get her thoughts in order, frowning in concentration. 'And we thought it was a cut-and-dried case. I guess we need to do a bit more probing into Quick's background. His friends and social life. Can I leave that with you? I need to see Barry about this. It might require another visit to see Pippa Chandler. But we need to get our facts right first.'

Lydia noticed the pensive look on George's face. 'What is it, George?'

'It's the girl, Jan. The body we found in that house. Do we know for sure whether she was an orphan or not? I keep thinking, poor kid, what a life.'

'Barry's team are looking into that. I think Tommy and Jackie are pursuing it as we speak, trying to find witnesses from way back then. We suspect she was a niece of this Bruce Greenfield character, and a cousin to Pippa Chandler. It won't be easy confirming all this. Meanwhile, I'm off to see Holly Evans again. I'm hoping she's remembered more. It's not just the spiking incident but what she found out about her background from Joshua Quick. She was still a bit woozy the last time I saw her, but I need to get it clearer. It's possible that what he told her got him killed.'

'Do you think he was followed when he met her? That someone was watching and listening?' Jimmy seemed intrigued by the possibility. 'It would explain a lot.'

'It's possible. Or maybe Quick blabbed about it to someone he trusted.'

'Pippa Chandler? She was his live-in carer, after all. He may not have known how closely she was linked to it all.'

'Well, that's what I want to find out.'

* * *

Holly glanced up from her bedside chair. She was looking perkier, Lydia thought. She was reading a textbook and had a notepad to hand.

'I'll be ready to be discharged the day after tomorrow,' she said to Lydia, a smile on her face. 'A couple more tests to make sure, but they don't see a problem.'

'That's good news, Holly. I'll need to get the protection officer rearranged. You'll be going to your family home in Basingstoke? Is that what's been decided?'

The young woman nodded, her freshly shampooed hair swaying around her face. 'Just for a few days. I hope to be back at uni as soon as I can, though.'

'Is that what you're spending your time on? Catching up on coursework?'

'Yeah. I don't want to fall too far behind. I'll have a one-to-one with my tutor when I start back, and she'll want to check that I haven't missed too much. She was on the phone to me earlier with some suggested reading. My friend Josie brought the stuff that I needed in for me.' She waved the textbook in the air before putting it to one side.

'You're on a Business degree, aren't you?'

'That's right. Second year.'

'Good luck with it. I did a degree in Maths before I joined the police, and I spent a couple of years with a financial fraud unit in Bath a while back. I had to get to grips with accounting principles, looking for the signs of someone fiddling the books.'

'When did you join the police? Straight after uni?'

It was Lydia's turn to nod. 'Fast track. Did the basics of policing then moved into a specialist unit as a DC. It was headed up by the chief superintendent you met last week. She was a DCI back then.'

'Wow. That's so impressive. And now you're a detective inspector. You must be pleased.'

'My life has changed beyond recognition. I was a quiet girl from a conservative Asian background. A bit timid. Wouldn't say boo to a goose. Now, well — I tell people what to do and they jump to it. My work's a bit like putting together a giant jigsaw puzzle, but where the bits have been hidden. You've got to find them first, then try to slot them together.' Lydia looked at the young woman. 'Anyway, enough of this chitchat. I'm here to see what else you've remembered and to ask a few more questions.'

Holly sat up straighter. 'Okay. Ready.'

'Was it only Joshua Quick you spoke to? Was there ever anyone else present?'

'Just him. He said he knew my probable biological father quite well, this man Phil, around the time I was conceived.'

'Do you think someone could have overheard your chat?'

'I don't know. I didn't think it was that important, what we were talking about.' She frowned. 'There was someone acting a bit suspiciously, one time.'

Lydia leaned forward. 'Tell me.'

'I went to the loo. A woman was in there and she looked at me a bit strange. Like she was fixing my face in her mind. I thought I was imagining things.'

'Can you remember what she looked like?'

Holly thought for a while before continuing. 'It's hard to remember exactly. She was short. Stocky. Quite red-faced. A bit angry-looking. She went out pretty quickly after I came in.'

'I'm going to show you a photo, Holly. Tell me if it's her.'

Lydia called up a photo of Pippa Chandler on her phone and showed it to the young woman.

A look of surprise crossed her face. 'Yes! That's her. Who is she? How did you know?'

'Her name is Pippa Chandler. She's currently on remand, awaiting trial for the murder of Joshua Quick.'

Holly's eyes widened in astonishment.

'She was Joshua Quick's live-in carer. But there's another connection. Gus Gibson left her a property in Crawley Terrace when he died. We've just found out that Joshua was left a share in that property too. We're wondering if he was aware of it. Did he mention it to you?'

The young woman frowned. 'He did say something about inheriting a house. Or a share of it. I was a bit confused by it all.'

Lydia could imagine how confusing all of this was to Holly. 'We're trying to get to the bottom of everything that's been going on but it's proving to be really complicated. It seems to be connected to things that went on many years ago, at about the time you were born. It might revolve around something Phil McCluskie was involved in, the man who might have been your biological dad.'

'Mum looked shocked. I could see she was upset by something, but she wouldn't say much about it. She did let slip that she knew the young girl you've been interested in. Then she clammed up after that.'

Lydia thought for a few seconds, then nodded slowly. 'It's probably opened up a lot of unpleasant stuff that your mum managed to forget a long time ago. Maybe I need to go and see her.'

Holly glanced at the time. 'She's coming in this afternoon to visit. Right after lunch.'

'That would work. I'll probably bring someone with me.' She paused for a few seconds, watching the young woman. 'Don't let all this get on top of you, Holly. You need to concentrate on your recovery and getting back to your studies. Leave it to us. Understood?'

Holly nodded. 'Of course. Dad says I ought to take a short holiday. He suggested Spain, but Mum didn't look too pleased. I guess she'd like me home so she can fuss over me.'

'Why Spain?'

'I have a vague memory of being there with Mum when I was small. I haven't been back since.'

Lydia gave her a smile before she left. Underneath, she knew there was little chance of Holly doing as she'd asked and avoiding thinking too much about the reasons behind the attack. Her thoughts would be in turmoil, and she'd be wondering non-stop about the complex network of strands that surrounded her. She must realise that she was like an innocent fly, trapped near the centre of a spider's web. The spider hadn't yet shown itself, but it would be on its way, carefully picking through the various obstacles between itself and some unknown juicy prize waiting for it. The problem for the police, and for Holly, was that they didn't know who that spider was. Nor had they much idea about the nature of the prize.

Lydia phoned Barry to update him on Holly's information and received some interesting news in exchange.

'Romy Mathieson's just phoned in, from Crawley Terrace? She's remembered a bit more about the neighbours who might have heard something the night of the row in number sixty-eight. They're Welsh and she thinks they moved to Swanage. Something about owning a sweet shop. I've allocated it to Tommy. He's got a bit of a sweet tooth.'

Lydia then had a few words with the police officer on duty outside Holly's room, warning her that things might be coming to a head. Forewarned was forearmed, after all.

CHAPTER 39: APPLE, PIP

'Hello again, Pippa.'

Lydia kept her voice neutral, giving nothing away. That's what years of interviews with suspects did; you learned good facial control. You became a master at not giving anything away unintentionally. She and Jackie Spring sat down opposite the glowering, silent woman.

'What do you want now?' Pippa finally asked.

'For a starter, we'd like to know a little more about your inheritance of that house, the one in Crawley Terrace. We have a few more questions for you.'

'What, again? You asked me all that stuff before. I don't know nuffin' else.'

Jackie spoke. 'When I was here last, I asked you for any other information about your inheritance. You claimed there wasn't anything else.'

'So?' Pippa stared at her challengingly.

'We've recently discovered it wasn't left to you alone.'

Pippa screwed up her eyes and sneered at Jackie. She said nothing.

'In fact, you shared ownership with Joshua Quick. Gus Gibson left it to both of you. Why didn't you tell us then? You must have known.'

'Well, you see, I didn't, Miss Clever Clogs. He'd talk to me, my Uncle Gus, but I didn't follow a lot of what he was goin' on about. It was all so boring. Why didn't he just leave me cash? Make it a lot easier.'

'He probably didn't know he was going to die. It was his home, wasn't it?'

'Yeah, well, he was a right awkward bastard.'

'Did you really have no idea that Joshua also had a share in the house?'

Pippa shook her head, looking wary. 'No.'

'Really?'

'I said no, didn't I? What the fuck's wrong with you? Deaf or summat?'

Lydia took over. 'It makes me wonder, Pippa, what else you know that you've kept quiet about.' Lydia looked her straight in the eye, this sullen, glowering woman who seemed full of malevolence towards her fellow human beings. Did she have any redeeming features?

'Did you ever follow Joshua Quick, Pippa? When he went out?'

Again, the piglike, narrowed eyes. 'What you getting at?'

'Did you secretly follow him to a café where he was meeting someone, then lurk in the shadows, listening and watching?'

'Fuck's sake. Why would I do summat like that?'

'We had another look at the contents of your phone, Pippa. A couple of the photos on it didn't mean much to us when we first arrested you, but they do now. They show Joshua Quick talking to a young blonde woman in the café I just mentioned. It was Holly Evans. Why are those photos on your phone, Pippa? The date was just a day before you killed him. And a week before Holly almost lost her life in the spiking incident.'

Pippa shrugged. 'Dunno about any of that.' She glanced around the bare room. 'I've had enough. You're just trying to trick me. I ain't saying nuffin' else.'

'We think you probably overheard what Joshua was saying to Holly. You sent those photos to Chalky Busby. We might not be able to see exactly what you sent him, but it was a large file of some sort. Your phone company account shows it.'

'Well, clever you. You know what? You make me sick. Both of you. I bet you come from posh backgrounds and had people looking after you when you was young. See, I didn't have anything like that. My life was a mess from the start. No one gave me the time of day. If I didn't look out for myself, no one else ever bothered. My life's been shit from the word go.'

Jackie leaned forward. 'That's where you're wrong, Pippa. I was an orphan. But I always wanted to do something with my life. And I did. That's where we're different, not in any of your twisted justifications for the terrible things you've done. What you said just there, it cuts no ice with me.'

* * *

Lydia dropped Jackie back at the incident room, then hurried across town to the hospital where she'd arranged to meet Sophie Allen before speaking to Holly's mother. It seemed that things were beginning to loosen up nicely, maybe allowing long-hidden secrets to spill out. This wasn't going to be pretty.

The two detectives ambushed Carole Evans as she approached Holly's room in the ward.

'We need to speak to you, Carole,' Sophie said, fixing her with a cold stare. 'With some urgency. Go in, say a brief hello to your daughter, and tell her you'll be back in a while. Then come straight back out here.'

'Do I have to? Can't it wait?'

'No. It's either that or we take you in to the local station, in a much less salubrious setting. The choice is yours.'

Carole nervously scratched at her head. 'Okay. Have it your way. I suppose I should have known when I saw you. You're the boss, aren't you? Must be serious.'

'Dead right, Carole. Five minutes only. Then back here. Right?'

In fact, Holly's mother was back with the two detectives well inside five minutes. They led her to a small meeting room, placed a Do Not Disturb sign on the door and settled around a small, central table.

'You've been keeping things from us,' Sophie said.

'I've been hiding things from myself,' Carole responded. 'For almost twenty years.'

'That's not what I mean,' Sophie replied, not attempting to hide the annoyance in her voice. 'You must have come across young Janice, the child whose body we found in an old house in Bournemouth. You can't possibly have missed the fact that we've been trying to build her backstory. It's been in the press enough, even on TV. Why didn't you come forward?'

Carole shook her head, her blonde hair swaying on her shoulders. 'It's stuff I've been desperate to forget all this time. It's so painful, horrific. I couldn't face raking it all up again, not after so long.'

'And meanwhile, the perpetrators of a truly terrible crime escape scot-free? Don't you have any sense of moral duty? She was a young child, for God's sake. No one deserves what happened to her.'

Carole looked ashen. 'I realise that now. I feel ashamed.'

'Well, you can try answering our questions now, and maybe you'll feel a bit better about yourself. As far as we're concerned, everything hinges on that young girl, Jan. Did you ever meet her all those years ago?'

Carole nodded slowly. 'A few times. I didn't get to know her well. She flitted in and out of those places around Crawley Terrace like a ghost. She'd be there, then she'd be gone.'

'What places are you referring to?'

'The pub, the Lincoln Arms. Gus Gibson's house. The local café. Gus owned that too, back then.'

'How old was she when you met her?'

Carole looked unsure. 'I don't really know. She was small-boned and thin-looking. She could have been eight, nine, maybe ten or even eleven.'

'Did you talk to her?'

'Not really.'

'That's too vague, Carole. Either you did or you didn't. Which is it?' Sophie wasn't letting up on the pressure.

'What I mean is, I probably said hello, and spoke a few words to her, but it wasn't anything substantial.'

'I don't really understand. Here was a young girl, clearly in the wrong place, somewhere totally unsuitable for someone of her age. Didn't that occur to you? Weren't you at all concerned about her presence in those places?'

'Look, I'm not proud of what I was involved in back then. I'd fallen out with my parents, badly. I was drinking far too much, I was trying to make some money to get my life back on track, and getting men to pay me for sex was a quick way of making some cash. Looking back on it makes me shudder. But it worked in an odd sort of way. I saved enough to wave goodbye to it all after a year or two. I had a holiday in Spain, then moved away when I returned and found a job. The only person I kept in contact with was Phil McCluskie. That's when I got pregnant with Holly.'

Lydia was intrigued. 'Why did you stay in contact with him and not any of the others?'

Carole shrugged and put a hand to her brow. 'I sort of thought he was a bit better than the others, but it's all relative, isn't it? They were all sad wasters in a way. I sometimes thought he might have had a soft spot for me and that we might have a future together. Sheer fantasy. More fool me.' She extracted a tissue from her bag, wiped her eyes and blew her nose.

Sophie felt that the subject had shifted away from the planned path. 'Let's not lose focus here. All this may be useful in its own way. But we need information about the girl. I know it was a long time ago. I know it'll be hard to remember. But the people who killed her are probably still alive and I need to identify them, then gather the evidence that will convict them. And you can offer vital help, Carole. You need to get those memories back. Who was around back then? Who was the type of person who could have burned her with cigarettes? Who could harbour such malice towards her? And why? I'm not expecting those memories to pop into your head just now, right this minute. It might take hours, even days. Something might flash up in your brain when you least expect it. Whenever, whatever, we need to know.'

Carole had her eyes closed. 'There was a weird teenage girl around then. She was about seventeen or eighteen. Not much younger than me. Really nasty minded, totally untrustworthy. She stole stuff from the pockets of the punters who visited. I can't remember her name, but it always reminded me of apples.'

'I don't want to prompt you, Carole. You need to come up with the name independently. But ask yourself, why would it remind you of apples? Think variety names. Bramley and the like. Think of apple parts. Peel. Core.'

Carole put her hand back to her head. 'God, this is so hard.' She suddenly jerked her head up. 'Pip. That's it. Pip.'

'Are you sure?'

'Yes, absolutely. Pip.'

'Okay, we'll note that. But keep thinking.' Sophie checked the time. 'I need to be off. You've got my number. You've got Lydia's number. Call us.'

With that, the two detectives left.

'Could it have been her, Lydia? Pippa Chandler? You've interviewed her for longer than anyone else on the team.'

'It fits. She's one of the nastiest pieces of work I've come across in recent years. Full of bile against everyone. Even so, it doesn't work entirely for me. It's the way the young girl was found, stuffed inside that suitcase and carefully hidden behind a false wall. That's not Pippa's style. It's too thorough, too pre-planned. Pippa has rages and acts on them instantly.'

'So it might not be her? Is that what you're saying?'

Lydia shook her head. 'I don't know what I'm saying. I'm speaking at the same time as thinking. I really need time to think it through, to be honest. And we've still got to find some evidence, haven't we?'

Sophie nodded. 'Well, let's get back. Maybe someone else has found something.'

They made their way across the car park towards Sophie's car. She spoke as she extracted the key from her bag.

'Of course, we've been side-stepping one of the key questions for too long. Who was Jan's mother? If she wasn't around, why not? If she was around, why didn't she step in? And if the girl's mother wasn't there, who was meant to be looking after her? The father? A guardian? Whoever it was, they were negligent in the extreme. But they've covered things up really well. It makes me angry and uneasy, Lydia.'

CHAPTER 40: I WANT A LAWYER

'There's something else we should check on,' Rae said. 'It was suggested some time back that whoever spiked Holly knew about her heart defect. It could have been a deliberate attempt to kill her. We're pretty sure it was Jerry Busby, though he hasn't been charged yet because we're still waiting for some final forensic evidence. Shouldn't we bring him in now? See what he has to say?'

Lydia agreed. 'I'm ready. I think we need to put the screws on him. George and Jimmy have just been tying up some loose ends to do with the DNA tests and some newly found CCTV from a bus, but I think we're ready for him now.'

'Okay,' Barry said. 'But several things still need to be chased up, and someone has to make another visit to Holly, and possibly her parents, to check. Firstly, who knew of her heart defect? And secondly, did she mention it in her two chats with Joshua Quick? Because if she did, and Pippa Chandler overheard, it would all fit together neatly, wouldn't it?'

'There's something else bothering me,' Rae added. 'I keep looking at the photo of Pippa on the incident board. She reminds me of someone, but I don't know who.'

She cut two pieces of plain white paper into rudimentary frames and placed them in turn around the faces of the women. The other detectives watched her with interest. She moved the paper frames so that she could concentrate on smaller or larger areas of the subjects' faces, comparing them each time to Pippa's.

Rae finally stood back. 'I thought so,' she said. 'Look. There's a definite similarity in her face shape to Doreen Butcher. Look at the nose. Do you see it?'

The others weren't so convinced but agreed that it needed to be pursued.

'Remember Pippa's spent most of her life addicted to booze and drugs, and picking fights with all and sundry. Try to take away the spiteful, snarling look she always adopts. Try to think of her looking calmer, placid even.'

Lydia snorted. 'What, Pippa Chandler? Calm and placid? You must be joking!'

* * *

Jerry Busby was arrogant and tried to bluster his way through the first few minutes in the police station, having been brought in by a uniformed unit.

'Why am I here?' he demanded. 'You got no grounds for hauling me in. I'm gonna complain.'

Jimmy and George regarded him coolly.

'You have that right, Mr Busby, as you have the right to a lawyer,' Jimmy told him. 'You can change your mind about that at any time. By the way, what name would you prefer us to use when addressing you? Jerry Busby or Curtis Murchison? We've opted for the former so far, but are happy to switch to your other identity if you'd prefer.'

Busby Junior looked at him through narrowed eyes but didn't respond. Jimmy placed a photo in front of him.

'This is a still extracted from the CCTV system at Suki's Bar on the evening that Holly Evans was jabbed in her upper left thigh. She collapsed shortly afterwards. That is you, isn't it?'

Busby stared at the image carefully, as if looking for something to dispute. 'Yeah, I was there. But it weren't me that jabbed her.'

Jimmy ignored the comment. 'We can't see your left hand, of course. But she clearly had to pass within touching distance of you to get to the dancefloor.' He pushed across a second photo. 'This is a waste bin, attached to a lamppost some hundred yards away from Suki's. And this—' he showed a third photo — 'is a simple hypodermic needle found inside it, wrapped in a piece of tissue paper.'

Jimmy then showed another still, this one rather fuzzy and indistinct. 'This is from the CCTV on a bus that passed along the road that evening, just a minute or two after Holly was jabbed.' The still image showed someone passing the bin, arm out, as if dropping something into it. 'Is this you, Mr Busby?'

The young man stared at the photo. 'Course not. You can't make it out, anyway. It's too blurry. What you take me for? An idiot? This shows nothing.'

'The DNA test from the needle was interesting, though. It obviously shows Holly's DNA on its tip. But we also got a tiny trace on the body of the syringe and on the tissue paper. Someone else's. Maybe that someone else was you?' Jimmy looked at him questioningly.

'I want a lawyer,' came the reply.

257

CHAPTER 41: SHE WAS NASTY

Tuesday

'How did it all happen, boss? I mean, drugs, prostitution, the works. And a young kid caught up in it all.' Tommy was deep in thought, clicking his pen absent-mindedly.

Rae shrugged. 'Something was going on. But what it was is still unclear. Our glorious former colleague Phil McCluskie managed to keep it all hidden in the shadows as far as the police were concerned. How he kept social services at bay, I'll never know.'

'Someone must have gained something, surely.'

Rae came alert. 'What do you mean?'

'Well, we're assuming that Jan was a kiddie from a poor background, with nothing to her name. What if that wasn't the case? What if someone gained from her death? Substantially, I mean. It would have to be someone the girl knew, though. Someone she was scared of, even.'

'Well, Greenfield owned up to knowing her when Jackie and I first interviewed him, even though he claimed that he was totally unaware of the family connection. And it would have had to be someone a good bit older than Jan, and that rules out Chandler, I would have thought. She would have been only a few years older than the girl at the time she died. I also wonder if someone found a way of keeping social services in the dark.' Rae was thinking hard. 'Who would have had that kind of influence? Let's see if we can find records dating back to that time. People who had that kind of access. Let's do some brainstorming.'

'Who was her guardian back then? Surely there's some way of finding out?'

'Not if it was all carefully hidden. But we can try. You take the guardian angle, Tommy, then do yet another check of child records and who had access to them. This time, though, you're looking for signs of who might have been able to keep the girl hidden.' She checked the time. 'Barry and I are just about to head off to see Greenfield and the Brogan woman. I'll ask them again what they know about Jan.'

* * *

'How long have the two of you been together?' Barry asked.

He and Rae were sitting in the living room of Bruce Greenfield's home in north Bournemouth. He was particularly interested in several photos displayed around the room, each showing a sunny Mediterranean scene with the couple centre frame.

'Two years? Closer to three, probably,' Greenfield answered. 'Why?'

Barry ignored the question. 'Did you know each other before that?'

Greenfield shifted slightly in his chair. 'Sort of. When we was a lot younger.'

'How did you meet back then?'

'At parties and stuff. Look, why is this important? What's it got to do with whatever you're poking into?'

Again, Barry refused to be sidetracked. 'And do you travel to the Mediterranean for a break fairly often?'

'Spain. Maybe twice a year.'

'Do you stay at the same location?'

Kim hesitated, and Rae thought that, for some reason, she looked trapped by the question. Why would that be? She was obviously hiding something. 'Well, yeah, sort of.'

A glance passed between her and Greenfield. Was it some kind of warning? A recognition between the two of them that caution was needed here? Barry remembered the photo he and Sophie had spotted in McCluskie's old flat, the one that now belonged to Doreen Butcher.

'A hotel or a villa?'

Again, a hesitation. 'A villa that we rent.'

'Whereabouts?'

'Overlooking the coast, south of Malaga.'

Greenfield interrupted. 'What's the point of this? It's just a place we like to go to for our holidays.'

Rae took over the questioning. 'When you went to Spain years ago, Kim, before you started your relationship with Mr Greenfield, who did you go with?'

Kim looked at her almost mutinously. 'A friend. A close friend. That's all you're getting.'

'Was it Doreen Butcher?'

A series of momentary reactions flickered across Kim's face. 'That's nothing to do with you,' she said in a near-whisper.

Rae realised she'd touched a nerve. She glanced at her boss. Barry was looking intrigued too. He glanced back at her and moved the hand he was leaning on, the sign that a topic change was coming. Clearly, he'd like time to gather more background on the Butcher woman before he delved any deeper. Rae knew Barry's methods. He liked to have all his facts ready before starting a new line of questioning about someone who might be of considerable interest. Better to pretend zero curiosity in case an unexpected alarm was raised.

'Mr Greenfield,' he said, 'have you thought any more about your DNA link with our long-dead child? You must be closely related to either the mother or father. I'm sure you've speculated about it. The likelihood is that you were either Jan's uncle or grandfather. That means one of her parents was either your child or your sibling. Which is it? We know you have a daughter, living in London. So could you enlighten us?'

'That's Susie, and she's not that girl's mother. Susie's only twenty-eight so would have been about eight at the time. Don't you think I'd have known if she was my own grand-daughter? It's got to be my brother or sister.'

'Details please, Mr Greenfield.'

The man glowered. 'Christ. You don't want much, do you? Okay, I had a sister and a brother. It couldn't have been my brother. He was gay. Kept it secret, though. He was in the army. But they're both long dead.'

Barry looked up with interest. 'Sorry to hear that. How long ago did your sister pass away?'

'Fifteen or sixteen years or so. Drug overdose, I think. But she left home as a teenager way before that, and we didn't stay in touch. A bit of a wild child. Don't remember much about her.'

Barry glanced at Rae, who nodded slightly. This sounded promising, particularly the wild-child sister. If she had given birth a year or two before she died, then Jan's age matched closely.

'Names please, Mr Greenfield. And any other information you have on them. You were asked to do this by my colleagues when they visited, and it bothers us that you haven't done so.'

'Okay, keep your hat on. I'll get it done as soon as I can.'

Barry glared at him. 'I don't think you understand. We're not leaving until we have that information. Get it now, please.'

Greenfield grunted and left the room. Barry turned to Kim Brogan. 'Tell us about your friendship with Doreen Butcher, Kim.'

'What about it? We're friends. What else is there to tell?'

'You've been on holiday with her. Spain, wasn't it?'

'Yeah.' She was glancing around nervously. Both of the detectives sensed that they'd touched on something important.

261

'Who owns that villa you use, Kim?'

'Doreen.'

'How long has she owned it for?'

'Ages. Dunno exactly, though. Fifteen, twenty years maybe?' She suddenly put a hand to her mouth.

Rae had been watching her carefully. A germ of a thought flickered in her brain. It needed checking out, though. Best not to push Kim too far at the moment in case word got out.

'You know, you've got a nice house here, Kim. I like the décor. Is that down to you or to Bruce?'

The ploy worked. Kim looked pleased. 'Me, mainly. Bruce hasn't got a sense of style. I bin in enough posh places to know what's what.'

Barry was looking bemused. Rae gave him a slight wink. She'd successfully drawn Kim's attention away from the Spanish villa.

'I like the colours. And the way they're picked out in the fabrics you've chosen.'

Kim looked even more pleased. 'Yeah, I really thought a lot about it. Bruce, he ain't got much idea of that kind of thing.' She was smiling now.

Greenfield came back in with a slip of paper. 'Names and addresses for you. I hope you're bloody grateful.'

'Does it include your late sister?'

'Yeah. She was the younger than me. Melanie. She was offbeat.'

* * *

Melanie Greenfield, born 1972, died 1995.

Barry and Rae looked again at the first line of text on the sheet of paper in front of them. Tommy had begun working his way through the names on Greenfield's list, his siblings, checking them against various registers and data sources. The only one of obvious interest was the wayward one. They read on through Tommy's summary.

> *Gave birth to child, Janice, in 1993 but died of an overdose in 1995.*

Rae felt depressed by the bleakness that lay behind those few words. That would presumably have left Janice orphaned at the age of two. What had happened then? How had she slipped through the social-care safety net? Rae could imagine it. A mother living in a series of squats, a young child left to fend for itself, taken in by others after the mother had died. It looked as though Jan might have been left to run wild, living on the fringes of a low-status brothel and possible drug den. And all this in the last decade or so of the twentieth century. How on earth did it happen? Why did it happen? It didn't make any kind of sense.

Barry turned to the junior detective standing beside him. 'Thanks, Tommy. Getting the dates pinned down like this helps enormously. Listen, do what you can to find who the father is. And find out where Melanie lived, if you can.'

'I already started on that,' Tommy replied. 'She was in the south of Spain for a few years with some Spanish guy. He died in a boating accident. Drowned.'

The two senior detectives looked at him. 'Right. Concentrate on him. Find out everything you can. I need to update the boss.' Barry reached for the phone.

* * *

Sophie Allen was in the incident room within the hour. 'Let me get this right. Jan's mother was this Melanie Greenfield, a sort of hippy-like free spirit. She was a regular on the London party scene for some years. Are you sure about this?'

'It's all been double-checked,' Barry explained. 'I put everyone onto it as soon as we got her name. As far as we know, she went to live in Spain with this man but came back after he died. It must have been about then that her own life went into a rapid decline. That's what it looks like.'

'Fell in with the wrong crowd?' Sophie suggested, indulging in her frequent habit of tucking some strands of hair behind her ear.

'Returned to them, more like. It looks like the same group of people she was in with before,' Rae said. 'Do the dates match up? Does it fit with the age we have for Jan?'

Barry nodded.

Sophie continued. 'Okay, that's good. I'm going to get in contact with my opposite number in the Malaga district. You know what would confirm it, don't you? The cleft palate. It's not always inherited, but there is a tendency for it to run in families. What's the name?'

'Romero. Juan Romero. My guess is that they were a wealthy family. Still are, I expect.'

Jackie shook her head. 'From what I found out, he was the last remaining family member.'

'Okay.' Sophie turned to Barry. 'We need more on the group of people this woman was in with. Was it a sort of commune or squat or something? We need to know who else was in the group. If Jan's mother inherited that villa but then died back here, in London, maybe she let slip about its existence. With her dead, presumably ownership would have passed to her child, Jan. And she was only two.'

Rae stated the obvious, in case anyone had any doubts. 'And we know someone who has a villa in that part of Spain. Doreen Butcher. It's the one Kim Brogan was being very coy about this morning.'

'Are they all in on it, do you think?'

Barry shrugged. 'Could be. That's for us to find out.'

Sophie had a faraway look in her eye. Clearly something had struck a nerve of some type. The others waited.

'Holly Evans. There's still something that's niggling me. What was it you said about her plans for a short break, Lydia?'

'It was a bit odd,' came the reply. 'Holly said her mum wasn't keen on her idea for a holiday in Spain. She also said she vaguely remembers being there as a youngster, with her mum.' She paused. 'Ah. Are you thinking what I'm thinking?'

Sophie nodded her head, knowingly. 'Exactly. Let's get to her before she leaves the hospital and goes home. I can see her mother trying to influence her once she's there.'

Sophie popped into the hospital shop, situated close to the entrance, and bought a small bag of fudge. Such a gift might work wonders, she thought. She was right. The young woman closed her eyes as if she was in paradise when the first chunk slid onto her tongue.

'God, that is just the best,' Holly said.

'I need to ask you something about your childhood, Holly,' Lydia said as she, too, savoured the sweet, caramelly flavour. She offered the bag to Holly again, then took a second piece herself before passing it back to Sophie, who refrained from taking another chunk. Instead, she placed it on top of Holly's locker.

'You mentioned going to Spain on holiday, back when you were a child. Can you remember any details? Where you stayed, for instance?'

'I was only about five, I think. I really have no idea of where it was in Spain. But we flew there. That's partly what stuck in my mind.'

'Did you stay in a hotel?'

A shake of the head. 'No. I think it was a villa of some sort. There was a pool. I don't remember much else about it.'

'Was it just you and your mum there? Did you have the place to yourselves?'

Holly was picking at her lip and frowning deeply. 'No. Someone else was there some of the time.' She closed her eyes as if concentrating hard. 'Two women, same age as Mum. And another, younger one. I didn't like her. Can't remember why, though. I think she was a bit nasty.' Her eyes opened wide. 'I think Mum knew them.'

There was another pause.

'One of the women drove us to the airport when we came home. Mum was really thankful. I remember now. She was a bit stressed.'

'Do you remember any names, Holly?'

The young woman shook her head again. 'No. It was so long ago. I can't even picture them in any detail.' She paused, gazing into the distance. 'There was something odd when we got back here, though. I've only just remembered. Mum told me to forget about them. Told me we'd never meet them again. It seems odd now.' Holly's forehead was deeply furrowed in puzzlement.

Sophie pondered on this for a few moments. What had been going through Carole's mind, causing her to say something like that? Was this the point at which Holly's mum had decided to cut all ties with her past? 'I need to ask you a big favour, Holly. Please don't talk to your mum about any of this, not until we've got it all sorted. We think that visit to Spain might be more important than it appears to you, and we need a bit of time to check some things out. We don't think your mum was doing anything bad, but other people might be watching her, and you. You're due to be discharged soon, aren't you?'

Holly looked upset on hearing the request. Clearly, she wasn't very happy. 'I'll be out tomorrow morning.'

Sophie thought fast. 'We'll send a car to take you home. When do you plan to go back to university?'

'Next week. Monday. Why? Don't you think it's safe?' She looked panic- stricken.

'No, I'm sure it'll be fine. We hope to have everything sorted by then. Not a word to anyone. Please.'

Holly was looking a little sheepish, embarrassed almost.

'Is there something else, Holly? Something you want to ask us?'

Holly hesitated but finally spoke. 'Umm, it's just that your protection officer told me that a couple of students tried to visit me yesterday, but they weren't on my friends list so they couldn't get in. He said they told him they were there when I got spiked.' She picked up a slip of paper that was on the top of her bedside locker. 'Their names were Dan and Ollie? They were hoping to visit and see how I was.'

Sophie relaxed. 'They've been helping DC Warrander a bit with information. Do you want to see them?'

'Well, I thought it can't do any harm if they're genuine and if you approve. It'd be nice to see someone different.'

'Leave it with me. I'll maybe get DC Warrander to message them. But wait until next week before you make any arrangements.'

Holly nodded and smiled, somewhat bashfully.

The two detectives left and had a few words with the officer at the ward entrance.

'You and your romantic shenanigans, boss,' Lydia said, laughing, as they made their way to the car. 'You're incorrigible.'

CHAPTER 42: PROTECTING VESTED INTERESTS

Jackie Spring joined Tommy Carter in checking through old records concerning Melanie Greenfield. Why was it proving so difficult to find information about her death? It was several hours before Jackie made the breakthrough.

'She got married,' she suddenly gasped, loudly enough to disturb her colleagues. They all looked across at her. 'In Spain. To that Juan Romero we talked about earlier, in 1992. Malaga. She was no longer a Greenfield on official records.'

Tommy instantly altered his search criteria and quickly found a coroner's report on her death. He read it aloud as he skimmed through it.

'Melanie Romero. Drugs overdose. 1995. Death by mis-adventure. Here in Bournemouth.' He paused, a look of horror on his face. 'Oh no. The police officer investigating the circumstances of her death and giving evidence was a certain DS Philip McCluskie.'

Silence fell on the incident room, broken by Sophie Allen, who was thumbing through messages on her phone.

'I can add to that,' she said. 'The local police chief in Malaga has just got back to me. The Romero family had one or two members who had cleft palates. Does that help to nail it?'

Jackie looked confused. 'Does that increase the likelihood then? Of Jan being Juan Romero's daughter? It isn't one hundred per cent reliable, is it?'

'No, you're right, Jackie,' Sophie answered. 'It's all a balance of probabilities when we're looking at a crime from twenty years ago. But it helps. We can make certain by carrying out some DNA comparisons, but that's likely to take weeks, if not months. It would involve identifying surviving Romero family members in the Malaga area, and we suspect Juan was an only child. Isn't that right, Tommy?'

'As far as I can tell, yes. So when he died in that boating accident, the ownership of his villa passed to his widow, Melanie, and his daughter, Janice. She could have been only a couple of months old at the time.'

'A catalogue of tragedy,' Sophie said. 'And it only got worse, didn't it? Melanie came back to England with the child, maybe fell in with the same rotten crowd as before, and all the rest happened. No wonder the kiddie slipped through the usual safety nets. She wasn't born here in the UK.'

Barry broke in. 'So how did Doreen Butcher get ownership of the villa? That's if it is the same one?'

'Presumably Melanie would have had the keys with her when she flew back,' Rae surmised. 'Do you think Doreen somehow tricked Melanie into transferring ownership? How could she have done that?'

Sophie's mind was made up. She looked at Lydia. 'I think you and I need to see Holly's mum, Carole Evans. We suspected she knew a bit more than she was letting on. Maybe it's a lot more. She'll be at the hospital by now. You go and pick her up and bring her in. We need to put the pressure on. Maybe we've been too gentle with her up to now.' She transferred her gaze to Barry. 'As for Doreen Butcher, maybe it's time to see her again too. Her name's been cropping up far too often for my liking. But wait until we've squeezed Holly's mum for the juicy stuff. We'll go in gently at first, and play our cards close to our chest. Remember, we have no real proof of her involvement yet. Somehow, we've got to get the facts out of her. Barry, it's over to you for that. How does this all sound? You're the SIOs, after all. It's your decision, in each case.'

Lydia snorted. 'We're not likely to go against your suggestions, are we? But you're absolutely right. With all the latest background we've uncovered, it's time to move.'

'Agreed,' Barry said.

Sophie smiled. That was as passionate a response as she expected from her number two, but she knew he'd be thinking along the same lines as her.

'You and your teams do the interviews. I'll watch from the observation room over a nice cup of tea. One of the benefits of my rank.'

* * *

'I don't know why I've had to come to the police station for this. It isn't as though I'm a criminal, is it?'

Carole Evans had been shown into an interview room and was looking around at the bare walls and plain furniture in obvious displeasure.

'Sit down please, Mrs Evans.' Jimmy Melsom pulled a chair out for her, then settled himself on the opposite side of the table. Finally, Lydia entered and took the seat directly opposite Carole, removing the folder that had been tucked under her arm.

'I heard what you said. In fact, it's become apparent that you haven't been entirely open and honest with us, Mrs Evans. We've discovered a fair number of discrepancies in what you've told us, and, more worryingly, you've kept quiet about several things that you must have guessed were of vital interest to us. That's wasted a lot of our time, something we don't take lightly.'

'I don't know what you mean.'

'Let's start with the discrepancies. You told us that you married Mark when Holly was a toddler. To me, that means about the age of two, maybe three. But we've discovered that she was eight when you married, and that Holly was bridesmaid. It's not something that's easily forgotten, Carole, so why lie to us about it?'

Carole's face turned pink, but she said nothing.

'You implied you never went on holidays until Mark was in your life because of a lack of money, but you visited Spain for a break when Holly was five.'

Carole stared at the tabletop but still said nothing.

'We also told you that we're investigating two murder cases, one of them a child whose desiccated body was found in the loft of a house in Crawley Terrace. The other, a man who was killed by his live-in carer and lodger. We have reason to believe that you knew both victims, but you've never told us this. We also suspect that you know the person we've charged with Joshua Quick's murder, Pippa Chandler. It seems that when you took Holly on that trip to Spain, Pippa was present for at least some of the time. Is that correct?'

'I was confused back then. Okay, I'd got myself clean from the drugs, but my mind was still all over the place. I don't remember who I did or didn't meet.'

Lydia was still angry. 'I'm not convinced, Carole. I think you remember a lot more than you're letting on. You went to that villa in Spain. We understand it belonged to Doreen Butcher and still does. She was there at the time you stayed, according to Holly. We strongly suspect that Pippa Chandler was there at the time as well. You must know we'd be interested in her because of her upcoming trial for the murder of Joshua Quick. You knew him as well.' Lydia paused and placed her hands flat on the table, fingers outstretched. 'Look, you may well prefer to forget about those people. I can understand that. It was back when your life was at a low point. But you must realise that a lot of these things were connected and still are. They've resurfaced. Quick's murder. The assault on your Holly. The child's body. Someone is clearly trying to remove loose ends. You must realise that. And to keep you all safe we need to know *everything* that went on, not just the bits that you feel comfortable enough to tell us. So, get real, please. Your daughter's life might be at stake here.'

Carole continued to stare at the table. Slowly, tears appeared in the corners of each eye and trickled down her cheeks. She started sobbing.

'I'm scared,' she murmured. 'They've threatened me. Keep quiet or we'll all suffer.' She looked up at Lydia. 'That attack on Holly. It was a warning.'

'Did they know about her heart weakness?'

Carol nodded her head. 'We didn't hide it. Family knew. Her friends knew. Maybe *they* knew. But went ahead anyway.'

She dabbed her face with a paper tissue.

'Okay, you're right. I should have told you. That Pippa Chandler is a nasty piece of work, always has been, even as a teenager. I didn't want her influencing my Holly. And the others manipulate everything. That's why I took myself away from them. I was lucky because I already knew Mark. I kind of threw myself at him. It all worked out better than I could have hoped. And then, after all this time, all that poison started bubbling up again. I just don't know how to deal with it. It's been horrible.'

'Well, tell me now. This is your opportunity. We need to know about Doreen Butcher.'

* * *

The bell on the sweet shop's door performed its jangling dance as Tommy pushed it open. He was in Swanage, a mere ten or so miles from Bournemouth as the crow flies, but a world away in many other ways, being cut off from the densely populated conurbation by the vast expanse of Poole Harbour. Tommy frequently visited the Swanage area, but usually on an off-road bicycle, riding across the byways of the Isle of Purbeck and admiring the coastal scenery. This time, of course, he was there on business.

He looked around. Fudge, and lots of it, along with other home-made cakes and sweets. The shop assistant looked up from her position behind the counter.

'I'm looking for Mr or Mrs Williams,' the detective said. 'But I'll be buying some fudge before I leave. I'm DC Tommy Carter.'

'Bronwen's in the back,' came the reply. 'She's been making a batch of rum fudge. Is she expecting you?'

'I hope so. I phoned yesterday.'

The young woman disappeared through a doorway but was soon back, accompanied by a middle-aged lady, wiping her hands on a towel.

'Come through,' she said. 'We'll use the office, though it's a bit small.'

They squeezed into a room not much larger than a walk-in closet. Maybe it had been a storage cupboard at one time, Tommy mused.

'I've been thinking about it since you phoned, you know, that house. We lived next to it for a couple of years back then. It was a strange place, with people coming and going at all sorts of odd times. I really didn't like it. We never knew what to expect.'

'Other people have told us that too. We're particularly interested in that Monday night in late August. I think it was a bank holiday weekend?'

'That's right. The weather was really good. Bournemouth was heaving with people. I suppose they wanted to enjoy a day at the seaside. The pubs were busy. There was definitely a holiday atmosphere. Even the local pub, the Lincoln Arms, was heaving, with people spilling out onto the street.'

'And when were you disturbed by the noise from next door, at number sixty-eight?'

'Quite late in the evening. Well after ten. It started with the sound of something getting smashed. Glass, or maybe crockery. That's when the shouting started. But it kept going. It really sounded as though it had turned into a fight. I could

273

hear loud noises like furniture being moved, maybe thrown. There was a child's voice, screaming. I thought maybe she'd been cut in the accident.'

'It was a girl's voice?'

Bronwen was beginning to look anxious, upset even. 'I think so. There was a young girl there quite a lot of the time. She had a cleft lip, poor little soul.'

'What was her name?'

'I think I remember it being Jan. I can't be absolutely sure, though.'

'How long did this argument go on for?'

'Long enough to stop me going to sleep. Both of us, in fact, and that's unusual because Bryn usually sleeps like a log. But then there was a loud shriek, and it all stopped. No more noise.'

'What did you do?'

'Bryn phoned for the police. We were worried, you see.'

Tommy sat forward, fully alert.

'And that was what was peculiar. We were watching from our bedroom window. A squad car arrived not very long after. The two officers climbed out but then another car drew up. A man got out and talked to the first two, and they got back in their car and drove away. Then he went into the house.'

Tommy felt a sense of foreboding creep over him. 'Did he stay long?'

'Don't know. We went back to bed.'

'Did you see Jan again after that night?'

'I don't think so. I kind of assumed the man was also from the police. Otherwise, why would the first two have gone away?'

'Did anyone come to see you? After all, you made a 999 call. It should have been followed up.'

'Someone did the next morning, quite early. It could have been the same man. He said he was a detective and that there was nothing to worry about.'

Tommy was holding his breath. 'How did that make you feel?'

'We thought it was a bit offhand, to be honest. But we didn't want to make a fuss.' She looked at Tommy warily. 'Was it that body in the suitcase?'

'It looks like it. We're still in the middle of the investigation.'

Bronwen's face had turned pale. 'It's just so awful. He told us not to worry. That it was nothing important. That's why we didn't follow it up, even recently when we saw the news. He seemed quite senior.'

'A detective sergeant?'

'Yes! How did you know?'

'It fits. Do you remember his name?'

'Not really. All I remember is it sounded Scottish. We know there was a bad-tempered teenage girl in the house. We saw her arrive earlier in the evening, along with an older woman in her late twenties. But the detective never asked us anything about them.'

Tommy thanked her for her help and said that a written statement would be needed. He then bought a luxury fudge selection to enjoy with Olivia, his fiancée, and a bag of the newly made rum fudge to share with his work colleagues.

When he reported back to Rae, what she said summed up everyone's feelings about the incident.

'Fucking Phil McCluskie.'

Tommy had rarely known Rae to swear before, yet this was the second time in a few days, and about the same person.

* * *

'Surely there's got to be a record of it somewhere?' Rae said to Sophie, who had just finished discussing the interviews with Barry. 'If there was a 999 call it would have to be logged and recorded.'

'I'll have another chat with Charlie Barrett. He's a magician when it comes to finding old records that no one knew existed, though it'll take him a couple of days, no doubt.'

Sophie was astonished at his response when she contacted him.

'I think I've got what you're looking for,' Charlie said.

'But how can you? Do you inhabit some kind of time warp? I'm only just making the request.'

She heard a guffaw down the line. 'I guessed you might want more. And I kidded the admin staff that the access you got for me would be for the duration of the investigation. I've been in and out a few times now.'

'You rascal, Charlie. You could get me reprimanded, you know. What have you got?'

'I pulled stuff from any file that involved McCluskie and Crawley Terrace. It's all secure, don't worry.'

'Can you bring it over here? Barry and I need to see it.'

'Sure thing. Get the coffee on.'

Within twenty minutes, Sophie, Barry and Lydia were huddled around a table while Charlie Barrett spread several ageing documents across the surface. He pointed to the first, a small sheet which looked to have been extracted from a memo pad.

999 call, made at 10 p.m., bank holiday weekend. Made by Mr Bryn Williams. A report of shouting and screaming from the neighbouring house, sixty-eight Crawley Terrace. Sounds of blows being made.

He then pulled a second sheet forward. 'This is the official report logged in the system. I quote, *Sounds of a minor altercation at sixty-eight Crawley Terrace. Neighbourhood policing team dispatched. CID already in attendance. Assured all was well. Team stood down from the incident.*'

A third incident sheet was then picked out. Charlie read this aloud too. '*No further action needed pertaining to the reported incident in Crawley Terrace last night. Neighbours probably over-reacted.* And the signatory? DS Phil McCluskie, Dorset Police.'

'But he was based in Blandford at that time. What was he doing across in Bournemouth?' This was Barry, always perplexed by evidence of a bent cop. Sophie knew that the concept of police corruption was so alien to him that he always struggled with it. She was about to answer but was beaten to it by Charlie Barrett.

'That's not hard to guess, is it? He was protecting his vested interests. Carrying out a damage limitation exercise.'

'Where's Lydia?' Sophie asked.

'Gone to visit Pippa Chandler,' Barry answered. 'Her and Jackie. It seems that Pippa is also set to tell all, in the hope of getting a lighter sentence. Coupled with the stuff that Lydia got out of Carole Evans, things are opening up nicely.'

CHAPTER 43: AIRPORT

'Well, here we are again, Pippa.' Lydia and Jackie were in the prison's interview room, looking across the table at the scowling woman. Lydia was taking the lead. 'Things have moved on. We're much clearer in our understanding of the events that took place in your Uncle Gus's house that August bank holiday weekend all those years ago. The one when young Janice was killed. I'd like to hear your side of the story. After all, with you getting all the blame, it's only fair to listen to what you have to say, isn't it?'

Pippa lifted her head, as if in surprise, staring hard at Lydia. 'What you saying? I'm getting the blame? That's not fucking right. You fucking with me?'

'No, I'm not. We've found witnesses that heard the shouts and screams. They stated categorically that your voice was one of them, shouting threats about killing someone. They heard the girl, Jan, screaming in pain. Then it all went quiet. We think you bundled her body into a suitcase and shoved her into the loft.'

'No. It weren't just me. I ain't taking the can for it all. That ain't right.' For once Pippa Chandler's facial expression showed a layer of worry over the fury.

'In that case, tell us who else was there and what happened. The ball's in your court.'

Pippa was almost snarling. 'Doreen. She was there. She's my cousin. And Chalky. Uncle Gus. We was all stoned. It's all a bit of a fog. But I didn't kill her. It weren't me. I hurt her but I didn't kill her.'

'Who was it, then?'

Pippa's face showed a mix of confusion, frustration and uncertainty. She still didn't speak.

'Look, Pippa. Get real. Can't you see what's going on here? They all know you're awaiting trial for Joshua Quick's murder. If they've been following the case and doing some probing of their own, they know it's pretty well certain you'll be found guilty. So it's in their interest to let you take the blame for this as well. You go down for a whole-life sentence. All over and done with. They get off scot-free. Do you want that? Is it really in your interest?'

'Bastards. It was her, Doreen. She smothered the girl with a cushion. Held it over her face. Chalky and Gus was laughing. They was all out of their heads. Bruce come in and went berserk. He took the kid and hid her.'

'Why him?'

'He organised the stuff we did. Drug shit. Cheap booze. Call girls. He was the boss. Planned stuff. Him and Doreen. And the cop.'

'What cop?'

Pippa leered. 'You mean you didn't know? He's dead now. Big Mac.'

Lydia pushed a pad and a pen across the table. 'A statement, Pippa. Right here, right now. I want it all detailed, what you've told me. I'll tell the chief superintendent. She'll have words with the judge at your trial, I promise.'

'She fucking better. I ain't doing this as some kind of favour.'

* * *

279

Rae Gregson had been to Bournemouth's main hospital, but not to visit a suspect or victim. Her partner, Craig, had suffered a sports-related injury to his shoulder and was receiving treatment. He couldn't currently drive, so Rae had volunteered to drop him off at the hospital, although she'd told him that he might well need to catch a bus to get back home. Instead of driving to the police station by the most direct route, she'd decided to make a diversion and carry out a quick check on Doreen Butcher's bungalow in Poole. The local police had been told to keep an eye on it with an occasional drive-by, but they'd been asked to keep it low-profile so as not to raise suspicions. The diversion to Poole would only delay Rae by half an hour or so, and it was the kind of thing she often did, just driving slowly by a location to check all was as it should be. Nosiness? Possibly. But she preferred to categorise such short visits as precautionary, looking out for something or someone out of place.

It was late morning. The sun was shining and the air was clear. It was a nice area, here, close to the harbour. Rae glanced right as she passed Doreen's home. There were two large suitcases outside the front door, which was ajar. She slowed her car. As she watched, Kim Brogan appeared with another, smaller case and set it down alongside the others.

Rae pulled in just past the house in question, swivelled in her seat and watched what was going on. At that point a taxi drove past Rae and pulled in outside the bungalow. Doreen Butcher then appeared with a second small case, quickly followed by Kim, carrying a shoulder bag. Doreen carefully locked the front door of her house and started to load the bags into the boot of the cab, aided by Kim and the driver. Within a few seconds the vehicle started to drive away, heading in the direction that Rae had come from. The local airport possibly, several miles north of Bournemouth hospital. Rae made a quick decision. She wouldn't stop the taxi just now; instead she'd follow it to check that her guess was right. It would give her time to report what she'd seen to Barry.

She made the call as she drove, receiving the advice she'd anticipated, then continued to trail the taxi as it drove northeast, the route to Bournemouth airport, a favourite setting-off point for many Mediterranean and European destinations. Spain, Greece, the Canaries. So where could the duo be heading? And for how long? Or did they have plans for a more permanent trip, heading somewhere that might take them out of reach?

She followed the taxi into the drop-off area at the airport and pulled into an emergency parking bay herself. She hurried into the departure building and looked around, trying to spot the couple. There they were, approaching the queue for a flight to the south of Spain. Rae approached a security officer standing near the door, showed her warrant card and explained what she was about to do. He followed her gaze to the line of people patiently waiting to check in.

'Just monitor them for a few minutes while I see your boss.'

Rae hurried to the airport's security office and spoke to the officer in charge. Within fifteen minutes a team of security staff were assembled and spread themselves around the airport. By now the target duo had made their way into the departure area. They were sitting in the first-class lounge, each clutching a large glass of wine, when Rae spotted them. A member of the security team approached them and asked to recheck their tickets, inspecting the paperwork closely.

The two women, already looking worried, glanced up in astonishment when Rae slid into a vacant seat beside them.

'Hello, Mrs Butcher, Ms Brogan. Planning to head off somewhere nice?'

The duo looked confused, glancing around as if considering possible escape options.

'I'll take those,' Rae said as she reached out for the documents held in a flight envelope poking out of Doreen's bag. 'We asked you to stay put, as persons of interest. And here you are, hoping to slip out of the country. Why? Is there something you haven't told us?' She looked around. 'The security office is just across there. That's where we're going. Bring your bags with you.'

Doreen looked at her watch irritably. 'Our flight leaves in an hour. You'll need to be quick.'

'Just be patient, Mrs Butcher. As persons of interest in an ongoing investigation, you may not leave the country.'

Kim snorted. 'That's ridiculous. You mean we can't have a holiday?'

Rae waved the paperwork she'd seized. 'These tickets are one-way, and the airline records don't show any return journey booked in your names. A holiday? I doubt it. Let's just wait. My boss is on his way.'

Barry and Tommy arrived some twenty minutes later, and Barry took over. 'You can't leave the UK. This is a murder investigation and we're still trying to link different aspects of the case. We can't have you disappearing off to Spain. Why didn't you inform us?'

'Why should we have to tell you?' Doreen said angrily. 'It's ridiculous.'

'If you were so desperate for a holiday, we could have come to some arrangement, as long as it was local and we had all the details for approval,' Barry explained. 'As it is, the very fact you've tried to sneak out of the country like this looks extremely suspicious.'

'I don't see why it should. I like the sun and a bit of warmth.' Kim sounded indignant.

'Well, you'll just have to enjoy sunny Bournemouth for a while longer. Think yourself lucky.'

Kim snorted.

Rae could see that Barry was thinking hard. He finally looked at her and jerked his head towards the door. She followed him out, wondering what was going on.

'Those missing photos from Doreen's flat make sense now. It's these two, her and Kim Brogan. There was a photo of a pub that we thought was the Lincoln Arms. That's the one we thought to be important. But the other one she removed was of two women by a pool, somewhere sunny. And no wonder. Too much of a giveaway.'

'It fits, doesn't it? She's a schemer, is Doreen Butcher. Very careful to cover her tracks. Isn't that the type of person we're looking for?'

They rejoined the group in the security office.

'We'll need to speak to you in more detail at the station, Mrs Butcher,' he said. 'DC Carter will take Ms Brogan back home.'

* * *

Doreen Butcher behaved entirely differently when she was interviewed an hour later, no longer the amiable innocent. She was alert and controlled. This was going to be a tricky dialogue to manipulate, Barry thought, as he led her into the meeting room. Rae followed on behind.

'Do I need a lawyer?' Doreen asked.

'Not as far as we're concerned. This is just a fact-finding interview. But you have the right to a lawyer if you feel you need one. If you don't opt for one just now, you can change your mind at any time.'

Doreen nodded her head and sat down, making herself comfortable on the hard chair. She glanced around at the non-existent décor and sniffed, then looked across the table at the two detectives, her face a blank canvas.

'We're investigating a number of cases that seem to be linked. Do you know a Pippa Chandler?'

'I don't think so.'

'Isn't that a bit curious? Isn't she your cousin?'

'I don't keep in contact with my family.'

'Bruce Greenfield?'

A shake of the head.

'Even though he's Ms Brogan's current partner? What about Alan Busby, often known as Chalky.'

'The name's familiar but I don't remember how.'

'His son, Jerry Busby.'

'No.' She shook her head.

'Jerry remembers differently. We found this photo on his phone.' Barry slipped across a colour print. It showed Chalky, two women and Jerry smiling at the camera.

'It looks to be a selfie,' Barry went on. 'Jerry is clearly holding the camera. That's you, along with Jerry's father Alan and his partner. We think it's in a pub near where you live.'

'You think? *Think?* That's just you guessing. Not very impressive. It could be someone who happens to look like me.'

'One of the cases we're investigating involves the death of a child found in a suitcase hidden in the loft at a house in Crawley Terrace, number sixty-eight. Her name was Janice Romero. She was the daughter of Juan and Melanie Romero. Melanie Romero's pre-marriage surname was Greenfield. Did you know any of those three people, Ms Butcher? Juan, Melanie or young Janice Romero?'

Doreen shook her head. 'No,' she answered firmly.

'You own a villa, a few miles outside Malaga in Spain. Is that right?'

'Yes.'

'Was it previously owned by someone from the Romero family? Possibly Juan, Melanie or Janice? Maybe a different member of the family?'

'I don't think so. But I bought it through an agency. They handled all the details. So I wouldn't have known who the previous owners were.'

'Why that villa? Did you look at others?'

'I left it to the agency. I trusted their judgement.'

'Was this the same villa that was shown in a photo you had on display in your flat on the occasion when I visited with the chief superintendent? The photo that seemed to have been removed when the DS here came to visit?'

Doreen shrugged, but, for the first time, there was a momentary flicker of worry on her face. 'Don't know.'

'Really?'

'Can't be sure. I might have visited other villas. It's a friendly kind of place, that part of Spain. We were invited out a lot, to neighbouring places.'

'Do you holiday there regularly?'

'Maybe three or four times a year. Look, what has this to do with the death of that child?' She sounded irritated.

'It was her villa, Ms Butcher. It became hers when her mother died, even though she was only two at the time. From what we can ascertain, the girl lived in poverty. Yet, in theory, she had assets worth well over half a million pounds. We suspect she was cheated out of those assets, Mrs Butcher. And here you are, the registered owner of that very same villa, having owned it for . . .' Barry paused while pulling a sheet of paper out of a folder. 'Twenty years. That's pretty much the timeframe since the girl's death. And as far as we can tell, you paid a pittance for it. Can I remind you, Mrs Butcher, that we strongly suspect the girl was tortured before being murdered and hidden in that house? We found her body crammed into a suitcase, hidden behind a cleverly constructed partition under the eaves. She had marks from what looked like cigarette burns on her skin.'

'I'd like my lawyer present.'

'As you wish.'

* * *

'What do you think, Barry?' This was Sophie's first question when the detectives met in the observation room.

'It's her. Clever and cautious. Subtle, even. Of course, she doesn't know how much evidence we have. She'll be wondering though, asking herself how thorough we've been.'

'Good idea just to show her the one photo and not the rest. And just the single slip of paper about the villa but taking it from that thick file. As you say, she'll be wondering. Good job we've got the Busby men in custody too. The son, Jerry, is the weak link.'

'All bluster and no substance,' Rae added. 'Jimmy says he's started spilling the beans about the recent stuff concerning Holly.'

'Good. Do we need to see Greenfield and his girlfriend again today?'

Barry answered. 'It would be a good idea. Just to verify some of the information. Kim Brogan's on the periphery. Greenfield himself seems to have got sick of it all, some years back. Busby runs the intimidation racket now, along with his son. They're not so good at it.'

'Well, it all worked when Phil McCluskie was alive. He, Gus Gibson and Greenfield had the various rackets all wrapped up nicely, it seems. But with two of them dead, Greenfield saw the writing on the wall and started cutting his ties. I wonder if he even knew what Doreen Butcher and Pippa Chandler were getting up to. He might not have known they were cousins. There's a big age difference, after all.' Sophie looked at Barry. 'You've got everything you need? Enough evidence to charge Butcher and Chandler?'

He nodded.

'And Lydia is charging the Busby duo today. The son with the spiking incident and the father with conspiracy. It's all good.' She sighed as she reached for her elbow crutches. 'God, I feel emotionally drained.'

* * *

Holly Evans' phone rang. 'Hello?' she said tentatively.

'Hi,' came an equally cautious male voice, that of a young man. 'It's Dan. I messaged you and you said it was okay to phone. I was there that night you got jabbed. Totally awful. Anyway, my friend Ollie and me, we wondered how you'd feel about meeting up sometime. No hurry. And we'd understand if you weren't keen. You probably want to forget about it all.'

'No, that'd be alright. The detectives said you and your friend had both been really helpful. I should be back at uni next week. I know this sounds stupid, but I might go back to Suki's just to convince myself that I'm back to normal. With my friends, of course. Shall we meet you there?'

'Great,' Dan said. 'And I don't think it's stupid at all. You obviously like it there. And everything's sorted, isn't it? Someone's getting charged. I think it's the guy Ollie and I found out about. We've both heard rumours that he's spiked other people, though it's always been just into their drinks before.'

'There could have been an extra reason why he jabbed me, but keep that to yourself. To be honest, I just want to forget it ever happened. It's like coming out of a nightmare at last.'

'Yeah, I'm sure. Just text me when you're ready. Bye, then.'

'Bye,' Holly replied.

Maybe things were looking up a bit, Holly thought. Now she just had to try and rebuild her relationship with her mother, whose deception was the reason she'd been targeted by that weirdo guy in Suki's. And that was not going to be easy, particularly with the DNA profiles that had recently arrived, proving that man McCluskie to have been her father.

* * *

Kim Brogan was confused. Why had Doreen been detained further? Was something else going on? No one was answering their phones. Bruce had been collected by a police car, whisked away to a police station somewhere, she supposed. Doreen hadn't picked up on her many phone calls and wasn't replying to the voicemails Kim had left for her. So, it looked as though she'd finally been found out too. She'd even phoned that dim woman who was Chalky's partner, and been told he'd been lifted by the cops, along with his son.

She used her phone to access her bank accounts. Thank goodness. Her secret nest egg was still there, the money safe and secure. It was enough to see her through the next year or two, though maybe she'd find a little job to tide her over until Bruce was free. He'd always told her that he'd never been involved in anything violent, so he shouldn't be away for too long. Then again, maybe there was another sugar daddy around somewhere, looking for a live-in housekeeper and provider of speciality services. She wasn't picky. Loyalty to one person was all very well in theory, but there were limits. The cops didn't seem particularly interested in her. Maybe she might manage a trip to Spain sometime soon, after all. She still held a set of keys to Doreen's villa that no one knew about. If the worst came to the worst, she could wait a year or two for Bruce, then move out there. And if he was in the clink for longer than that? Well, she could go anyway. Any time she felt like it.

Kim made herself a nice cup of tea and settled back in her favourite armchair. No rush. She had plenty of time to think through her options.

CHAPTER 44: FUNERAL

A month later

Sophie Allen glanced at the other people dotted around the parish church close to Crawley Terrace. There were rather more mourners than she'd expected. It looked as though everyone with anything to do with the investigation had chosen to attend, along with a large number of local residents. No wonder. A tragedy like this would often bring out the best in people, even if the events had happened almost twenty years earlier.

She looked again at the small coffin, almost completely hidden under a huge pile of flowers. Flowers of every colour imaginable, and of every type. Janice's tragic story had obviously touched the heartstrings of the local community. She'd been failed by everyone. The very agencies that had been set up to protect vulnerable young children like her had, ultimately, failed in that task when it came to young Jan. And the responsibility for that had fallen on a now-dead detective, abusing his power and influence in order to line his own pockets rather than protect the communities he was meant to be serving.

McCluskie had partly owned up to, and even regretted, his serious failings in that letter to his daughter, but it could never make amends for the harm he'd done in his life. And to one young girl in particular, who was now inside the flower-covered coffin. She should have had a life. A proper chance to live, love and prosper. A chance to reach her potential as a human being.

Sophie thought of her own daughters, now grown up and living a full life. Jan never had that chance. It was snatched from her by the selfish actions of a handful of people who'd exploited her vulnerabilities and then murdered her.

One thing was for sure. Now that she had contacts in Malaga police, Sophie wouldn't rest until she'd found the rightful person to inherit the Spanish villa that Doreen Butcher seemed to have misappropriated. It may well be that there were distant members of the Romero family still living in the area. If not, would one of the charities that had tried to support Jan be interested in it? Wouldn't it be just perfect if groups of orphaned children had access to such a place for holiday breaks? There might even be a Romero family member who might be interested in such a scheme. Would George Warrander want to help? After all, it was his sharp eyes that had spotted Jan's hastily scrawled note in the dusty loft of an old house in Crawley Terrace, the note that had helped to initiate the case. She'd talk the idea over with him.

THE END

GLOSSARY

Bloke: guy, man.

Environment Agency: the body charged with overseeing the environment, offering advice and tackling pollution. It monitors river pollution.

Malaga: popular holiday destination on the south coast of Spain.

Mobile phone: cell phone.

R & R: rest and recuperation time.

RSPB: The Royal Society for the Protection of Birds. Probably the UK's most effective wildlife charity. Arne is one of its most famous reserves because of its use in many BBC wildlife programmes. It's a promontory that juts out into the Poole Harbour mudflats and has become one of Europe's top birdwatching sites.

School, Primary: usually the first school a child attends between ages 5 and 11.

School, Secondary (high school): provides education between ages 11 and 16 or 18.

Uni: university.

UK Police Ranks (in descending order of seniority):
Chief Constable (or Commissioner in London's Metropolitan Police force)
Deputy CC (Deputy Commissioner in London)
Assistant CC (Assistant Commissioner in London)
Chief Superintendent
Superintendent
Chief Inspector
Inspector
Sergeant
Constable

Detectives hold the same ranks but with a prefix before the title (DC, DS etc.). There is sometimes career movement back and forth between detectives and uniformed ranks.

ACKNOWLEDGEMENTS

Writing a novel such as this can be, at times, rather lonely. But lots of people help in many different ways and deserve a mention.

Thanks to all the staff at Joffe Books for their help, particularly the editorial team for working on my original text so thoroughly. They always do a great job. Special thanks to Kate Lyall Grant and to my meticulous editor, Rachel Malig, along with Kate Ballard and Matthew Grundy-Haigh. Jasmine Callaghan always deserves a mention. The biggest thanks go to the boss, Jasper Joffe, to whom I owe so much.

Any errors in this book are mine. If you spot a typo, please email Joffe Books and they'll do their best to correct it.

A big thanks to fellow authors (and friends) Joy Ellis, Janice Frost and Helen Durrant. Thank you for your continued friendship.

At home in Salisbury, thanks are due to many friends, those who help to keep me going just by being around. Thank you all. Above all, to my darling wife, Margaret.

I need to mention again that I really dislike social media, the misuse of which causes so much harm to so many people. I like email though, and I'd like to reassure readers that if they email me I will always respond as quickly as I can. Please visit my website at www.michaelhambling.co.uk. It went through a bit of an overhaul a while ago, though I need to remember to post stuff on it more regularly! It does carry relevant information and a selection of free-to-read short stories.

You may like to read the novels I've written for teenagers, the Misfit books. The stories are about a small group of unorthodox young people in Dorset who try to solve low-level, antisocial crimes that have a habit of escalating into something more serious. Rae Gregson, who appears in the Sophie Allen novels, tries to keep an eye on the group in her spare moments, and acts as an unofficial adviser. Available from Amazon.

Email me with any comments at michael@michaelhambling.co.uk

* * *

If you enjoy quality crime mystery books set in Dorset and the surrounding area, then please consider the two novels recently written by Carol Cole: *Murder in the New Forest* and *Straw in the Wind*. I can also recommend *Murder in Arundel* by Ruby Vitorino Moody. Both are fellow Salisbury-based writers.

AUTHOR'S NOTES

Gaia Pope-Sutherland

You'll have noticed that this novel is dedicated to the memory of Gaia Pope-Sutherland. Gaia was a free-spirited young woman who lived in Swanage, close to where we have a flat. She disappeared from her home in autumn 2017. It was known that she was extremely upset when she went missing, but it took a lot of time to get to the truth of the matter, far too late to save her life.

It would appear that Gaia had been given spiked drinks in the company of a couple of young men in Bournemouth some two years earlier, as a sixteen-year-old. While she was unconscious from the effect of the drug, she was raped. Gaia had no immediate memory of this but a short while later she started getting flashbacks of her ordeal and began to experience spells of trauma. Mental health support was patchy, and her feeling of desperation grew. Some of her attempts to contact the police and other services were handled inappropriately and, on occasion, her calls were callously ignored by emergency call-handlers who labelled her as a time-waster. It was this combination of factors, the flashbacks coupled with her unfeeling treatment, that caused her immense stress. She probably felt ignored by the world. It is possible that she ran away in an attempt to escape the confused thoughts that were crowding her brain.

Unfortunately, Gaia suffered from epilepsy and didn't take any medication with her when she ran away from home. Despite mass searches from the authorities and by organised volunteers from the local community, she was not found in time to save her life. Her body was found curled up under a bush on the edge of a lonely field near Dancing Ledge. The coroner's report into her death identified weaknesses in the mental health support that Gaia had access to, as well as deficiencies in the police response once Gaia went missing. The cause of death was hypothermia.

A stone memorial bench dedicated to Gaia can be found on the upper coast path at Spyway Hill, overlooking the steep slope down to Dancing Ledge.

A BBC documentary was made about her tragic death, and a shortened extract can be found on YouTube. As one of the characters in this novel says, the perpetrators of spiking can never know the detailed health issues of their victims. They can never be sure that the spiking they've inflicted on someone doesn't initiate heart failure or an epileptic attack that might be fatal.

My sixth Sophie Allen novel, *Evil Crimes*, was originally due to be published on Friday 24 November 2017, after spending several months passing through the various stages of editing. That story starts with a dramatic death at Dancing Ledge, followed by careful police-led searches along the coast path. Gaia's body was found just a few days before the planned publication date after just such a set of searches. I immediately contacted Jasper Joffe, the CEO of Joffe Books, and asked for a publication postponement of a week and he was happy to agree.

Location

Bournemouth, one of the largest seaside resorts on the south coast of England, hardly needs a description. I've used it a couple of times in earlier novels. It's often perceived as being genteel and sedate. Not in recent years! Since it gained a university several decades ago, it has been transformed. Its town centre is now a vibrant place, but that change has brought with it some social problems. It still has its great beach though, along with lovely gardens. The Russell-Cotes Museum is worth a visit, while the renowned Bournemouth Symphony Orchestra has its regular home in the Lighthouse arts centre in nearby Poole.

My favourite pub in the town is the Goat & Tricycle on West Hill Road. It's a beautifully kept Victorian pub that serves really good food and has about eleven hand pumps for real ale on the polished bar. The beers on offer are mostly from the Butcombe and Liberation (Channel Islands) breweries.

THE JOFFE BOOKS STORY

We began in 2014 when Jasper agreed to publish his mum's much-rejected romance novel and it became a bestseller.

Since then we've grown into the largest independent publisher in the UK. We're extremely proud to publish some of the very best writers in the world, including Joy Ellis, Faith Martin, Caro Ramsay, Helen Forrester, Simon Brett and Robert Goddard. Everyone at Joffe Books loves reading and we never forget that it all begins with the magic of an author telling a story.

We are proud to publish talented first-time authors, as well as established writers whose books we love introducing to a new generation of readers.

We won Trade Publisher of the Year at the Independent Publishing Awards in 2023 and Best Publisher Award in 2024 at the People's Book Prize. We have been shortlisted for Independent Publisher of the Year at the British Book Awards for the last five years, and were shortlisted for the Diversity and Inclusivity Award at the 2022 Independent Publishing Awards. In 2023 we were shortlisted for Publisher of the Year at the RNA Industry Awards, and in 2024 we were shortlisted at the CWA Daggers for the Best Crime and Mystery Publisher.

We built this company with your help, and we love to hear from you, so please email us about absolutely anything bookish at feedback@joffebooks.com.

If you want to receive free books every Friday and hear about all our new releases, join our mailing list here: www.joffebooks.com/freebooks.

And when you tell your friends about us, just remember: it's pronounced Joffe as in coffee or toffee!